BELLE
BREZING

The execution of innocence is silent.

BELLE BREZING

MC PRICE

authorHOUSE®

AuthorHouse™
1663 Liberty Drive
Bloomington, IN 47403
www.authorhouse.com
Phone: 1-800-839-8640

Published by AuthorHouse   10/21/2014

ISBN: 978-1-4969-3246-4 (sc)
ISBN: 978-1-4969-3247-1 (hc)
ISBN: 978-1-4969-3248-8 (e)

Library of Congress Control Number: 2014913883

Madam Belle Brezing in black dress

DEDICATION

I dedicate this novel to my mother, Peggy Kingsley Price, whose love of poetry and history ignited a fire in my imagination as a child and who still today inspires me to seek portals to Wonder and Magic. I write because she gave me a powerful wand – the gift of believing in my dreams.

And also – to my father, Charles Price, a peacemaker, whose wonderful sense of humor and wisdom (often shared on scraps of paper with a bag of peanut M&M's) reminds me not to take Life, or myself, too seriously . . . and always to speak my Truth.

NEW YORK TIMES
Front page
"Died. Belle Brezing. August 11, 1940. Famed Ky. bawd."

LIFE MAGAZINE (August 1940) paid tribute to Miss Brezing, whose house of pleasure on Lexington's Megowan Street was known as the "most orderly of disorderly houses."

LEXINGTON HERALD NEWSPAPER (July, 2013)
"Belle Brezing was the model for Belle Watling in Margaret Mitchell's novel **Gone With the Wind.**"

Child Belle, about eight years old

One small star . . .

"Willie always says that lightning bugs are the eyes of angels watching over us. And if you catch one, ya got to let it go – so it can give its light to a star. Then when you get to that bridge between heaven and earth, the lightning bugs will be waiting there for you. I reckon when I get to that bridge, Jesus and the lightning bugs and Willie will be there waiting for me – waiting for me to give my light to one small star."

Child-Belle, age 8
June 1868

"59 Megowan Street"

Belle's last paperboy . . .

Belle Brezing belongs to my childhood in the same way as B&B Bat suckers, tiger eye marbles and Moon-pies. Like those things I bought with the two pennies I was supposed to put in the basket at the First Methodist Church, Belle Brezing was deliciously decadent. A comfort food thinly disguised as forbidden fruit. And in the summer of 1940, with the Great Depression breathing on our heels and another war in Europe looming on the horizon, a lonely paper boy needed as many comfort foods as he could muster up. That summer gave us "Gone With the Wind" and "The Wizard of Oz" at the picture shows and a new roller coaster at Joyland Amusement Park -- the Wild Cat.

Belle Brezing left this world the summer of 1940. But I believe her spirit lives on in that roller coaster. Fast. Dangerous. Exhilarating. Belle Brezing was a roller coaster in a fancy Charles Worth gown.

But at six a.m. on August 11th, Belle Brezing was still very much alive. I know because I was Belle's last paper boy.

Gil Mabon
August 1940

INTRODUCTION

The Paperboy

Cicadas sing in the coming dusk. Fireflies pulse, then, like magic, melt into stars. It is hot. Powerful hot. The air is liquid and sultry, hanging like rain soaked laundry in a sky too tired to spit rain. Not a lick of wind stirring. Only heat lightning. Angels puffing on fat cigars. The only sound is the eerie clattering of the cicada wings. And the painted ladies of Megowan Street loom large — over-dressed, over-rouged and powdered in the dusk; they wait as street magicians to show their tricks - their flawless beauty - in the shadows of night.

Sometime after the cicadas tire of their ceaseless chatter and the wind has faded down to a whisper, twilight illumines the garden of a once grand Victorian house with a second floor sunporch. (59 Megowan). Bathing the roses in a light that hints of something hauntingly beautiful but lost. And in this twilight, another sound rises above the stirring of creatures whose playground appears only in the time of shadows. It is the distant sound of whistling. The kind of whistling that comes straight from the heart of a loyal, fearless paper boy.

Only a street away from Megowan, Gil Mabon, skinny and freckle-faced, flies past the town's 5 & Dime store on his bike, tossing papers out with a practiced grace. A lone maverick on a pony made of tin, he straddles his seat, kicks out his legs and flies. He catches his reflection in the glass windows of a florist shop where a sign, in large, sprawled script, reads "Yep, these are Pete's pups." And seconds later, as Gil pedals hard and fast, taking the turn at the corner of Limestone and Main, he slows, saluting the stray dog staring at him from a cardboard box. Gil winks at Smiley Pete. The dog, with a black patch around one eye, winks back– expecting the hard cinnamon biscuit, broken in half and then tossed from the paperboy's hand. It is their morning routine.

Gil rides on, spinning figure-eights through the rising mist. He flies past the Kentucky Theatre where *Gone With the Wind* and *The Wizard of Oz* are on the marquee. Then he makes his way to the corner of Megowan and Main where another paper boy, taller, with a cap pulled down over his eyes, waits.

"Tinsley, call it." Gil straddles his bike; his short legs barely hit the ground.

"I ain't callin' it, Cotton."

"Heads or tails?" Gil takes a coin out of his pocket and jangles it, tossing it high.

Tinsley shakes his head. "Jest hit the porch with the paper and run."

"Call it."

"There's no way I'm callin' it because I ain't going up there." Tinsley slips a B&B bat sucker on top of the paper he pulls out from the pile. He ties it with a string.

"Heads or tails."

"She's still up there." The older boy moves towards his bike.

"Who?" Gil flips the coin, back and forth. Feeling the fear as the sweat heats up on his hands.

Tinsley's voice drops low, "Belle Brezing."

Suddenly, white heat-lightning splinters the sky. Tinsley swallows his gum.

Gil scoffs his shoe in the dirt; dust rises. "Ah, it's jest heat-lighning. Jest call it, Tinsley." He tosses up the coin. It sails high. "Ain't nobody seen her for twenty years."

"Oh yeah, then who you think you're delivering the paper to, yeah? Ya ever think about that? Who's reading the paper?"

"Heads or tails?" Gil stares into Tinsley's eyes.

"Heads." Tinsley suddenly swerves his bike and shoves a newspaper at Gil who catches the paper and drops the coin. Tinsley takes off; Gil gets off his bike, leans down and picks up the coin.

"Tails." His voice catches as he slips the coin into his pocket and for the first time brings out a tiger-eyed marble. Then he mutters under his breath, "I ain't scared of her; and besides I got something I got to do." He places the newspaper in the bike basket – real gentle like; then he takes out a small bundle of letters. "This is for you, Uncle Billy." He tucks these inside the newspaper. And in a low, solemn voice he says, "All right, let's' do this." He unwraps the sucker and sticks it in his mouth. "Ah shucks, horehound." He spits out the candy, wipes his mouth and slowly turns his bike up the hill.

At the top of the hill, a red brick Victorian with a second floor sun porch rises up. Overgrown with roses, the garden boasts a trellis, with a small seat. And on the lawn, silky and mist-enshrouded, there are some tables. A sign in the yard says "AUCTION". Gil is drawn to the tables. The boxes and spilled out belongings (lace napkins and old shoes, dusty books and tarnished jewelry) appear surreal in the morning mist. He sets down the bike, forgetting the paper and glances at the initials on a crate: *BB*. Something about the box gives the paperboy the shivers and he backs away.

Gil makes his way through the tall grass towards the porch. For a split second, he considers just throwing the paper up onto the house porch, but changes his mind. Curious, he climbs up onto the dilapidated porch; the railing isn't worth holding onto a lick. The rotting floorboards creak beneath his footsteps; he glances at a stained glass window and suddenly remembers the newspaper (with the letters folded up inside) left in the bike's basket. He's about to go get it when the front door opens and a caramel colored hand reaches out and grabs his wrist.

"Boy, git in here and eat you some flapjacks."

Gil stares up into the sizzling black eyes of a woman wearing a scarlet turban. He knows then that he doesn't have a chance of turning around.

"You like flapjacks?"

It isn't really a question. Miss Flora, who is about as tall as she is round with gold bracelets jangling on her plump wrists, escorts the paper boy inside. And in that moment, time slides to a sudden stop. Gil has to remember to breathe. They walk into a front hall with a staircase that's missing some steps. He catches his reflection in a parlor mirror, off to the left. The room dazzles. Everything is gold with accents of red. But it is a gold that has long since lost its luster. At the tall windows, heavy curtains hang down. Velvet and hinting of secrets kept in their heavy folds. There is a chilling sense that time in this once grand parlor has stopped.

Gil sneezes.

"Bless you. I ain't had a chance to dust yet."

"No ma'am, it ain't that. I think it's goin' rain."

She turns and looks at him. Hard. "It ain't goin' rain till morning." Something in Miss Flora's eyes gives Gil the shivers. He catches on that Miss Flora is not really talking about rain. She runs her tongue around her mouth, puffing out her cheeks. A curious gesture, Gil thinks. He follows her – trying not to stare through the beads hanging down – separating the hallway from the parlor; but in the parlor there's a life-size portrait of a nude above the mantel. And it's like a magnet or one of those funny mirrors in a circus side-show. He can't not look.

And so he stares. He's never really seen a naked woman. He's surprised about how white her skin is – and well, she's kind of fat. Gil catches Miss Flora eyeing him. She's got eyes in the back of that red turban he figures. Maybe she's some kind of circus gypsy. Gil blushes. He thinks for a second that she's smiling at him with those eyes. She ushers Gil through another door into a kitchen.

He smells the wonderful, delicious intoxicatingly rich smells of a distant time. Smells of fried bacon and warm syrup and skillets frying up grease. It is a memory that hurts and so he doesn't go there. Instead he slips off his cap, staring at the ladies who are just now comin' into focus. They wander into the kitchen, dressed in skimpy negligees and silky things that don't cover much of anything. One of the girls, tall and black-haired, lights a cigarette. Others sit at the large oak table, sipping their first cup of Sunday morning coffee. Gil, mesmerized, blushes.

"Girls, this is . . . ?" Miss Flora turns to the paper boy.

"Gil." He's surprised at the sound of his own voice. He figured maybe he'd left it outside, with his bike and dag-gone it – where's the paper? He'll have to look for it. But not now.

"Gil's from over at the Short Street Orphanage. Where's that other boy?"

"Ah, well . . . Tinsley's probably wondering where I'm at." Gil tries to figure out where to look so he won't be lookin' at bare flesh. Flesh that's different shades – the color of coffee or the liquid amber of sweet tea, and the caramel color of delicious butterscotch toffee. A hand, with red nails, reaches in front of his plate, picks up a slice of bacon. Her skin glistens, like cracked walnuts drenched in September sun. Gil glances at his hands, still ink-stained and decides he looks kind'a pale. Too white. He puts his hands in his lap. Then realizes that he can't eat; so he slowly reaches for a fork.

"Too scared, huh? Tell ya not to go up to that bad house on the Hill?" Miss Flora laughs. It's a deep infectious laugh. "Gil, you're acting like you've never seen a flapjack before. Lets' get some of that ink off your hands." Miss Flora lifts Gil up onto the edge of the sink, washes the ink off of his hands and then gestures over to the table. "Sit." She puts down a plate filled with steaming hot flapjacks. "Butter and syrups on the table. Pass the bacon to Gil, Sally."

Gil sits. Staring at the plate in front of him. Someone passes him a plate piled high with bacon.

"Mornin', blue eyes. Ya want some bacon? I'm Sally."

"Uh, mornin', ma'am." Gil says this without looking up. Sally, a ginger-haired young woman with freckles, moves in closer; he can smell the bacon she's eating. She leans an elbow on the table, looking into his eyes. He glances up; Sally nibbles the bacon then licks it, like she's licking a lollipop. It makes Gil's cheeks tingle. She is intoxicatingly beautiful and practically naked.

Another whiff of perfume and then a voice, "Gilbert, you goin' down to First Methodist? Maybe I'll see ya after I git my face on." Gil glances at another girl, smaller, in a cream negligee with roses. "I'm Rose."

Miss Flora puts down another plate of flapjacks, motioning to the girls. "Eat up."

"Baby, you got the bluest eyes."

"Leave the boy alone, Rose." This comes from a larger, darker skinned woman. She lifts her leg up onto a chair next to Gil and laces up her shoe. He's never seen a shoe quite like the one she's lacing; it's gold and has open toes and black laces.

"Where'd you get those shoes, Lacey?" Rose glares across the table at the expensive and very sexy shoes.

"She won't be needin' em any longer." Lacey licks her fingers, wetting the laces so they tie up nice and tight.

Gil picks up a fork; he considers asking for the syrup. Changes his mind.

"Miss Flora, Lacey's stolen Miss Belle's slippers."

Miss Flora, at the stove, pours grease into the iron skillet. "I know I didn't hear you right cuz none of my girls would be stealin' from . . ."

"They were out on the lawn. With the other auction stuff. Why should some skinny white lady git Miss Belle's slippers?"

"Those came from an admirer in Paris. You put them back." Rose's voice quivers. "Miss Flora . . ." Rose stands, hands placed firmly on her slim hips. Lacey puts her leg down off the chair and faces Rose. Gil stares at his plate of flapjacks, now swimming in – nope, drowning in hot, bubbling maple sugar. "Put 'em back, Lacey!"

"I ain't goin' put 'em back. What – ya'll don't git it do ya? The skinny white girls got folks lookin' out for them. They got lawyers and politicians – making sure they don't turn tricks no more neither. Look at us. We're the poor colored girls who've got to turn the tricks cuz the law protects the skinny white girls' asses." She glances at Gil. ". . . ya know, from being respectable seamstresses. So now it's Miss Flora and a house of colored girls. Colored bathrooms. Colored drinking fountains and colored girls turning tricks for the white boys." She blows rings of smoke – staring at Miss Flora. "You know I'm right. And Miss Belle's been up there on that sun porch with all them scraggly black cats – makes me want to scream something fierce." She practically swallows the smoke she's puffing so hard and fast. "So - what are you goin' be able to buy out there when they get that Auction goin'? Huh?"

"I'm goin' buy Miss Belle's bed. But she ain't dead yet."

"Well, I ain't buyin' nothin'. I saw these first and I'm takin' them."

Rose rises up on tip-toe; her fingers shape into a small fist, "Miss Flora!"

"She'll put em back or she won't eat." Miss Flora spits the words; grease crackles.

Furious, Lacey kicks up her leg and unties the strings on the fancy slippers. "I don't care if I eat your flapjacks or not; they got flies in 'em."

Gil puts down his fork.

"They come in with the fan – jest swooshes 'em right into the batter." Lacey is getting even. Miss Flora's face is about to explode. She smacks at a fly on the counter.

Lacey, dangling the expensive pair of slippers, raises an eyebrow with a "I told ya so" expression in her eyes.

Another younger woman, Lily May, wanders in; raising her arms over her head, she stretches, exposing her bare thighs. Rose, sitting, introduces Gil.

"Lily May, this is Gilbert. From over at the . . ."

Lily May sits down next to Gil, "Mornin'." She takes a flapjack, reaches for the syrup. He glimpses a flower tattooed on her breast. "Shew, it's hot. Oh, ya want something to drink?" She says this very casually, and Gil wonders if she's asking him. Lily May reaches for the syrup; her fingers brush against Gil's hand, rough and still ink-stained.

"Miss Flora, pour Mister Gil some of your hot chicory coffee?"

"Oh, no thanks, ma'am. I don't drink coffee."

Miss Flora rubs her tongue around her cheek. Then she opens a cabinet, painted white with see through glass, and takes out a cup. Gil notices that the shelf has a sign, marked "Colored".

Miss Flora spits in the cup, wipes it clean with her apron. "You ain't never tried it."

"Sweeten it, Miss Flora." This from Sally who is now all excited about the chicory coffee and Gil. She winks at Rose.

"You want some cream, Mister Gil." Miss Flora turns to the black stove and pours a cup from the coffee pot. "Ya want some?"

Gil shrugs his shoulders.

"Well I'll take that as a 'yes'." Miss Flora pours some rich, thick cream into the coffee. Then, she opens a flask and pours in some whiskey. Then, slowly, Gil lifts the cup to his lips and the aroma is powerful strong.

Sally takes a deep breath, smelling the coffee from across the table. "Sip it real slow so you don't burn your tongue, Gil."

Gil hesitates.

"Ya got to sweeten it, sugar." Sally leans over and spoons sugar into Gil's cup. She licks the spoon with her tongue and for a second, Gil thinks he sees something glittery – silver – pierced in her tongue. He sips the rich chicory coffee, and licks his lips. All eyes are on the paperboy. He knows this; takes another sip. Then another and licking his lips, he grins up at Miss Flora. He holds up his empty cup for more.

"Humph, boy don't drink coffee."

"Well, I reckon I do now."

The girls, gathered around the table, burst out laughing. Miss Flora laughs and takes Gil's empty cup. She pours another cup of the chicory, and is about to set it down in front of Gil when a deep wailing seeps down through the ceiling. It is an almost inhuman sound. Filled with anguish and pain. The moaning permeates the hush that settles over the kitchen. The sound has a chilling effect on Miss Flora and the girls who pull their robes tight, staring silently into the coffee cups or at their unfinished breakfasts. Suddenly, Miss Flora places her strong arms around Gil's thin shoulders, "Sing with me, Gil. Sing out now." It isn't a request; it is an order.

Miss Flora's black eyes dart back and forth from Gil to the other girls. Her voice sings out – "'Amen. Amen.' Sing with me, Gil. Miss Belle always loved to hear my mama sing."

Lacey grinds out her cigarette, "Pearl's dead."

"Sing with me, Lacey. Now." Miss Flora bursts out – "'Amen. Amen. Amen. Amen.'"

And the other girls, all except Lacey who lights another cigarette, join in. They sing; holding each other's souls, if not their hands. Lacey's cigarette smoke wafts around Gil and the girls, and as she smokes, she seems to disappear. But the other girls hold on tight to one another, forming a circle around Gil as he stares at his second cup of chicory coffee. They sing the old spiritual out of key, like a familiar church hymn banged out on a piano that's missing some of its keys but still plays – hitting the melody every now and then. And their voices drown out the other sound. The haunting sound of human despair. There is a moment when Gil hears something hard hit the floorboards upstairs. Then the moaning stops. And Flora stops singing. One by one, the girls push back their plates. And Gil catches on that it's his cue to leave. Miss Flora picks up his plate.

"Miss Flora, ma'am, I got more papers. Thank ya, ma'am. It was nice to meet ya'll. It was a pleasure to meet such nice ladies."

Rose reaches over and sips his coffee, "Bye, blue eyes."

"Bye, Gil." Lily May's voice is soft, a whisper. "Come back now."

Lacey slings the slippers over her shoulder and blows Gil a kiss, "Don't you grow up too fast. Maybe come back for the auction."

Miss Flora's eyes shoot Lacey a look. She pouts, moves towards a back door. "I'll put 'em back." She waves good-bye to Gil as she slips out the screen door.

Rose leans over and smiles into Gil's eyes, "Bye, paper boy."

Miss Flora's small slippered feet shuffle towards the front doorway; Gil follows her into the front hall. Light streams in from a stained glass window; Gil turns and glances up the stairs towards the window. For a second, he thinks he sees something. A wisp of long hair. A figure – standing in the light. But then she is gone. He turns towards the front door and suddenly hears Miss Flora clear her throat. He catches on that he still has his napkin tucked into his shirt.

"Oh, sorry, ma'am." Embarrassed, he slips it off, offering it to Miss Flora.

"Keep it. If anyone asks ya over at the orphanage . . ."

"I ain't an orphan, ma'am."

". . . you tell them it belonged to Miss Belle Brezing. She'd want a nice young paper boy like you to have something from her house." Under her breath she hisses, "Better than goin' to them buzzards."

Gil's not sure he heard her but he isn't really interested in the auction. He wants to clear up something. "Miss Flora, ma'am, thank you for the coffee and all. But I ain't an orphan. My mama's jest restin' awhile till . . ."

Miss Flora wraps her strong warm arm around his shoulders. "I knows. 59 Megowan knows a heap of secrets, Mr. Gil. And it don't breathe a word. No use troublin' the living with secrets of the dead."

Her words open his heart; a rush of feelings explode. He feels the tears coming to his eyes but he's powerless to hold them back, "My mama ain't comin' back, but I don't tell anyone that. They got no reason to know."

Miss Flora lets him cry. "You're a mighty fine paper boy, Mr. Gil. Mighty fine."

Suddenly, the light falls across Gil's face. She lifts his chin. "You any kin to a Mr. Billy Mabon used to work up at the Water Company?"

"Billy Mabon was my uncle."

"Well, I reckon Miss Belle would be mighty proud to have you takin' one of her embroidered napkins. Miss Belle always liked her paper boys." Miss Flora smiles and then the smile spreads into a laugh that lightens her whole being. In that moment, she seems to grow younger, filled with a vibrant energy that in a curious way empowers the paper boy to give her a hug. It is a spontaneous gesture of affection; she folds the napkin into his hands, then opens the front door. As the light floods the hallway, Gil sees what the darkness covered. The glaring light destroys any illusion of grandeur. There are gashes in the walls, holes in the floorboards and cobwebs floating mid-air. A scratching sound comes from behind the thinly papered walls. And then, from upstairs, there is a faint sound, soft like a hungry kitten, crying.

"Good-bye, Mr. Gil." Miss Flora steps back into the shadows.

"Good-bye, ma'am."

"We have flapjacks pretty near ever' Sunday." The door closes behind her. And only then does Gil notice the words on the faded knocker, "Family Entrance."

Gil turns and makes his way back down the porch steps, seemingly more ravaged and dangerous than he had noticed before and picks up his bike. Then, he senses a presence. And for a split second, he sees a light coming from the second floor sun porch window. A woman's face presses against the glass.

Heat lightning flashes. Gil takes off on his bike, disappearing into a dawn spun with images that only vaguely catch his attention - a spider's web glistening in the orange kissed lilies, the long wooden tables with boxes spilling out gowns, the Auction sign, slightly bent, and the curious man wearing a white tunic, smelling of sweet cake, waiting at the corner. He is aware of a palette of colors – the deep fusia, the lavender blooms of the wild lilac and the rusts of hard dirt thirsty for summer's rain.

He rides, spinning the pedals of his well-loved pony made of tin.

Fireflies

CHAPTER ONE

Girl With the Ribbon

Alone on the second floor sun porch, Belle Brezing watches the paper boy take off on his bike. Disappearing into a sea of fireflies. Flickers of light, dancing on the lawn. Then she catches on that fireflies don't come with the dawn. Time is playing tricks. Or is it she – is she confused? Or are the fireflies confused? It is unnatural. Wind whispers across the windowsill, disturbing the once fine lace curtains. Lace from Brussels; gift of an admirer.

She leans in closer to the window and wonders at the reflection of the stranger with white hair, sunken cheeks and eyes that hold no light. This woman in the glass is small and frail, more bone than flesh. An unfamiliar visitor who has slipped into her beautiful kimono and stolen the soft silken threads, the glistening buttons and the embroidered white lilies that once mesmerized gentleman, old and young alike. Newspaper publishers, senators and horse racing kings; red-faced boys in pantaloons looking for their first taste of the female charms. And men, lonely, but loyal, worn down from taking care of wives that no longer smelt of lilac or jasmine. Belle shivers and tries to shut the window. But it is too hard. She forces herself to look through her gaunt face – out towards the hill where they are setting up tables for the auction. A chill settles over her heart.

And in that moment, she knows. She can feel her. The little girl. Out in the mist. Coming up the hill. A shadow child – unseen by everyone else. A child beyond the edges of memory, taunting her with vague feelings and dreams forgotten. Belle knows. She knows the little girl is out there, with the scavengers and scallywags comin' for the auction. Coming to pick at her things like black birds with broken wings. The little girl is looking for her. In her mind's eye, she sees the child. Staring hard. Staring up at the sun porch. A little girl with green eyes that betray nothing. She holds a burlap bag – all soggy and dirty. And she takes the tired white ribbon out of her hair - wildly disheveled, and a crown of tangled curls – and she ties up the bag. And looks up at the window, taunting Belle with the lost memory - the secret that is tied up in her rain soaked bag.

Frightened, Belle screams, "Mama".

Then she reaches for the needle, hidden in the folds of her kimono and pushes the shot of morphine into her bruised arm. Stumbling out of the wicker rocking chair, she makes her way back towards her bedroom. It is a shadow-box of memories, disappearing into nothingness. The fading grandeur suffocates beneath the ravages of time. What remains is papered walls with peeling roses and rosewood chests scratched by mice. It is a bedroom disappearing as quickly as the emaciated body of the woman who desperately tries to make her way to the bed, falls, and then rises, and curls up beneath the sheets.

Alone, desperately afraid, she does not see the tireless scorching of sunlight on heavy curtains or the rotting floorboards. For 59 Megowan Street is her sanctuary; untainted by Time. She sees the golden angel suspended mid-air above her great walnut bed. Her fingers brush across satin sheets, scented with lavender and a hint of rosewater. And her eyes shape beauty out of nothingness. She remembers 59 Megowan as the New York Times will soon describe the house on its front page, - "a gold-gilded mansion for men." For this is her palace. This is all she has between her and the little girl swinging the burlap bag, taunting her with the nursery rhyme, "Hush little baby, don't say a word. Mama's gonna buy you a mocking bird. If that mockingbird don't sing . . ."

Anxious, she reaches for one of the stray cats, eyeing her from beneath the rocker. His claws scratch air, narrowly missing her cheek. She loosens her hold and he escapes; retreating back behind the scattered piles of books – where the other cats, thin, misfits – one who walks with a terrible leaning to the side – all watch. Hungry black shadows with green and amber eyes. Watching.

Then suddenly, she hears footsteps on the stairs, coming up onto the landing. The door opens. Miss Flora searches in the dim light for the powerful mistress of Megowan. But that woman is gone. Vanished. Almost. And all that remains lies, like a discarded paper doll, beneath threadbare covers. Sweating from the fever. Emaciated and worn thin by the excruciating pain. Flora's keen eyes take in the room; Belle, in her silk black kimono, takes shape – lying in the big four poster bed.

"Pearl, shut the window."

Miss Flora shakes her head, muttering under her breath, "Now why you want me to do that, baby? You burnin' up with fever and ain't a lick of cool air stirring."

"Shut the window." There is something in Belle's voice – a desperate, almost shrill gasping of sound that catches Flora by surprise. She shuts the window. Locks it. "Shew it's hot. Nothin' but heat lightning. And those damn cicadas, clattering their wings. Gives me the chills, don't it now."

Belle struggles to raise her head, "She's comin'."

"Who baby? Ain't nobody comin' for you, Miss Belle." Miss Flora smoothes the cover, reaches behind Belle and lifts her head, real gentle like, back down on the feather pillow. Under her breath, she mutters- "Lordy, ain't nobody out there except a bunch of scallywags comin' to pick, pick, pick at the auction." Flora takes Belle's hand, gnarled and twisted by arthritis into her own strong hands and rubs the boney fingers, "Hush baby, you're safe."

Belle's eyelids flicker, a fluttering that seems to take the eyeballs back into the sockets. It unnerves Flora. She hums; small sips of air escape through Belle's parched lips. The pain is scorching her insides. Flora strokes Belle's thinning hair, damp from the raging fever, "Sh, sh, baby. Jest squeeze my hand when the pain gits too bad."

"Pearl? Pearl, don't leave me."

"Miss Belle, Pearl's gone. You know that. I'm Flora. Miss Pearl's girl. Mama's done passed." She lowers Belle's emaciated arm, trying not to see the scars; the popped blue veins, the blood scabbed over old scars. She leans in, smelling of flapjacks and bacon grease . . . of cabbage slaw and sugar beets. "Remember – we used to catch lightning bugs. You remember now. We'd put them in glass mayonnaise jars." She laughs. "Remember, we'd watch 'em glowing all yellow and flappin' their wings. It was jest like catching magic in a jar. Then you'd whisper, 'Let 'em go, Flora.' And I'd open the lid and let 'em out – so they could give their magic to a star." She turns slightly, looking out the window. "You reckon one of those lightning bugs is shinin' up in heaven – turned into a star?"

"Is it night, then?"

"No ma'am, morning. You rest. Sleep, Miss Belle. And when you wake-up, there will be a whole sky full of lightning bugs."

3

"Pearl sing. Please sing."

"Mama's done passed, Miss Belle. But I reckon she'll be waiting there. On that bridge between heaven and earth. Waitin' with Jesus and the lightning bugs to welcome you home."

Flora hums; her voice is raspy and earthy. She waits until Belle is breathing more calmly; then she goes out. The door creaks shut on rusted hinges.

CHAPTER TWO

Undelivered Papers

Gil flies down the hill, past the grand old painted ladies. He's almost to the corner when he slows the bike. Something's wrong. He can sense a tingling on the inside of his left palm. The hand that tosses the newspapers. The hand that still has the ink, which Miss Flora tried so hard to wash off. And Gil stops. He's got this feeling that he's being watched. He dares one look back up the Hill. At the house. But there is no one. His imagination is playing tricks. Still, he doesn't move. He waits, knowing that there's something he's forgotten to do. He slips the napkin out of his pocket and for the first time, notices the initials. *BB.*

And then he sees it: The newspaper still lying in the bike's basket. He hesitates; he doesn't want to go back up to that house on the Hill. He swallows hard. He's a paperboy. Delivering papers is what paperboys do. He'll just hit the porch with the paper and take off runnin'. No flapjacks. No chicory. No lookin' at naked ladies. Just hit the porch with the paper and the envelope and take off. Plain and simple. He can do it.

But once he's on the porch, the door opens. As if pushed by some unseen hand.

It just opens. And he steps back inside. Clutching the newspaper with his now sweating hand, he stands still in the entrance way. Listening. Not sure what he's listening for – but then he hears it. The same chilling lullaby, reverberating through the floorboards, the paper thin walls – the shadowed stairway. The singing/moaning comes from above; it is unnatural in its soft almost sing-song lilt. Gil, curious – more curious than he's ever been in his life – decides to risk being caught by Miss Flora and climbs the stairs. He pauses on the stairwell, staring up into the purple light streaming in through the stained glass. Something about that window is comforting to the paper boy; he feels as if he might be going up the steps to the First Methodist Church. It's kind of sacred like.

The lullaby comes from a room towards the end of the hallway. He walks slow, real slow down the floor, careful so as not to alarm Miss Flora or some of the other girls (whom Gil figures might be on their way to Church.) When he reaches the doorway, he stops. And stands quietly. Waiting. But the sound doesn't repeat.

Gil dares one quick look into the bedroom. Eerily quiet, suffocatingly hot, the room seems to be empty. He steps inside. And almost gags from the wretched smell of cats. Too many cats locked inside a bedroom without fresh air. He looks, but can't see a single cat. Slowly, holding his nose, he dares one step into the silent chamber. The bedroom's grandeur fades slowly in the iron grasp of Time. But everywhere there are Angels. Glass angels on the mantel. And angels swinging down from the ceiling. He steps around piles of books, touches the horn of a Texas Longhorn Chair and stares at a lamp shaped like a woman's leg. He blushes, turns and steals a glance at the large walnut bed. Above the bed hangs wall-paper decorated with images of a naked woman. Her wild red hair falls over her naked breasts; she holds a sword in one hand and a scepter in the other. She looks both powerfully fierce and comically sad. Slowly, Gil lifts up a piece of the torn wallpaper - filling in the missing "face".

Suddenly, he hears a loud thud. And then glass breaking. And a shrill, piercing scream. Gil, paralyzed by fear, realizes that he is not alone in the bedroom. Someone is in the room. He considers getting out of there . . . and then he sees something. The faintest movement of a small door. It's a closet, he figures. And he goes towards the closed door. He can feel his heart lunging against his rib-cage; but he leans down and stares into the closed door's key-hole. Clearly visible is a woman, shooting a needle into her badly bruised arm. She's standing in broken glass; and a chair tilts forward, blocking the door. As if sensing his presence, she raises her eyes – and looks straight at him.

Gil gasps.

The woman shoves the chair out of the way.

Suddenly the closet door flies open.

A woman, dressed in a kimono, her wild hair falling over her face, lunges towards the boy. "Wait. Please . . . help me."

Gil can't get out of there fast enough; he's almost to the door when she cries out again "Please, help. Help me." Something in her voice makes him turn around.

"The needle's broke off in my arm. Please . . ." She stretches out her boney, needle-punctured arm. Gil stares hard. A tiny trickle of blood stains her wrist where the needle lies half-buried in her parchment like skin.

"I'll git Miss Flora."

"No. She won't understand. Please."

Gil stares into the woman's eyes; they are light green and mesmeric. He turns, calls out, "Miss Flora!"

Suddenly, as if she has been listening just outside the door, Miss Flora enters.

Gil steps back, "She's . . . she's got . . ."

"Flora, the needle's broken off in my arm." Belle speaks, without emotion.

Flora goes immediately to Belle; she tries to loosen the needle; it's deep in the skin. Impulsively she leans in and bites the needle with her teeth. Spits it out. Gil, pale and frightened, stares. Hard. Miss Flora firmly takes the woman around the waist, calmly holding her, "You're safe, Miss Belle. You're safe, baby."

Belle tightens her grasp on Miss Flora's strong arm, "Thank you, Pearl." She catches her reflection in a mirror above a vanity table and sweeps her gnarled fingers through her wet hair, "Oh, my rouge. Please - and a comb."

Miss Flora brushes Belle's hair out of her face, "Now Miss Belle, you know who I am." She turns, looking at Gil as if actually seeing him for the first time, "I'm Pearl's daughter, Flora. Mama's done passed. I been fixing you flapjacks pretty near twenty years now."

Belle leans in, "I want to go to my dressing table. Please." She straightens her back slightly, letting Flora guide her over to the small chair in front of the vanity mirror. Then, with an attempt at dignity, she sinks into the chair, facing the mirror and winces. She is in agonizing pain.

"You just squeeze my hand when the pain gits too bad." She glances at Gil, whose face is now also reflected in the mirror. "Gil, you better go on now."

Belle stares into the glass, "No, Pearl. No. I don't want him to leave." She whispers, "Pearl, where's my rouge?" She sweeps her fingers across the table, as if unable to see clearly - picking up a powder box, silver brush.

"My lipstick? Her red-painted nails flail wildly in the air. Then she sweeps everything – old nail polish bottles, compacts, lipsticks onto the floor.

Miss Flora remains calm; she leans down and picks up the fancy rouge box. Belle's hands are shaking; she can't apply the rouge. Miss Flora puts some rouge on Belle's face; she paints Belle's face as if coloring a paper doll.

Belle sees Gil looking at her in the mirror and turns. "Do you know who I am?"

Gil shakes his head – uable to speak.

"I'm Belle." She smiles, and a flicker of light appears in her eyes. "Madame Belle Brezing." She gestures with a refined sweep of her hand, "Take something. The spoils of War."

Gil shakes his head, "No ma'am, I don't want nothin'."

She looks him straight in the eye, "Don't be so proud. All this will be gone soon enough. 'Gone with the wind, Flung roses dancing... lost lilies out of mind . . .'" The lines of the poem hang in the air – as if waiting for the poet to come and place them back in proper order. Like neatly folded pieces of laundry. "Please, I'd like for you to have something."

Gil suddenly sheds his shyness; he seizes the moment. This moment. Why he came here on this particular morning. His voice surprises him. "No ma'am, see it's the other way round. I brung you something." He holds out the newspaper; carefully folded inside the paper is an envelope; he slips out several letters tied with a ribbon. "My Uncle Billy wrote these letters when he was real sick; he asked my mama to deliver these to you - but she forgot and so now . . . well, here."

He holds out the letters.

Belle stares at the letters; unable to speak. Only her eyes betray the deep abyss into which she is sinking. And the perfectly made-up face, the mask that betrays so little of the real woman, cracks. And Gil sees this. Belle drops the lipstick but not before smearing the red across her lower lip; she shivers and her eyes dart back and forth, uncomfortable seeing what she is being asked to see. Finally, she turns, staring back into the mirror. At Gil's reflection – only not at the boy. It is as if the letters cast a spell on her; she seems to disappear into the smoky glass – disappear into whatever strange portal those letters had opened before the dying woman. When she does speak, after a considerable silence, she says simply "I - I can't read them."

Miss Flora holds out her hand to Gil, "Why don't you just leave them here and . . ."

Gil, surprised by his own courage, steps past Miss Flora and stares straight at Belle. "Ma'am, I – I don't mean you no disrespect ..."

"Mr. Gil . . ." Miss Flora isn't used to being stepped around; she clucks her tongue and reaches again for the letters.

Gil keeps talking, "Uncle Billy wrote these letters to you when he was real sick; and he made my mama promise, cross her heart and swear on the Bible that she'd make sure you got them. So they've just got to be real important or Uncle Billy wouldn't have made my mother swear on the Bible, but she – she let Uncle Billy down. A whole lot of folks have let my mama down and she let Billy down by forgetting. And he was too sick to deliver them himself. You just got to read 'em so my mama can get something right. Please, don't let it be too late. Can you just read them? Please, ma'am." He holds out the letters.

Belle finds the lipstick; she uses it to stir the ice in a tarnished mint julep cup holding some amber liquid. And she sips the drink, slowly. "No . . . my eyes aren't good anymore. I - I can't read." She lets the bourbon take effect. "Take them back. Please thank your mother. It's Mary, isn't it? Tell her that I . . . I'm sorry if I hurt her. If I hurt Billy."

Gil feels the anger rise up in his throat, "Ma'am . . . sorry ain't goin' fix nothing." He can't believe he's saying the words; they fly out of his mouth. The words seem to be swimming out there in the air – swimming with the sound of the ice clinking against the hard silver rim of the mint julep glass. He feels his legs shaking against his knickers.

And then, unexpectedly, all the emotions that have been pushed down – all the whippings at the orphange and all the plates of cold potatoes and the look of his mama in her grey dress sitting in the concrete room at the Asylum – they all come shooting up, pouring out of his skin and his soul and he speaks. "You broke my Uncle Billy's heart. He died and now my mama's nerves ain't good and she's in an Asylum and I'm stuck in an orphanage with a mad woman who beats me and all the other boys. And starves us. You're sorry?" He slaps the letter hard against his open fist – a little too hard. He winces from the sting.

She, however, stands perfectly still -"You have Billy's eyes."

Something in her voice - not a plea - but rather strength, catches Gil by surprise. He looks at her. As if seeing her for the first time. Standing in front of him, in her black kimono splashed with flowers, and a blush of pink on her cheeks (from the fever or perhaps rouge), he feels sorry for her. "My Uncle Billy wanted you to hear something pretty bad . . ."

She whispers, "I could tell you things about your Uncle Billy."

". . . so I reckon the right thing for you to do is . . . please, just read them."

Gil holds out the letters.

Belle reaches out her hand. There is a moment when their fingers brush. When she feels the warmth, the life-force flowing through his ink-stained hands and realizes that he is so young, so terribly terribly young. And at that exact same moment, he feels the icy chill of her fingers, reaching across twenty years of anguish and loneliness – reaching for this unexpected gift from a mere boy, a paper boy.

"Perhaps you could read them to me. Pearl could fix you a cup of her chicory coffee."

Gil sighs, grateful that he's accomplished what he came there that morning to do. But he sure as heck is not going to risk another cup of that chicory coffee; he figures it could be some of that *black magic* he's heard some of the other boys at Short Street talk about. The kind of *black magic* that makes you do things you wouldn't ordinarily do – like *basket making*, or *playing St. George* or havin' an *amorous congress*. But he's not going to lie to Madam Belle Brezing, so he just says, "Thank ya, ma'am, Miss Flora makes a real good cup of chicory coffee but I got to deliver more papers or I'll lose my paper route and boys at Short Street don't usually get paper routes." He wonders where on earth he's coming up with all these little white lies and he finally just stops talking. "Thank you, ma'am." He glances at Miss Flora who's staring at him. "It was real nice to meet ya'll."

Gil walks to the door; and then he hears something. A loud rapping against glass. He turns and sees a red bird. Pecking hard at the sun porch window. And almost without thinking he says, "Uncle Billy always said you were a lady."

Miss Flora suddenly throws up her arms, shews the bird away – "Go on. Git. Git out'a here."

Then, she follows Gil out the door.

As the door closes behind them, the bird flies closer to the glass, pecks hard and disappears.

CHAPTER THREE

Falling Feathers

Belle holds the letters. Silent. Still. For a long long time. Then she makes her way towards the sun porch, towards her faithful rocking chair. But she's weak; unsteady. Frightened, she stumbles back towards the bed. Exhausted, she sinks down. Burning up with fever, she waits. Staring at the letters that seem suddenly very heavy. Weighted down with a life-time of regret. Of words left unspoken. Secrets left untold.

Alone in her bedroom for the past twenty years, she now feels as if the face in the wallpaper is looking at her. Judging her. She is aware of the letters, slipping from her fingers. She is utterly and completely alone. Alone. In a bedroom of mirrors catching the light of glass angels. On the fireplace mantel. Hanging on the wall; near the bed. In her morphine-induced sleep, Belle knows the glass angels are staring at her. Waiting and watching. Watching for the little girl with the tired white ribbon. Outside. On the lawn. Staring up at the sun porch.

Restless, she struggles to shed the blanket and opens her eyes. The faces of girls – her girls, her lovely, long lost girls appear in the mirror over the mantel and take shape in the collection of crystal angels. The girls' faces distort; she turns away, staring at the figure painted on the wallpaper. A thin, red-haired figure, wearing ribbons and slippers tied up with gold laces. The woman's face is ugly, Belle thinks and yet, vaguely familiar. She turns away, restless, frightened. Then, from outside, closer now – perhaps right beneath her window, Belle hears the girl, whispering the lullabye. She reaches for the morphine and needle, hidden behind the Bible and accidentally sweeps her hand against a photograph of a dark-haired man, smoking a cigar. The glass frame shatters as it hits the floor. She grasps the needle, pushes it into her raw skin, "It's not enough. It's not enough."

From outside, in the wind there is the voice of the child, singing in a soft, sing-song lilt, "If that mockingbird don't sing, mama's gonna buy me a diamond ring." The little girl, swinging the burlap bag, is coming towards the window. Closer and closer. And then, Belle sees her. The child is slipping through the window and staring at Belle. Then the little girl slowly, oh so slowly, makes her way towards the bed. Terrified, Belle shuts her eyes. Tight.

"Oh God, please. Billy! Billy! Oh God, why did you take my Billy?"

In excruciating pain and fear, she sinks down, cradling her head with her hands, she cries out, "Oh God, help." As she lies there, she slowly opens her eyes and sees a single feather float down – from seemingly out of nowhere. Then she hears whistling. It is the kind of whistling that comes straight from the soul of a tireless, loyal paperboy. And magically, a dusty, elegant grandfather clock takes shape in the shadows. A hidden door in the clock opens. An intense white light floods the bedroom. And into this light dances Billy Mabon. Dressed in tails with a dead corsage on his lapel, he carries the morning newspaper. He leans over and whistles; it's a jaunty, playful tune and the whistling seems to play with the light. The chandelier glows. There is a brilliant light around Billy – not so much an aura but rather a field of energy that is dazzling. An effervescence that transforms the energy inside the bedroom. His very presence raises the vibration. And Belle's pain disappears.

He glances at the broken phonograph player near Belle's bed; the lid lifts; the arm moves out over and then down. And suddenly, a jazz piece plays. Pleased with this little magic, he slides down the banister and lands with great style. He walks over to the bed, gazes lovingly into Belle's face and then lightly kisses her on her lips.

"Hello, Kitten. Missed me?" His voice is strong, masculine with an engaging southern charm.

Belle, eyes closed, breathes shallow sips of air; she is restless. But does not waken at his touch.

Billy, undaunted, walks over to the mantel, removes a brick inside the fireplace and takes out a tarnished silver case. He blows off the dust and takes out several Cuban cigars and slips one inside his coat pocket. He sniffs the cigar, delights in the memory of its delicious scent, and then lights it by simply placing his left palm directly above the cigar tip. He takes a puff, enjoying the cigar with relish.

Belle, restless, gasps.

"Wake up, Kitten. It's time to dream the life you've forgotten. Wake-up, my beautiful Belle. I'm here. I've always been here. So close." He gently brushes his hand over her head; rose petals fall down over her hair and cheeks. The wrinkles soften, then disappear. Her hair glistens; and her mouth, rose-tinted, quivers. "Come, sweet Kitten, awaken to dance."

Belle relaxes but does not awaken.

Billy turns to the mantel; he blows dust off photographs of several young women; he smiles, as if he knows them. Then he sees a photograph, turned face-down. He lifts it, turns the picture towards the moonlight and stares for a long time into the face of a girl with long, auburn hair, smiling from a distant past. He steps back, sighs and makes his way over to a sewing box on a bedside table.

He takes out a dusty bottle of whiskey and holds it up to what little light is filtering through the heavy curtains. Then grins, relishing in the expectation of what lies in this bottle. Fine bourbon whiskey, bottled in bond, 1917. He considers opening the bourbon. Why not. This is expensive bourbon – the finest. Unlike the cheaper, imitation whiskeys aged in wood chips to mimic the color. Just one drink. He looks for a glass.

Belle suddenly cries out in pain. Billy walks over to the bed and again looks lovingly down into Belle's face. Slowly, he holds out his palms. A white light emanates out from his fingers; he moves his hands in small circles directly above her heart and breathes deeply, calmly. "Kitten?"

And Belle awakens. She doesn't see Billy at first. She senses his presence. Slowly, she reaches up her fingers and touches his face. There is a tingling sensation; she stares at the gold light that connects her hand with his face. "Billy? Billy? My Billy! Is this possible?"

Billy grins.

"I've missed you so much." She fingers the corsage. "What's this? Oh my god, last time I saw you in this coat and tails, darlin', you were lyin' horizontal."

"You saw me lying horizontal a'lot, sugar."

"Billy, am I . . .?"

"Belle, darlin', you're beautiful as ever." He leans down, kisses her and holds out his arms. His gesture is very empowering. He invites her spirit up out of her body. "Come Kitten, awaken to dance."

Belle, as a radiant, luminous spiritual being, rises out of her former physical body. Her old, discarded body, like a coat that no longer serves a purpose on a surprisingly warm day, slips back down onto the bed. Spirit-Belle, who looks as if she might be in her early or mid-thirties, is exquisite, with hair the color of a summer's sunset (a shade all its own worthy of christening magnificent thoroughbreds bred just for that color!), fine features and luminous skin. Belle holds out her arms to Billy, "Is this the last dance?"

"Remember, you always promised that one to me." Billy gestures to the phonograph player, and as he takes her into his arms, a waltz plays. And they dance beneath the crystal chandelier, spinning slowly, ever so slowly. Turning back time.

Around her, Belle senses, rather than actually sees, the familiar bedroom fade. It does not completely disappear but rather seems to exist in a different dimension. Only faintly visible. The room expands and grows ever more translucent. Then, another scene takes shape. Belle, still held in her lover's arms, hears the music box melody disappear into a waltz played by a full orchestra. And suddenly, she is no longer dancing in Billy's arms.

She is slightly younger than her Spirit, late twenties, gorgeous with her auburn hair pulled up in pearls. She stands on a half-moon stairway outside the Phoenix Hotel. A light rain is falling. Guests, in elegant attire, step around her, past her, entering through the glass revolving door. Belle moves away from the door and stares through a large glass window.

Inside the hotel, the guests, in their gowns and black tie tuxedos, enter a ballroom. There's a large banner above the dance-floor, "Lexington Charity Ball For Our Orphans". Belle curls her gloved hand into a fist and starts to hit the glass pane. Suddenly, Billy, also in a tux, comes up behind her and kisses her shoulder.

"Dance with me."

Young Belle, flushed with anger, shakes her head.

"Come on, Kitten, dance with me." He leans in closer, whispers, "They're not worth it." He pulls her towards him, down the stairs and then whirls her out. Her black cape falls open, revealing her girlish figure, her stunning gold gown glistening with crystals. Music from inside the hotel seeps out through the revolving door as more guests arrive – raising eyebrows at the dancing couple. Billy whistles along; and as they dance, the rain turns to snow.

"Belle, open your eyes."

She does. And gazes in wonder at the snowflakes, swirling around her. "How do you do it?"

"What?" He gently kisses a snowflake on her hair.

"This." She reaches out her hands and catches the snowflakes. "Always make me forget who I am."

Billy turns her into him, pulls her close. "Some tricks are easier than others." They dance for a moment. And then he lifts her face, gazing into her green eyes, "Promise me something, Belle."

"What?"

"No matter what happens, you'll always save the last dance for me."

She tries to kiss him; he looks straight in her eyes, "Promise."

"Promise."

As they kiss, the snow falls. And slowly, the orchestra fades back into the tinny waltz on the phonograph. Billy whirls her around; her bare feet touch the wood floors of her bedroom. The Phoenix Hotel, a memory, closes into the past.

Belle, furious, stomps her foot. "I gave five hundred dollars and a dozen new sheets to the Short Street Orphans' Home but the snobby old Lexington bitties wouldn't take a cent or the sheets."

Billy considers his cigar, changes his mind. "Now Belle, honey, that was forty years ago." He takes her hand, moves her towards the long, petticoat mirror, "Will you look at her?"

Belle catches her reflection. She stares, then backs away from the mirror, turns around and stares again. Delighted with her youthful body, she gazes at her reflection with approving eyes. Impulsively, she slips the white gown over her head and stands naked in front of the mirror. Admiring her body. She turns, catching Billy watching her in the mirror.

"Don't get too stuck on yourself." He throws her a kimono.

"Billy, is this a dream or the morphine?" She slips into the kimono, ties the sash and turns away from her reflection.

Suddenly, the grandfather clock, dust-covered, in a far corner of the bedroom, chimes. Belle glances at the clock, "Why – it hasn't chimed in twenty years."

"Time to move on."

The clock continues to chime. And in the night-wind there is another sound. A chiming of church bells. "Is that Christ Church bells? Damn, so it's as bad as all that."

"Change of costumes; that's all." Billy steps back, bows slightly and gestures towards the dusty grandfather clock "Ladies first."

Spirit Belle hesitates, as if she doesn't or can't see the Grandfather clock clearly. Then, slowly, the moon shaped face and stars take shape on the glass door. She catches her breath. Glances at Billy and then with absolute fearless resolution, she ties the ribbon on her kimono and marches straight to the mysterious Clock. Billy lets out a soft whistle, admiring her style. Belle places her hand firmly on the small knob on the clock's face. And turns the knob.

CHAPTER FOUR

Kitten

"Damn, Billy, the Door's locked."

"Well, honey, maybe you're early. What time is it?" Billy glances at a pocket-watch and nonchalantly opens the newspaper.

Belle's green eyes flash, "Billy Mabon!"

"Yep, ya don't die until four thirty. You might jest as well come on over here. Ya ain't dead yet. You don't die for another couple of hours."

"You knew damn well 'I ain't dead yet.' Just why have you come back, Billy Mabon."

"Calm down, Kitten. Come on down here and sit beside old Billy for ole time's sake."

"Old time's sake, my ass." She tries the door knob; shakes it.

"Hey careful, Kitten, just cuz it's locked don't mean someone isn't listening."

This gets her attention; Belle steps back from the Clock. Billy sits down in a chair with long-horns attached to its arms. He smoothes his hands along the horns, grinning up at Belle who sits down on the bottom stair. Staring at him.

"Just why have you come back, Billy?"

He looks at her, "Perhaps love is a way of leading someone gently back to self."

"What the heck does that mean anyway? Have you gone and got religious?"

He gets up and goes over to sit beside her on the chaise, "Death has that effect." He leans in to kiss her. She gets up, walks away.

"Under the circumstances, Billy, I think a "tiff" is in bad taste."

"What circumstances?"

"My death." She kicks out her leg; he catches her ankle, playfully and she pulls away but not before giving him a small kick, carefully aimed.

He scoots back, "Whoa, I'd forgotten what a hell-cat you are, Kitten." He whistles.

She smiles at him, flirting, "You still have that little scar?"

Billy starts to roll up his pants leg, "Yeah, some things– old scars and broken hearts – they slip through from one life to the next. Ya want to see?"

"No thanks, I'll take your word. But you brought that on, Billy. You never could hold your bourbon."

Billy leans back, stretches his arms up over his head, "Hey babe, I thought you closed Megowan – what's with Miss Flora and her girls?"

"You're changing the subject."

"They're not your style – remind me of rather flamboyant flamingoes if you get my drift. Of course, you've been stuck in that bed like roasted hot corn husks for the last twenty . . .?"

Spirit Belle arches an eyebrow, "I could make you disappear. Just like that." She snaps her fingers.

"Yeah, but you won't."

She sighs, "Those black hearted officers gave me orders to close Megowan; they thought my girls would be too much of a distraction for the boys who needed to be soldiers focused on saving the world for democracy. So I did as I was told. Miss Flora must have moved in those other girls while I was powdering my nose." She sulks.

"Well times change."

"I wish you would stop referring to me as if I were almost dead. I'm very much alive and looking marvelous."

"The only woman I ever loved, darlin', is lying in that bed. I've waited twenty years for our last dance. I figure I can wait until dawn breaks."

Billy smiles; it is a smile without judgment or acknowledgement. An expression only of holding her in love. "Hey, cheer up, sugar, you're gonna be famous. A southern belle from Atlanta named Margaret Mitchell put you in her book, **Gone With the Wind**. That was several years ago and now, the book's been made into a movie. It's playing at the Kentucky Theatre."

Curious, Belle leans over Billy's shoulder and massages his neck.

He takes her hand and pulls her down onto his lap, "The movie opened last Saturday."

"Really? Am I the belle?"

"No, that's Scarlet O'Hara, honey. You're Belle Watling. The Madam. She's kind of a big woman with red hair – voluptuous and . . ."

"I don't think so. You're mistaken. She used some other madam for the ..."

"No, you're the inspiration. There's plenty of evidence linking you to the madam. Margaret Mitchell's husband, John Marsh was a reporter for the paper here in Lexington and he . . ."

"I have never heard of him in my life!"

"Well he heard of you, kitten. He was a reporter here a few years back; assigned the red light district. And well – Ms. Watling and you got a whole lot more than the first name in common."

"Oh? Charismatic and rather foxy?"

"Yeah, something like that I guess. Red hair and a child stuck in some institution."

Belle grabs for the newspaper and tries to hit him; Billy gently takes it out of her hand. She reacts to his strength and retreats over to the window. "Mr. Marsh should have made his intentions known." She winks at Billy.

"Always got to get the last shot."

Belle curls up on a chaise lounge. "I'm going to take a little cat nap until it's time."

"Hey, curious, darling? You make the paper again. Front page. Lexington Herald. All copies are going to be sold out by 10:00 am. August 11th." He throws the paper; Belle catches it – but barely.

"Billy, even as my paper boy, you never could throw the paper straight." She opens the paper, "Isn't there a picture?"

"Course now Time Magazine gets the parting word." He pulls a Time Magazine out of his coat and opens it. "Died. Belle Brezing. August 11, 1940. Famed Kentucky bawd."

Belle springs off the chaise and grabs the magazine. "That's my obituary? Eighty years of amorous congress, romance and *clicket* and all I get is 'bawd'?" She tosses the magazine back over her shoulder and rummages through her wardrobe, taking out moth-eaten but once glamorous gowns. "Oh well, what difference does it make now? I'm discarding that old body and . . . hey, I do get to look like this? Right? And in a few hours that Door will open and . . ." She holds up a black taffeta dress then turns to an emerald green dress with pearls sewn into the bodice.

"Maybe."

She's still musing over the gowns, "Maybe?"

"Maybe not."

She puts the gowns back in the wardrobe and turns, facing him, "I'm no good at guessing games, Billy."

"All I know is if that Door's still locked by half past nine, well, ya don't get in."

"I don't die August 11th . . .?"

"No, you die all right. You just stay here."

Spirit Belle drops all the gowns and stares into the mirror on the back of the wardrobe – "As a ghost?" She shivers, then turns. There is something very child-like and innocent in her face. "Oh but I won't be alone, Billy. You'll be here. It will be like old times. Lets' go to New York!" She starts to wrap her arms around Billy; he gets up, moves towards the clock. His look unnerves her.

"No, Belle. I'm sorry. Regardless of what happens to you, I still go back."

Belle stares at him, pulls up her hair off her neck and clasps it with a brooch ripped off the emerald gown. Her mouth closes in a firm, almost stoic expression. "I should have known someone like me wouldn't get to heaven." She sweeps the gowns off of the chaise lounge and sits down in the middle of them. Billy holds out his hand to her. She refuses.

"You're wrong, darlin'. It's not that. It's something else."

"How do you know?"

"Well, they've got a few madams up there already. Look, all you got to do is tell the truth."

Spirit Belle closes the lids on the polish. "About what?"

"Yourself."

Spirit Belle slowly rises up out of the taffeta and satin gowns; she throws back her head and laughs. The laugh catches Billy by surprise. "Oh, so that's why you've come. You – nothing more than a wisp of memory- a dream gift from a drug? You're not real, Billy – anymore than that ugly woman in the wall paper is real. You and she – you're just something imagined. You died. You're dead. But I – I had to live. Don't you – whoever you are – whatever being sent you – dare judge me."

"I'm not judging you, Belle."

She suddenly begins to rip the wallpaper – peeling away the roses and the woman's scantily clad body. "I decided my life. I owned this house and this town. I owned all the judges and the lawyers. I never spent one night in jail. Once a week, I got in my carriage and Joey and two bay horses drove me to the bank where I delivered my week's earnings in a paper sack. Every week I went to a different bank; I had accounts in every bank in this town." Her voice rises, shaking with emotion. She stands back and admires her work; she has stripped the wall bare. The paper lies in curls around her bare feet. "Bawd! Who the hell writes the obituaries?!"

"Hungry reporters."

Billy hands her a pillow; she turns on him – hitting him hard with the pillow. Feathers fly. He ducks. "Bawd! The dying should be allowed to write their own obituaries. 'Died. Bewitching Belle Brezing. Exquisite Mary Magdalene of a repressed southern town. Husbands, fathers and sons whispered their sexual fantasies and my girls gave these up-tight, morally righteous, sexually repressed gentleman what their wives wouldn't. Sex. Bawd, my sweet ass!"

She hits the bed with the pillow, over and over again. Nearly hitting the frail body of her former self. Only when a feather floats down over dying Belle's mouth, does Billy intervene and grab the featherless pillow. "Whoa, easy Kitten. You also spent the last twenty years of your life rotting away on a dilapidated sun porch. The rising Phoenix of the first fifty years doesn't fit with the recluse – the victim – of the last twenty."

"How dare you accuse me of being a victim. I am not a victim. I have never been a victim and I will never be a victim. My life was my choice. I simply lived with the consequences of my choices."

"You actually believe that?"

She retreats to the long-horn chair and curls up with Time Magzine, ripping out the obituary. Billy goes to her; his voice is gentler, "You didin't live with the consequences, Belle. You buried yourself in booze and morphine." He takes the magazine out of her hands. "Come on, Kitten, I wouldn't be here if you didn't want some peace with you past."

Spirit Belle puts down the magazine. From downstairs, in the kitchen, Flora's humming seeps into the bedroom. It has a strong effect on Spirit Belle; she dares a darting glance at her old body, lying, feverish and yet so very still, beneath the bed sheets.

"You're scaring me, Billy. Stop it." She suddenly opens a drawer and muses over nail polishes. She brings out two polishes and holds each up to the light. "Poppy pink or sunburnt . . ."

"Belle, honey, what are you doing?"

"I want to look nice for tomorrow."

"Kitten, there ain't gonna be nobody there except for a couple of grave diggers."

Spirit Belle dips the tiny brush in both colors and paints her nails – polka dot pink and orange. She waves her fingers dramatically – drying them with her breath, "What! Nobody comes to my funeral? What about doc . . . oh, what's his name? And Pearl?"

"Doc's wife won't let him and Pearl's been dead for the last fifteen years. You didn't even bother to go to her funeral."

Spirit Belle is genuinely surprised. "Really? But who's been singing?"

"Flora Hudson. She's moved in downstairs."

"Oh yes. I knew that. I simply forgot."

"You're forgettin' a whole bunch of things, Belle."

She gets up, restless, circles the room. "I'm no good at guessing games, Billy. Just shoot straight with me!"

He only looks at her; his eyes filled with compassion.

"Oh what is that look now. Pity? Don't feel sorry for me, Billy. It's an unbecoming look on your handsome face." Spirit Belle impulsively opens the window – letting in sounds of the cicada, clattering their wings. She has a strong reaction to the sound and turns to face Billy. "If I had a pistol, I'd shoot those god-damn cicadas."

His voice lowers; he casts a glance at the door at the Door. "Sh-sh, just because the Door's locked, Kitten, doesn't mean someone ain't listening."

She whispers back, "Yeah – like who? God?"

A solitary white feather floats down. Billy catches the feather and gently places it in Spirit Belle's hair.

"It's gonna be a long night."

Spirit Belle, her hair now wildly falling around her face, walks over to the sun porch and opens the window. "Pearl's right. It's hot." She shakes her hair – "Miss Flora . . . . Flora's right. It's powerful hot." From outside, the clattering of the cicada wings beats the air, fast and deliberate, like a gavel rapping wood. She leans out the windowsill, breathing in the night air. And then sees the tables set up in the lawn. She digs her fingernails into the wood sill. "Why those yellow bellied, blood sucking buzzards. What's in those boxes, Billy? Is that . . . oh my god, they're auctioning off my gowns." She glances back at the pile of gowns lying on the floor. "What's going on? I don't understand . . . how can something be in two places at the same time?"

"Time is an illusion, Belle. Things exist – in different dimensions, sometimes simultaneously."

She looks at him. "I don't know what the hell you're talking about. But I'm going to take care of this now." She runs back to the pile and scoops up the gowns. A black taffeta dress slips out of her grasp; she clings to it. "I wore this the night we opened Megowan. The Senator said I looked like "starlight swept up . . ."

Billy finishes the sentence ". . . in a bed of roses."

Spirit Belle turns to Billy; her eyes are filled with a deep longing, a longing for something not even she can put in words. A secret from herself. "I'm lost, Billy. Please, get me out of here before that Auction. I don't want to see people who shunned me in life laughing and mocking me – pawing my belongings after I'm gone."

Billy closes the window. He shuts out the eerie beating of the cicada wings.

"Help me, please."

He holds her, lovingly smoothing her hair out of her face and looks into her eyes. "Easy, Kitten. You don't have to be here. It's up to you." He offers her a sip of the "elixir" in the mint julep cup. She starts to take a drink, then notices the cup. She takes it out of Billy's hands and holds it up to the light, 'To Kitten.'

"No – wait. I'm ready but just wait. I only need a minute or two." She turns away, and impulsively opens the wardrobe. Rising up on her toes, she feels the top shelf and brings out a package wrapped in lilac scented tissue. As she unwraps the tissue, Billy waits, watching. Spirit Belle holds up the two delicate glass perfume bottles, with flowers painted on the outside. "These are from Paris. I'm going to hide these with the mint julep glass. You understand, Billy. I've got to do this." She marches over to the mantel, lifts a secret brick.

Behind her, the crystal chandelier begins to fade. And as this light grows dim, Billy also begins to disappear. He glances at the grandfather clock, then says in a voice that is both calm and compassionate, "Belle, this is your choice."

She doesn't turn around; she's wrapping up the perfume bottles, slipping them into the secret hiding place. Then, she feels something. A chill. And she whips around – terrified that Billy has left her. He's still there – but fading in and out of the twilight.

"Billy!"

"Maybe I was wrong. Maybe you just haven't tasted loneliness long enough."

Spirit Belle drops the mint julep cup; it hits the floor, with a ringing sound against the wood. "How dare you! I've tasted loneliness all my life.

After you died, I thought I couldn't bear the loneliness or the silence. That's all death is, Billy. Silence."

"I can't help you. You're still clinging onto life." Billy starts towards the dusty grandfather clock, becoming more and more translucent.

Spirit Belle runs after him, grabbing hold of his shoulders which seem to disappear beneath her grasp. She holds nothing more than moonlight and air. Terrified, she looks up after him, "Billy, don't you dare leave me again."

He doesn't turn around. "You're not ready for that Door to open."

"Don't condemn me to this . . ."

"To what?" He stops; turns and looks at her. "This pretty doll house. Or just how long has it been since you played dolls, Kitten. Take a good hard look at the rats, the stinking garbage, the rotting . . . Stay here. Have tea with the mice. They look rather scrawny."

"Billy, get back here."

CHAPTER FIVE

A storybook

Billy turns around.

A white feather falls slowly down; it lands on a tattered child's story book, lying near the rocking chair. Billy walks towards Spirit Belle and as he does, he materializes into clearer physical form. He casually picks up the book and holds it out, "Here read yourself back to sleep."

Belle goes after him, "Billy, wait! You know damn well I called you back here tonight. Why can't that clock just chime or that Door open or do whatever the hell it's supposed to do for me to be with you?"

"My beautiful, darlin' Belle, will you trust me to lead you gently back to self?" He places the second feather in the storybook.

She reaches up, gently touches his face, "Billy, you've changed. I don't remember you being this smart."

Billy grins. He waves the storybook; a few worn pages slip out. Belle leans down, gathering up the pages, "I thought Mama burned this book."

"Recognize it?"

"Yes, it's my storybook. The one I had as a child."

"Close your eyes." He places the storybook in her hands.

"How can I read with my eyes closed?"

"Read from the heart."

Spirit Belle closes her eyes. She tries to remember; slowly, the memory washes over her – in waves, "Once upon a time, there was a duckling."

The chandelier casts a prism across the faded storybook. Slowly, the bedroom disappears into a different dimension of time. There is the sound of new-born kittens, meowing, softly.

Spirit Belle holds the storybook closer to her heart. Images – only wisps of form appear. Rain soaked sheets flapping in a strong wind. A wicker basket . . . a wild-eyed hen, pecking hard earth. Then the bedroom completely disappears and Spirit Belle, still holding the storybook, stands next to Billy in a muddy yard where sheets rise and fall on a clothes line. They billow out, then slap the hard ground. It is an eerie sound.

"What do you see, Belle?"

"Sheets. White sheets rising and falling in a strong wind. Slapping the ground. There's no grass, only mud." As she remembers, the sheets and clothes line take shape. The memory slowly materializes into shadows that then sharpen into substance and form.

"What else?"

"Behind the sheets . . . there's a house. It's all tired out. Nothin' but scraped white paint and broken window panes . . . And there's a child."

"A happy child?"

"Yes." Belle stares at the child. "No."

And the memory unfolds.

The little girl walks away from the house, towards the edge of a circle of pine trees. There, in a field, she kneels down beside a freshly dug grave. Her small fingers sprinkle dirt on a burlap bag, lying in the shallow grave. The bag is tied with a tired white ribbon. As she gently gathers the dirt and throws it on the grave, she whispers, half-singing, "Hush, little baby, don't say a word. Mama's gonna buy you . . . mama's . . ." Suddenly, her voice quivers. She stops singing and firmly presses wild violets on the mounded earth. A strong wind blows, scattering white blooms from a giant catalpa. The leaves shiver, revealing a boy's face. He watches, hiding in the tree branches.

The little girl tries to fold her hands in prayer over her heart, but she can't do this. She closes her eyes, holding back tears.

Around her, a sea of iridescent fireflies take shape in the coming dusk.

The little girl opens her eyes; she holds out her hands, capturing a lightning bug. And she watches the firefly, glowing a green yellow and hitting its fragile wings against her fingers. Slowly, she opens her hand, freeing the lightning bug. It slips into a cloud of fireflies, spinning their light, disappearing into the stars.

Then a woman's piercing voice shatters the stillness, "Belle! Mary Belle Cox git in here. Belle!"

And the memory disappears into nothingness.

Spirit Belle closes the storybook, "I – I can't remember." Her hands shake; there is a wild, terrified look in her eyes.

"Belle, you're safe." Billy takes the storybook out of her hands and holds her. "We'll let the gentler memories come first."

CHAPTER SIX

Angel wings

Seemingly unaware of the memory's paralyzing effect on Spirit Belle, Billy casually lights a cigar. And blows smoke rings. Then pops his finger through one of the rings of smoke, and pretends to juggle the rings. Holding the cigar between his lips, he leans down, pulling dust bunnies out from under the bed.

"Billy, what are you looking for?"

He pulls out an old travelers' trunk. Takes a key out of his pocket and opens the lid. It's papered with roses. An intoxicatingly sweet aroma fills the room. Spirit Belle, frightened, steps back. Staring at the trunk.

"I told Pearl to give that trunk away."

"Pearl did." Billy holds out the key to Belle. "She hid the key in your soul, Belle."

"Well aren't you religious now? I should buy a pew at Christ Church and engrave your name on a plaque." She turns away; he reaches for her arm and holds her with the most loving expression in his eyes. "Belle."

"Who are you? What have you done with my Billy? Are you - an angel?"

"Angels always come if ya ask. The trick is to remember to ask." He shuffles through papers and ribbons and lifts out a scrapbook, tied with a faded ribbon "You should think of me more as a guide – kind of like a spirit guide. But I'm no angel. Remember this?"

"It always makes me sad – looking at old photos and things. Please, I'm . . . you're givin' me a head-ache." Spirit Belle tosses back her head, letting her hair fall loosely about her face.

The gesture makes Billy grin, "You always reminded me of a circus pony when you did that. Now that I think of it, you were kind of a trick pony at times." He winks and holds out the scrapbook.

Spirit Belle turns towards the window. She gazes out at the still twilight, "The cicada's are gone. Pearl must have shot them."

"Pearl's dead." He slips a piece of paper out of the scrapbook. "Lets' let the cicadas be. 'Kisses, sweet. Well I remember.'"

She stares at him, "It's a silly school girl's poem."

"Do you remember it?"

"No . . . yes, yes, a thousand "yes's"." She takes the poem, holds it to her heart. "Kisses, sweet kisses. Well I remember."

The familiar bedroom disappears and Spirit Belle stands in her childhood home.

The house on West Main with the crooked wrought iron fence and the gate leading into a yard more mud than grass appears.

Child-Belle, in a dress too fancy for a school girl, hurries up West Main, carrying a book satchel. Behind her, a skinny boy in knickers and a cap follows, always staying out of sight. Child Belle pushes open a rusted wrought iron gate leading into the yard. There's a crooked shotgun house within spitting distance of the Lexington Cemetery.

Spirit Belle stands beside Billy, outside the house. She stares at sheets, billowing out, hung on a clothes line. Spirit Belle pushes through the sheets and sees Child-Belle, slightly older, dragging a school satchel. She's dressed in a fancy, white dress with a bow, a bow way too big for her delicate features. As she pushes through the sheets, her voice cries out – "Mama?" Then, she throws up a sheet and runs to Sarah, pinning up laundry. "Oh Mama!"

Spirit Belle steps in closer. "Mama?" Her voice catches, as if she's not sure that what she's seeing is possible.

Billy lets out a soft whistle, "Belle . . . what are ya doin'?"

Spirit Belle, still holding the poem, steps closer to her mother. "I didn't remember – she had such brilliant blue eyes."

As Spirit Belle remembers, Sarah Brezing becomes more distinct. Her hair, a soft brown with hints of gold, falls over her eyes; she is still young, maybe early thirties. Sarah holds her hand up, cupping her fingers to catch the soft rain. She holds out her arms to her little daughter, "Belle, sh-sh." Sarah wraps her arms around Belle, hugging her tightly. Then they fall, laughing, on the ground and lie stretched out on the grass. And curiously, there is grass. Thick, green grass with dandelions popping up. Sarah points up at the sheets, placing a finger over Belle's mouth – "Sh-sh . . ."

Child-Belle turns over on her stomach and stares at her mother who is mesmerized by the sheets, rising and flapping in the warm wind.

"What are ya doin', mama?"

"I'm listening." She closes her eyes.

Child Belle closes her eyes; then peeks through her cupped fingers. "Listening to what, Mama?"

"Angel wings, flappin' in the wind." Sarah Brezing wraps her strong arm around Child Belle. They wait, breathlessly watching, as the sheets transform into luminous winged beings.

CHAPTER SEVEN

Sarah Brezing

"Belle, you're not playing fair."

Billy suddenly waves his arm; the memory fades. The house, the sheets and the wrought iron fence disappear into an iridescence that then settles on the chandelier. Spirit Belle throws back her hair, as if to laugh. He catches her arm, and hands her the discarded scrapbook.

"You got a mighty convenient memory, Belle."

Spirit Belle retreats to the chaise, "What difference does it make? They're all gone. They're all dead."

"Even that little girl who imagined angels in the sheets, flappin' in the wind?"

"It was 1868. A breath away from the Great War Between the States. What harm could a little girl's longing for something pretty – something prettier than mud and dirty laundry – What difference could it possibly make if a little girl imagined angels in those sheets? That Door isn't closed because of lies my mama taught me."

"You have to tell the truth."

"All right. You don't have to be so pushy. I'm sure not all Spirit Guides are nearly as pushy. Why didn't I get an animal spirit guide. A dog or a pony or something. I think I'll send you back."

"You're wasting time. Now your mama, Sarah Brezing?"

"Mama was a laundress." She stares at Billy. Her eyes flash.

He points to the poem, reading "Kisses. Sweet kisses."

Spirit Belle holds the poem close to her heart, "Well I remember."

As she remembers, the chandelier glistens. And the room again loses shape, slipping into that other dimension that exists outside past, present and future. A time shaped by memories. Spirit Belle opens her eyes – staring into the bedroom of her childhood. There is a little girl, a little girl far different from the child imagined in the earlier memory; this little girl, dressed in a fancy dress way too old for her, with a big, tired bow, sits on the dirt floor. Playing paper dolls made out of leaves and the petals of flowers. She hears something – a sound from outside. A haunting, eerie wind seeps into the room. The little girl listens, then opens the door.

Spirit Belle follows the child, her former self. As she goes out into the muddy yard, the sound of sheets, flapping in the wind, crescendos into a woman's scream. Child-Belle, frightened, pushes through the wet sheets – searching desperately for her mother. She sees Sarah, lying on her back; her bruised legs are covered with mud. Beside her, stuck in the mud, is a bottle of whiskey. Child-Belle drops her paper dolls, and leans down to her mother, "Mama, Mama! What happened?"

Spirit Belle reaches down to pick up the paper dolls, shaped from flowers. She holds them, watching the memory unfold.

Sarah looks up into her small daughter's eyes; she pushes a lock of Belle's wild hair out of her eyes, "Ain't you a shaggy pony, baby? I fell. Sh-sh . . ." She laughs, trying to lift herself out of the mud and then suddenly grabs up a chicken, pecking at the hard dirt. "Me and Tinny Penny fell. We're like two hogs in the mud." The chicken protests loudly before escaping.

Child Belle holds out her hand and tries to help Sarah lift up. "It's all right, mama. Sh-sh, don't talk."

Sarah is almost halfway up when she sees the broken whiskey bottle. She suddenly grabs for the bottle and despite the glass, brings it close to her lips, already bleeding from earlier sips. She steadies herself, as if trying to bring Child Belle into focus. "Hold me, baby."

Child-Belle wraps her two small arms around her drunken mother; they rise up, suddenly hit by one of the soggy sheets. "Mama! Look out."

Sarah falls into the sheet, laughing and drinking more of the whiskey, despite the bleeding lip from the bottle's splintered glass. Child Belle tries to pull her mother's hand away from the bottle, "Mama, look, don't it look jest like angel wings, flapping in the wind?"

Suddenly, a tall, plain girl with lank blonde hair framing her thin face, pushes back the sheets. Her eyes flash angrily. "No, they're sheets."

Child Belle looks up, surprised, "Hester."

"And they're getting soaked. We'll have to wash them all over again. And look at you – filthy. Get up out of the mud, Belle." Furious, Hester pulls up her younger sister; sees the child's scraped chin.

"What'd ya do now? You're too wild, Belle." She looks back at Sarah, "Mama, get up. Can't you do anything right?"

Sarah lets the sheet fall off of her shoulder, exposing her torn, soaked dress. "Well, I'm your mama, Hester. Don't that count for something."

"I wish you weren't my mother. It's humiliating. Being talked about, laughed at – everyone whisperin' behind my back. I'd like to git out of this town."

Child Belle tries to smooth her mother's hair, her muddy dress, "Ya look pretty, Mama."

Sarah rolls over. A small hen darts out, pecking wildly at the rain-softened dirt. Suddenly, Sarah lunges for the terrified hen, "I'm stuck. Me and Tinny Penny is stuck like hogs in the mud." The hen squawks madly. Sarah laughs; letting the hen escape. She flutters her wet, useless wings and disappears behind the sheets.

Hester turns to Child-Belle, "Help me git the sheets down. Oh Belle, look at you. Is mama dressing you like one of Mr. Megowan's fancy girls now?"

Child Belle goes up on tip-toe to unpin the sheets, "What's a fancy girl, Mama?"

Sarah struggles to stand, falters and leans in against the sheets, "Mr. Megowan takes the pretty girls of color and dresses them up - real fancy."

"Why, mama?"

Sarah holds onto the sheets, swaying in and out as the wind gathers them up and lets them back down, "So he can sell them at Cheapside."

"But the War's over, Mama."

"That war ain't over by a long shot." Sarah suddenly lets go of the sheets; the bottle slips out of her hand. "Damn. Looks like it might rain."

The rain falls harder.

Hester grabs Child-Belle's small hand, "Oh for God's sake, stop talkin'. Fancy girls? Really mama? Belle's a child. The whole town's talking about you. Us. Dragging us into court. A divorce – why couldn't you just . . . oh, I don't know – just . . . go away."

Child Belle slips one of the sheets over her head, staring up at the leaves of a giant ghinko. The tree's roots have broken through the hard ground, searching for the rain which now comes in large, hard pellets. The tree's branches open to the sky; and with the rain comes a whirlwind of golden leaves, swirling around and over the sheets. Christening the sun-parched grass with rain. Puddles quickly form. Child Belle splashes a bare foot in the puddle. Behind her – around her – Hester struggles violently against the wind; trying to rescue the sheets.

Sarah picks up the broken bottle, hides it under her torn petticoat. "I know you don't approve of me but reckon you could let Belle pretend for a little while longer." The rain comes in torrents. Hester gathers the sheets in her pale, thin arms.

"Pretend to read when she cain't."

Child Belle pushes forward, "I can read." Child-Belle helps Sarah, brushing her fingers through her mother's hair as she gently guides her towards the house. She has the door open, "Come on, Mama. You're gonna git . . ."

Sarah whirls, facing Hester; her voice, with its thick Irish clip, rises above the wind. "No Hester, pretend happiness for as long as she can. Because pretend happiness is all that you and Belle can ever hope for. There ain't nothin' else and the sooner you figure that out, darlin' Hester . . ."

Hester whips up the sheets, "You're wrong. Pretending happiness is worse than seeing life the way it really is. Belle can't live her whole life in a fantasy world, mama. Can't you see that in the end, pretend happiness will hurt her. She'll never know what real love is or . . ."

"Come inside, mama. Hester – help her."

Sarah lunges forward, trying to hit Hester and falls; she sinks down into the mud, clinging to the broken bottle.

Child Belle runs back, tugging at her mother's dress. "Git up, mama. Mama! "Mama, I am happy. I'm a happy girl."

Sarah laughs, takes a swig from the broken bottle and cuts her lips. She wipes the blood from her mouth. She sits down in the mud. Glaring fiercely at Hester, still trying to rescue the sheets – "Leave 'em be. Hester. Leave the god-damn sheets alone. Ya have to spoil it all, don't ya? You're so smart, but you're soft." Her voice lowers, "But Belle ain't soft. She ain't no victim, She's like her sweet mama."

Hester throws the wet sheets into the mud, "Belle's sweet mama is a . . ."

Child Belle reaches down and tries to gather up the rain-soaked sheets.

"Say it Hester. Say it real loud so Belle can hear ya good."

Hester covers her face with the sheets; she bends forward, crying.

"Cry. You jest cry. Cry baby. Cry. But Belle don't cry . . ." She glances over her shoulder at Child Belle who is staring. "It's a sign of weakness. Sarah Brezing doesn't ever cry. And neither does Belle."

Sarah gets up and yanks Hester's hands away from her face. Hester swallows; her face is red from the crying. "Crying . . . is God's way of washing away the hurt, mama."

"Where'd you hear that? You still seein' that preacher's son. "Go on. Go on now. Git."

Hester turns and runs for cover, inside the house. Child Belle calls out "Hester, please, please . . . help mama." Her voice is lost in the rain.

Sarah coughs, tries to catch her breath and falls forward. "Let her go. I don't need her help." Child Belle runs to her. Sarah spits out blood. Her weak, tired eyes try to focus on her youngest daughter, "Don't you ever cry, baby. My grandmamma used to say 'Sarah, pull yourself together.' She laughs; well, I reckon I'm tryin'. I'm trying but there's jest so many pieces of me done broke apart." Her voice breaks; she slips into a drunken, coarse fit of laughter. "Sing to me, baby. Sing me a lullabye, baby."

Child-Belle gathers up a sheet and sits down beside her mother, holding up the wet sheet over Sarah. The sheet billows up, then falls. Child-Belle leans in and sings "Hush little baby, don't say a word. Mama's goin' buy you a . . . mockingbird."

Child Belle looks towards the house; she sees Hester, crying, staring at her through the glass pane. She whispers, "I love ya, mama."

Spirit Belle sees the forgotten book satchel, lying face down in the mud. She shivers, letting the wind whip around her. "Kisses, sweet kisses. I remember."

Billy pops open an umbrella, "Go inside. Careful not to puddle water on the floors."

She grabs the umbrella and walks towards the house; the door opens and closes in the strong wind.

CHAPTER EIGHT

Painted paperdoll

Billy's voice is close — somewhere in the rain-soaked yard. He is a shadow figure, watching her. "There's another memory. Open the door."

"No, I'd rather not."

"Go." He blows softly on her neck. "Your mama's inside."

"No, I've forgotten the poem. It was a long, long time ago. I've forgotten . . ."

"You'll remember the kisses."

Slowly, Spirit Belle opens the door and enters her childhood home. The room is all shadows; a hard dirt floor materializes beneath her feet. Child-Belle, soaking wet and still carrying the sheet, slips off worn ankle-boots and holds up the laces in front of her. "Mama always told me to take off my 'golden slippers' in the house. There wasn't a floor; just dirt. And she didn't want me to get my shoes dirty — so I had clean shoes and dirty bare feet."

Spirit Belle steps in closer; she leans down and starts to brush a tangled lock of hair out of the little girl's eyes. The little girl suddenly tenses; Belle follows the child's gaze. Sarah struggles to sit down before a crooked mirror, in front of a small table cluttered with powders and rouge boxes. She desperately tries to brush out her matted curls.

Child-Belle's voice is calm, "Are ya all right, mama?"

"I'm sopping wet. How the hell do you think I am, baby?" In a sudden flare of temper, she throws the brush. It hits hard against the hard dirt floor. Child-Belle looks at the brush; and then suddenly holds out her arms and as if releasing some wild and wonderful spirit within, she begins to spin. Faster and faster.

"Stop that, you're goin' make me dizzy." Sarah Brezing leans forward, trying to paint her eyebrows. She squints, arches the brow and blackens it much darker and higher than the one on the other side. "Now look what you've made me do – I'm cross-eyed lookin' at myself." Child Belle laughs, dizzy. "Ah Belle baby, ya always can make me laugh." She laughs, catching Belle's face in the cracked glass. The little girl creases her own brow, as if mimicking her mother.

"Don't do that baby. Worry gives the face age . . . way too soon." She takes a lady-like sip from a flask. Coughs and spits out the liquor. She wipes her mouth; and there is nothing lady-like about this gesture.

Belle drops down off her toes. Sarah pushes the stool closer, then stands and almost touches the glass with her face as she tries to see to paint her lips. "Go on, dance. Dance for me, Belle."

The little girl smiles, pleased to have caught her mama's eye. She blows Sarah a kiss, then rises and dances. She's quite natural, turning with an easy grace. "I love you, Mama."

Sarah tries to fasten a cheap trinket around her wrist; she can't get the clasp. "Belle, honey, stop that now and help me." She holds out her wrist.

Child-Belle walks over and turns her mother's wrist over so that she can fasten the clasp. It's hard for her small fingers but she tries; again and again. Sarah looks at her, "Oh, can't you do nothin', baby?"

Child-Belle steps back, staring down.

"Oh it's just a cheap trinket – Dutchy gave me." She throws it into a pile of other broken trinkets on the vanity. Then, she reaches into the pile of tangled bracelets and cheap pearls, letting her pale fingers move through them, prowling for the one that's not broken.

"Mama."

Sarah glances up at Belle, holding out the hairbrush.

"Come here, baby." Sarah sighs. Belle steps forward. Sarah turns her to face the mirror. She takes out the large hair bow and brushes out Belle's long hair. "God, you got enough hair for a circus pony. Maybe I'll have to put you in the circus – parade you around with all this mane just a'flying. Put little bows and ribbons in it. You're sure a pretty little wisp of nothin'."

Sarah holds the bow in her mouth, pulls Belle's hair up from her neck and then secures the bow. Sarah's hands are rough; the little girl winces. Belle grips the vanity but doesn't move. Sarah looks at Belle in the mirror; rather than liking what she sees, a strange, shadowed expression crosses Sarah's face. It is a look of a woman who knows she is growing old; jealousy quivers about the tiny curves of her painted red lips. And then the jealous expression is gone – it is as if Sarah reconsidered Belle, not as a threat, but as a possible means to get something. Something she desperately desires; a chance to be free, to be rich . . . to be something other than Sarah Brezing.

"Baby, read to mama."

There's something in Sarah's voice – a catch – something that is edged with a dark energy. The little girl looks down; Sarah lifts Belle's chin – baiting her. "I said, read to me, baby."

"Mama, I cain't read."

Sarah starts to let the little girl go, and then suddenly grabs her and twists her arm, pulling her towards her. "Baby girl, you listen to me. You look at me." She turns Belle to face the broken mirror; there are double reflections of both Belle and Sarah.

Suddenly, Spirit Belle steps back as if she might also see her face reflected in those shards; with a chilling sigh, she looks at Billy – "Billy, my mama never hurt me." She faces Billy; behind her, Sarah and Child Belle fade into a tableau – faintly colored; frozen in time's forgotten moments.

Billy motions for Belle to face the memory, "Belle, ya ain't playin' fair."

Spirit Belle holds tight to the poem, "I don't know the rules. I think you're making them up as we go along."

"There are no rules, Belle. Just remember."

She turns, staring at herself as a child. "I'd forgotten my hair was that color. Mama said it was the color of sunburnt poppies – but I think it's more of a chestnut. What do you think, Billy?"

"What I think doesn't really mater, Kitten. But there's probably something in this memory that's more important than remembering the color of your hair."

Spirit Belle murmurs softly, "Kisses. Sweet kisses. I remember well." She stares at Sarah and Child-Belle, bringing them back to "life." And then she sits down on the floor, playing with the little girls' paper dolls, made from flowers.

Sarah braids Child-Belle's hair. "Belle, it don't matter if you cain't read. Don't you ever say that. Of course, you can read."

"No mama, I cain't. I don't go to school and I cain't . . ."

Sarah yanks Belle's hair, pulling her closer.

"Mama, you're hurting me."

"Now you listen to me. Belle, baby . . ." She smoothes Belle's hair, straightening the crooked bow. "Belle, it doesn't matter if ya cain't read.

Just pretend. It's the illusion; nothin's real. Ain't nobody gonna know the difference. You just act as if what you want is already right here. Like makin' a wish on a fallin' star. You jest got to believe. Now throw back your shoulders and smile, smile with those eyes of yours' – oh baby, you got your daddy's green eyes. Irish witch you are! Now give your mama a kiss."

Sarah grabs Child-Belle and kisses her, full on the mouth. The little girl tastes the liquor and her mama's foul breath and closes her lips. She accidentally bites her mother. Sarah, furious, slaps the little girl – hard. "You bit me. Don't you ever, ever bite me again."

Tears stream down the child's reddened cheeks. "I'm sorry, Mama." She throws her arms around her mother, "I'm sorry."

Sarah faces the mirror; then, coldly takes the child's arms off of her waiste. "Stand over there. In the dark. Stir the laundry. I don't want Dutchy seein' you when he comes in."

There is loud knocking on the door. A man's voice cuts against the shadowed quiet, "Sarah, me darlin'."

Sarah, half-dressed, pulls a shawl around her shoulders; there are holes in the shawl. She fusses over the tear, "Be out in a moment, Dutchy."

"Mama, please don't go."

Sarah's face is flushed from the fire. She tries to pin the hole in her sweater, "What baby?"

"Sarah!" His voice sounds harsh, edged with anger. "Git out here. What are you doin'?"

"Dutchy, I'm comin' . . ." Sarah turns the shawl around, flipping it wrong side out. She smiles at her reflection, "I'm a'comin'."

Suddenly, Child-Belle drops the stirring stick and clings to Sarah's skirt; her small fingers pull at the shawl, causing it to rip further. "Mama, don't go."

Sarah pushes her away, kicks her back. Child-Belle falls hard on the dirt floor. Sarah, realizing what she has done, reaches down to the little girl, "Baby, sh-sh. Mama's here. Look. Take mama's locket." Sarah unfastens her locket and places it around Belle's neck. "It'll keep the dragons away."

Child Belle looks straight into her mother's eyes. Fearless. "I ain't afraid, Mama. I ain't afraid of dragons or nothin'. You go on now. You look so pretty. You're gonna be the belle of the ball, mama."

Sarah takes Child-Belle's face into her hands, "You got light in them eyes of your's, Belle. Jest like the fireflies . . ."

"Sarah!" The Dutchman's heavy boot hits against the door.

Sarah throws a kiss to Belle and opens the door and goes out. Child-Belle, fingering her mother's locket, walks over to the window, and presses her face up to the glass. Waiting. Watching for the lightning bugs. The fireflies who carry their magic to the distant stars.

Hester enters the dark room, "Git back from the window, Belle. Someone might see ya."

Spirit Belle closes the scrapbook.

Billy steps in closer. "I don't think we're finished here."

"We're finished here."

CHAPTER NINE

The Dutchman

"No, you've forgotten some kisses."

Spirit Belle looks at Billy, then at the silent grandfather clock. She opens the scrapbook, staring at the poem. "Kisses, I remember. Sweet kisses."

Suddenly, the room spins into pitch black. There is a dizzying sensation as if objects were flying. A sliver of yellow moonlight illumines the black stove, the bed. Child Belle, wide awake, lies next to Hester. They are listening – not to the soulless quiet but to something else. A hoot owl. And the eerie "hooting" rises above the sound of the the tree branch scraping against the window pane. And then, there is the other sound. A gunshot.

Child-Belle grabs Hester's hand. They stare, wild-eyed, terrified, as a wildly disheveled Sarah dashes into the bedroom and grabs a pistol out from under the bed.

Hester sits up, "Mama?"

"I spit on the bastard Dutchman." Sarah cocks the pistol, waving it at the door. "Go on, George. Git. Git out of here."

A man's ominous form appears in the window. He waves a gun and a bottle. A curious, dark smile creases his face. "Sarah." He spits out the name.

"George, you're drunk."

"I am drunk. Damn drunk. And I got a damn bloody nose."

"I'll shoot ya, George. Don't think I won't."

The man's voice changes his tone; he lowers his own pistol. "Sarah, sweet Sarah put the pistol down. I won't hurt you. Just open the door."

Sarah hesitates, as if she might be going to open the door.

Hester grabs for her mother's arm, "Mama, mama don't."

Suddenly, the door opens. Hester screams. Sarah raises her arm and fires a shot. Hester pushes Child Belle down, throwing pillows over their heads. Then she rolls to the side and quickly helps the little girl under the bed. In the dark, the two girls wait. They see Sarah's bare feet – moving around the bed. And then, there is another shot. And heavy footsteps move towards the bed. Sarah screams. From beneath the bed, Child Belle stares at the man's shoes, thick and soleless, as they kick again and again. And she hears her mother's body fall – lying limp just a few inches from Child Belle.

The man picks up Sarah, throws her on the bed. Hiding, Hester and Child Belle cringe in terror, listening to the thrusting of the man as he brutally overpowers Sarah. As she hides there – in the filth and dark beneath that bed – Child-Belle twists the locket, tight around her neck. She stares at a candleflame, flickering higher and higher.

Then, Spirit Belle begins to hum, softly at first – a lullabye. She sings this almost as if she were hiding beneath that bed – so many years ago. A lullabye to drown out her mother's scream, to drown out the slapping sheets and then, the Silence . . . a lullabye to keep Child-Belle safe.

The rain pelts down outside. Hard and fast. The outside shutter flies off; rain seeps in through the window. Child-Belle gets up and walks towards the window. For a moment, she sees a boy, standing in the rain. He sees her and suddenly steps back into the shadows.

CHAPTER TEN

Flickering candles

Spirit Belle stands beside Billy in her bedroom. She reaches for his shoulder, "Billy, the boy … that boy watching me. Who was that boy?"

Billy steps back, "You shouldn't really touch me. You could get shocked."

Spirit Belle grabs his shoulder, as if to turn him towards her. She cries out; an electrical charge shoots through her hand. "Stop the magic tricks. Was that boy - you?"

"Lets' just say there are things you missed, Belle."

"Then let me see what I missed?"

"You sure about that?"

"Are you?"

Billy grins, "You're forgetting that I've already crossed through the portal." He waves his hand and the walls of the room quietly fold back. Belle starts to take hold of his arm, then changes her mind. He looks at her, "The skin between the worlds is thin. Sometimes, Belle, if you're real still, you can eavesdrop on the Past. Listen."

Rising above Miss Flora's humming from downstairs in the kitchen, there is another sound. Someone is crying.

As Spirit Belle listens, images appear. At first faint. An historic mansion. Set back from a winding road; there are giant pines that over-look formal gardens. And then she sees the boy and recognizes him, "Billy."

"Sh-sh, just watch. Just listen." Billy moves closer to the porch of the mansion.

"Where are we?"

"Fox Hollow."

Suddenly, the young boy, soaking wet, pushes past the invisible Spirit Belle. She watches as he hurries up the drive, towards the wide veranda. A young African-American girl, her hair pulled up in a red turban, sits on the steps, barely out of the rain. She sees Billy and stands, wiping tears.

"Pearl, wh- why . . . are you cr-crying?"

"Mr. Billy, I know where you go . . . where you been."

He looks young Pearl straight in her sizzling eyes and starts to say something, but his voice catches. "She . . . she's." Embarrassed by his stuttering, the young Billy pushes open the wide mahogany door. The brass knocker reads "Fox Hollow". Pearl follows him inside; her words slip out under her breath, "Her mama's white trash."

Billy turns, slightly, "She – sh-she's not . . . like her m-mother. People should g-give her a ch-chance." He steps into the hallway, filled with portraits. The eyes of all the past Mabons – the former gentlemen and gentle-ladies of Fox Hollow stare down at the rain drenched boy.

If Pearl is about to say something, which isn't likely given that they have now stepped back into the halls of the great former plantation, she misses her chance. A voice from the top of the wide stairway booms out – "Son!"

Billy glances up at Colonel William Mabon the Third, as he makes his way down the stairs. A southern aristocrat with a thunderous voice, he smokes his cigar with relish, "Billy! Wipe your boots, son. You're making puddles all across your mama's new Oriental."

Pearl hands Billy her apron; he dutifully wipes his boots. As Colonel Mabon comes down the stairs, the full force of his stature becomes more apparent. He curls his fists; his face reddens. "Do you know who's died?"

Billy looks up. "No-n- . . ."

"President Lincoln's been shot."

"Who - who . . . sh- shot him?"

"Damn idiot. Confederate sympathizer. John Wilkes Booth."

"Sic semper tyrannis. *Thus always to tyrants.*'" The man's voice catches both Billy and his father by surprise. Billy turns and stares at a young Catholic Priest, pale, with soft features, staring at him. The priest holds a silver mint julep glass in one hand; beads of water form on the outside of the cup. He sips the drink, "Booth's words to Lincoln - not mine. I only speak Latin in Mass."

The priest's gaze is unsettling for the boy. He smiles, turns his attention to Billy's father. Colonel Mabon takes his cue, "Son, your mama's invited Father McPhearson to join us for supper. He's the new priest at your mama's church. And evidently, he noticed you last Sunday and wants you to be a . . . What the hell, pardon me Father – what is it that you want the boy to be?"

"Acolyte. They light the candles." Father McPhearson stares at the boy without blinking; his liquid cerluean eyes are framed by white lashes; Billy realizes this – wondering if that is what gives the priest a white, pasty look. His skin seems unnaturally pale; and there is a moment when the boy, whose artistic sensitivity provides great insight despite or perhaps because of his stutter . . realizes that the priest is wearing powder on his cheeks. There is even a slight hint of painted rouge on his cheeks.

Billy steps back. His father pushes Billy towards the priest. "Shake his hand, son." He turns to the priest, "Billy's always retreating. Ya'd think he deserted in the war but he's just eight."

Father McPhearson steps in closer to the boy; smiling with his yellow-stained teeth. His breath smells of licorice, "I did notice you, Billy. The church is always looking for bright young boys to give service to Our Lord. Your mother tells me that you have an artist's soul. You like to draw."

Billy tries to speak; his face reddens. Colonel Mabon fills in the awkward silence, "All the McPhearson's are lawyers. Speak up, son."

Billy's hands curl into tight fists, "Y-y-s."

"Boy's got a stutter, Father. Maybe you can coax that out of him while he's lighting the candles." Colonel Mabon laughs; the edges of his lips, however, do not smile with the laugh. He tightens his hold on the boy's thin shoulders.

Suddenly, there is the soft rustle of satin and Mary Collins Mabon enters from the parlor, accompanied by her daughter, a dark-haired beauty of six who fidgets with her mother's sash. The quintessential southern belle, Mary Collins smiles at the Priest, "Father, we're so pleased you've come to Lexington. The Athens of the West!" A child-like gasp escapes her heart-shaped lips, "I know you'll have a lasting influence on our son." Her periwinkle eyes flash at her timid son, "Billy, why don't you light the candles for tonight's dinner."

Relieved, Billy escapes into the adjacent dining room. Pearl follows him into the room, with tall windows over-looking the garden. She hands him the box of matches, then turns to pour water in the crystal glasses. Billy carefully lights the candles in the silver candelabra on the table, then turns to the white candles in the wall sconces. As he reaches up, Billy feels a touch on his shoulder. He tenses; smelling the sweet licorice. His hand freezes mid-air. The priest's hand guides Billy's hand up to light the candles.

CHAPTER ELEVEN

West Main

"Billy, I – I didn't know."

"Sure you did. You just chose to miss seeing things. But now you know."

"I always wondered why you never liked to light a candle." She smiles, and forgetting, again reaches to touch his cheek.

He puts up his hand, in a warning gesture "Babe, not yet." And then suddenly, all of the white candles in the room burst into flame. Candles that have long ago melted down; candles hanging from the chandelier (no longer lit by electricity) now burn. Lighting up the bedroom. Giving the room a brilliance that is unnatural. And in another instant, a wind from seemingly out of nowhere – blows across the room.

Extinguishing the candles.

Belle's bedroom disappears into blackness.

Spirit Belle is unexpectedly back in her old childhood home on West Main, staring at a white candle burning low on the bedside table. She looks for Billy; but he is not in this memory. She stands alone. Staring at the sunlight, spilling through the shattered glass pane. Child-Belle lies asleep next to Hester; the paper dolls lie scattered on the dirt floor. There's a soft moaning, coming from a figure lying face down. Child-Belle pushes back the cover, "Mama?"

Sarah, badly beaten, tries to lift her head. "Belle." Her voice is painfully weak. Her blood-stained dress lies across her naked back. Child Belle goes to her mother, kissing Sarah's hair. She looks up at Hester, who sits in bed, her legs curled up. Stoic.

"Hester, is mama dead? Hester"

Hester shakes her head "No."

Child-Belle leans in closer to her mother, "Don't die, mama. Please, don't die."

Hester gets out of bed, and begins picking up the broken whiskey bottles. Disgusted, angry, she turns to Sarah, lifts her head and spoons some whiskey into her mother's mouth. Sarah's eyes blink, open. She grabs hold of the bottle and drinks, covering her naked breasts with her torn dress. She turns away from her daughters, burying her pain in the amber liquid that rushes through her, deadening her feelings. Hester hands a brush to Belle.

"Brush your hair, Belle." She splashes some water on a cloth, and washes Child-Belle's face. "You don't have to end up like her."

Child-Belle takes the brush and tries to untangle Sarah's curls, "I love you mama."

Sarah looks at her daughter, as if seeing her for the first time, "Hush baby girl, don't cry. You ain't cryin', are you?"

Child Belle shakes her head, "No. But mama, when I grow-up, I'm going to kill the Dutchman."

Hester turns away. She slips into a fresh dress, splashes water across her face.

Sarah suddenly sets down the whiskey bottle and takes Child-Belle's face into her trembling hands, "No baby, no. When you grow-up, Belle, you're going to bewitch the Dutchman and all the other bastards. But don't ever fall in love, Belle…" She coughs, staining her hands with blood.

"Mama, are you all right?" She wipes the blood from Sarah's mouth.

Suddenly a school bell rings loudly.

Hester picks up a book satchel, "Come on, Belle. We got to go to school."

Child Belle stays with Sarah, "Go on. I'm not ever going back to Dudley."

Hester holds out the satchel, "Get up."

Sarah smoothes a stray lock of hair out of Child-Belle's green eyes, "Go on, baby. I'm fine. I'm going to be just fine. Go on now." She kisses Child-Belle on the cheek. "Your mama's going to be just fine."

Child-Belle takes the book satchel and follows Hester to the door; she turns, smiles at Sarah, "I love you mama." And blows her mother a kiss.

"Belle! We'll be late. Now." Hester holds open the door; Child-Belle hurries out. And the sound of the ringing schoolbell is deafening.

Left alone with Sarah, Spirit Belle leans down and blows out the candle, "Kisses, well I remember."

CHAPTER TWELVE

Willie

A little too casually, Billy slips a harmonica out of his pocket and plays a whimsical melody. The music has a chilling effect on Spirit Belle.

Spirit Belle backs away from Billy, towards the bed where she sees the little girl with the ribbon, holding the bag – staring at her fragile body. Spirit Belle shivers, turns to Billy with a frightened look in her eyes. "I forgave my mother a long, long time ago." She tries the door knob on the face of the clock. Disappointed, she turns to Billy, "I thought . . ."

"You ain't thought hard enough, Belle. There's something else. Someone you've over-looked." He holds up a scrapbook. "Here. This belong to you?"

Spirit Belle stares at the scrapbook. "You're quite the sorcerer, aren't you? But you're playing with Dark Magic, Billy. And there's nothing in that scrapbook that can unlock that clock's door."

He opens the scrapbook, "What is all this darlin'?" He pulls out a paper doll chain.

"Memories." Spirit Belle takes the paper doll chain, gently as if afraid it might crumble into dust. She wears the paper dolls like a favorite, forgotten necklace.

"I didn't know you were such a packrat. Paper dolls. Fancy little handkerchiefs." He sniffs the faded paper, "Poems on rose-scented scraps of paper stolen from a junkyard."

As Spirit Belle holds tight to the paper dolls, Billy flips through the pages in the time-worn and tattered scrapbook. "Well look at this – you got some photos in here. Who's the freckle-faced kid in the overalls?"

Spirit Belle's eyes soften; she leans over Billy's shoulder, staring at the photograph for several seconds before she whispers, "Willie. Willie Sutphin."

Billy takes out a faded piece of paper and starts to hand it to her but she catches his wrist, "I know that poem by heart." She closes her eyes, holding the faded poem close to her own heart, "If kisses sweet you'll give to me."

There is the sound of a jump-rope turning, faster and faster. Spirit Belle opens her eyes, staring at a little girl, Child-Belle, about eight, jumping rope. She trips, catches herself and spins the rope around her bare ankles. She dances with the jump-rope, a wild gypsy princess, spinning around in the dust of a lonely playground. Then she stops, staring at a chain of paper dolls. She picks it up. One of the paper dolls has her name, Belle's mama. The face is colored black. Child-Belle hurls it on the ground, then takes the jump rope firmly in her small hands and walks over to a group of girls, sitting quietly, coloring paper dolls.

"My mama is not colored."

The other little girls, in white dresses with perfectly tied bows, turn their backs to Child Belle; then they lean forward and whisper, giggling. Child Belle rips apart the paper doll chain. The girls hurriedly get up and skip across the playground, retreating inside the school.

Furious, Child Belle picks up a rock. "I hate you! I hate this school. I hate . . ." She hurls the rock straight at the school window. She throws it. Hard. The window shatters. Her hair falls in her face; her white bow slips down, giving her the look of some untamed circus pony escaping from the Big Tent. Escaping from the glare and tormenting ridicule of all the circus patrons.

"I am not a trick pony!" She hurls another rock, and then another, "And my mama is not . . ." Suddenly the horrified and completely fascinated faces of the Dudley School properly mannered children appear around the broken shards in the window frame. They appear as faces captured in a photograph; their eyes wide with fear. Enthralled, drawn to the wild child throwing a tantrum outside their school. Charlotte Clay, a plump little girl with blonde ringlets, points a finger at Belle, who is now madly ripping apart a paper doll colored black.

"I guess she didn't like her paper doll." Charlotte's cold eyes mock Belle. The corners of her lips quiver in mock disbelief. Behind her, several other of the well-dressed, well-heeled, little girls of "old Lexington" gather round. Staring over the jagged glass, glaring at Belle. They whisper and giggle.

Unexpectedly, a boy's shadow falls across Child-Belle. Billy, in his usual knickers and cap, says quietly, "P-put it d-down."

Child Belle whirls; her face is scraped and dirty. In her eyes there is an expression of hope. A yearning for love – for a friend. But the girls are watching. Glaring. Taunting Billy with their cruel giggles. Trapping Billy.

Charlotte's voice is edged with sweetness, "Billy Mabon, are you still sweet on Miss Belle Brezing? Do you like her bows?"

Child-Belle gazes intently, earnestly at Billy. He is her Knight in Shining Armor.

But he steps back, "N-nawh . . . I'm – I'm . . . n-not sweet on . . ."

Charlotte throws the gauntlet, "Good. Because Miss Brezing is white trash and her mama is . . ."

Sally, a tall, thin girl, leans in, "Say it Charlotte." Her small eyes flash.

"I can't, Sally. I'm a lady." She glances at Billy, "You say it Billy. You're a boy."

Child-Belle digs her white boots in the soft playground grass. Waiting. Daring Billy to humiliate her further. The children's voices rise in a chorus, "Say it, Billy. Say it."

Billy's face reddens. He opens his lips but he can't find his voice. Stuttering, he finally bursts out – "C-c-colored. Her m-mama is c-colored."

Disappointed, Charlotte turns to the other children, "Not colored. Billy's too much of a coward to say it. Lets' call him Stutt for short." The other girls laugh.

A teacher appears in the window. She shakes her fist at Billy, "Get in here right now, Billy Mabon." She sees Belle. "And you, you're no longer a student in this school. Do you understand? Leave the premises now."

Child Belle, hurt, looks straight into Billy's eyes and then takes off, running fast and furious. Leaving behind the torn paper dolls, lying face down in the parched dirt. Spirit Belle walks over to the forgotten paper dolls, and gently picks up the chain. She brushes off the dirt, holding the torn paper doll with the black face close to her heart.

Billy picks up the scrapbook, reading the poem, "If kisses sweet you'll give to me."

Spirit Belle recites the poem, without emotion "If dreams unsung you'll dream with me."

Billy taunts her deeper into the memory, playing the harmonica and slowly, the schoolyard disappears. A lonely dirt path leads away from town, winding into an ever more secluded trail. Evergreens sweep low, then rise, revealing footprints in the dirt. There is the sound of someone running, hard and fast up the trail. A shadow appears, cast in the pine needles, and then disappears. Slowly, as Spirit Belle calls up the memory, the sounds become more distinct.

A child is running. Fast. Up through waiste-high grasses, wind-blown and sun scorched. Her breathing quickens, coming in quick gasps. She pushes further into the grasses, making her way towards a distant train trestle, looming high above the yellowing sea of grass and wildflower. And suddenly, the child stops and Spirit Belle recognizes her former self, a little girl in a dress far too old for her eight years. Her pretty face is smudged with dirt and tears. She heads towards the train track, climbing the sudden rise of earth. And then, as she finally reaches the trestle's edge, she stops and furiously unties the ribbons on her pigtails. She shakes her tousled hair free – then rips off the bows and buttons on her tight bodice. She steps out of her crinoline skirt, kicks it hard. And then she tackles the white lace boots. As she kicks off the last boot, she throws up her arms and stands, barefoot, bare-skinned, hair flying wildly about her face and screams, "I hate you Mama."

Her foot finds the crinoline and kicks it hard. It floats up, then caught in the irons of an invisible wind, the crinoline falls over the tracks, downward. Another kick sends the bodice flying, and then the white boots follow.

"Ouch! Hey! Ya almost took off my freckles." The boy's voice is close. Suddenly, a dirty-blonde haired boy emerges from under the trellis. He looks up – wearing the crinoline like a crown and dangling white leather boots around his neck.

Spirit Belle gasps, "Willie!"

"Willie Sutphin, are you spying on me?" Child-Belle, standing in her cotton petticoat, folds her arms around her chest and glares at the boy, now grinning up at her. He steps into the light, a comical apparition in crinoline crown and over-alls.

"I ain't spyin'." He takes the crinoline off his head, and holds it out to Child-Belle. "I come here most ever' day."

She takes the crinoline and throws it on the ground. "I ain't never seen ya."

"I've seen you. Plenty of times."

"Ain't ya scared to talk to me?"

"Nawh, I ain't afraid to talk to you. Why should I be?" He slips a harmonica out of his pocket and sits down on the edge of the track.

Spirit-Belle steps up onto the train track, hesitant. She glances back at Billy, sensing that she is perhaps an intruder coming by chance upon a moment that is the stuffing of fairytales. Still holding the scrap of paper, she stares at Willie. She is deeply touched by his presence. Old playmates separated by time. She whispers with great feeling, "Willie, I'd forgotten how young – how beautiful my Willie was." She stares at the freckle-faced boy with his cocky grin and boyish swagger and for a moment, he sees her. Almost.

Willie gazes out over the edge of the trestle, staring at the view of church spires and the courthouse square and the old Cheapside slave market. Then, he glances up at a blistering blue sky, "Ya see that hawk. He's tame. Ya can feed him."

Child Belle finds the hawk, a thin speck circling in the coming of dusk light. "Oh."

He doesn't look at her, "Ya ought to git ya a baby hawk or a baby raccoon. Ya wouldn't be so lonely."

"I ain't lonely."

He looks at her. And sees her. Really sees the child so desperate to give love. "Yeah, ya are, Belle." He slips a harmonica out of his pocket. As he plays, the tune rises over the distant, eerie whistle of an approaching train. The trestles begin to reverberate.

She stares at him, sizing him up with her eyes, sea-green in the spring light. "They ain't gonna let me go back to school cuz a'what I done."

"What'd ya do?"

"I threw a rock." She bites her fingernail. "It broke a window. At school."

"Why'd ya do that?" He sticks out his arms, balancing on the tracks.

"Because I'm trash. I'm poor white trash." She bites her lip, fighting back tears. "She colored this paperdoll all black and scribbled Belle's Mama on it and I . . ."

"Hey, ya ain't crying are ya?"

She looks straight into his eyes, pools of light and innocence, "I never cry."

Willie turns the harmonica over in his hand, then he plays. It's a catching tune. Child-Belle suddenly sticks out her legs, rolls up her pantaloons and dangles bare feet over the track. She unties her hair, and shakes out the touseled wild curls. Listening to the wind and Willie, playing the harmonica, she suddenly smiles, "You play good, Willie."

He looks at her, "I come up here quite a'bit."

"I ain't never been up here."

"It's kind'a dangerous. There's a dragon lives up here. When it spits fire – a star will appear. It isn't a bad dragon but it really, really doesn't like . . ."

"What?"

"Quitters. It eats 'em."

"I ain't a quitter."

"Good. Ya don't want to end up dragon spit."

She isn't quite sure if he's teasing her, but she takes a chance and answers from her heart. "No, but I reckon it would be all right to end up a star."

"Yeah, I reckon. "He looks at her, holds out his hand and helps her up. Then he walks along the tracks, arms held wide and she follows. They balance on the trestle, moving towards the sound of a train whistle, distant but moving close. His voice is calm, truthful. "If ya fall off this trestle, Belle, you'll disappear into the River of No Return. And you'll be lost forever."

"I'd like to be lost forever."

"Would ya now?" He glances back at Child-Belle, walking behind him, "So would I."

Suddenly, the train's light sweeps across the bridge. Child-Belle grabs Willie's hand and they jump. Seconds later, the train explodes onto the bridge, breathing smoke and fire. From a safe distance, Willie and Child-Belle roll, tumble down the slight hill and then lie, sprawled out – staring up at the sky where elephants and giant mushrooms take shape. And Willie takes Child-Belle's hand and traces the shapes until they disappear into wisps of white . . . and a solitary star appears.

Willie is quiet; then he picks a slender blade of yellowing grass and gently takes Belle's hand. He winds the grass around her ring finger, smiling into her eyes and asks, quite serious, "Belle, when we grow-up, will ya marry me?"

She giggles; gathers up a handful of grass and throws it into his hair. Smitten with her, Willie lies back in the grass, smiling. Then, he steals a kiss.

Spirit Belle watching, smiles and whispers the poem she knows by heart:

"If kisses sweet you'll give to me.
If dreams unsung you'll dream with me.
Then all my life I'll be your friend
And marry she who gave me first
Her kisses free."

Slowly, the childhood memory slips back behind the mists of time. The sound of a train's whistle, shrill and eerie, disturbs the quiet. And a solitary white feather floats down, landing beside Spirit Belle. She ignores the feather.

Billy places a strong hand on her shoulder, "There's more, isn't there?"

The lights of the approaching train sweep across the track, casting the woods and hillside where Child-Belle lies next to Willie in an unnatural light. Then, pitch black covers the memory and Spirit Belle is no longer standing by the trestle bridge, but back in the hard-dirt floored house on West Main.

CHAPTER THIRTEEN

Hester

Child Belle sits on the floor, near the coal black stove. She pastes a poem into her scrapbook. She hears a hesitant knocking and as the door opens, Hester, older, in a plain brown coat that barely conceals the pregnancy, enters. Visibly anxious, Hester stares at Child Belle, holding out a scrap of torn paper, "Belle."

Child Belle runs to her sister, "Oh Hester. Hester! I've missed you so much." She tries to hug Hester, but she steps back.

"Belle, this . . . this is for you. They found it in his pocket." Hester's voice catches with emotion. "Willie wrote it."

Child-Belle takes the poem, "Willie?"

Without warning the door opens. Sarah Brezing appears in the doorway, swinging a bottle. Her eyes are bloodshot; her hands shake as she puts the bottle to her lips, and stares hard – trying to find Child Belle in the muted light.

"Mama?" Child Belle, confused, turns towards her mother. Hester steps back towards the stove.

"Oh baby, sweet baby, don't cry."

"Mama, what's happened?"

Sarah walks towards Child-Belle, falters and catches herself. Her words come out in short gasps of breath, "Baby, they was playin' . . . he was shot. It was an accident."

"Mama . . ."

"Baby, Willie and the O'Hara boy was foolin' with a pistol up at Dudley School – in the yard." Sarah reaches out to smooth Child-Belle's hair.

Child-Belle catches her mother's wrist, "Mama, I don't understand what you're saying."

"The pistol went off and Willie . . ." Sarah, hysterical, tries to hug Child-Belle.

Child Belle reaches up and turns her mother's face towards her, "Mama, is Willie hurt bad?" Her mother slinks back. "Hester, is Willie . . ."

Hester, crying uncontrollably nods "Yes."

Sarah stands, "They don't think Willie's gonna make it, baby."

Child-Belle rushes at her mama, curling her hands into fists, "Look at me. Look at me, mama. Where is he? Where is Willie, mama?"

Sarah moves towards a chair, "Ya don't want to see him, Belle. The bullet went through his left eye. Try and remember Willie the way he was the last time ya saw him. Here, baby." She offers the bottle to Child-Belle, staring at her mother.

"Mama, is Willie dead?"

Sarah shakes her head, "No . . . not yet. But Belle, the bullet- they say it blew out his . . ."

Hester covers her ears, and leans forward. Child-Belle stands frozen. Only her bottom lip quivers; she slowly unfolds the scrap of paper and reads Willie's poem. Spirit Belle watches, reciting from heart "And when grown up, I'll marry she who gave me first – her kisses free." Your friend, Willie Sutphin.

Sarah starts to undress; she flings off her petticoat and slips into a man's trousers. Her wild behavior frightens Child-Belle who tries to hide the bottle of whiskey. Sarah circles the room in crazy, spinning motions, "Where is George's other shoe?" She holds a man's boot over her head, hopping from one foot to the other. She is pathetically comical.

Hester, glaring hard, holds out the other shoe.

Sarah, as if seeing her for the first time, curtsey's in thanks, "Why Hester darlin', I didn't see ya there. How sweet of you to come for a visit. Course with Willie getting' a bullet through his brains, it ain't the best time for a social call."

"Oh hush-up mama, I didn't come for a social call."

"Well, I'm glad ya still remember who I am. How's that husband Pickett of your's?" She laughs, a coarse, wildly uncontrolled laugh, "Piggy-faced Pick! I'm surprised he let you out." Sarah swings the boot threateningly over her head; her eyes flash. There is something almost alien in her bizarre behavior. Frightened, Hester backs up. Sarah impulsively throws the shoe and then grabs Child-Belle, "I'll say a wee prayer for you wee Willie Winkle." She kisses the little girl hard on the lips. Child-Belle wipes off the kiss and stands still.

Sarah retreats for the still open door. A cold draft of air blows into the room, extinguishing the one lit candle. Her coarse, drunken laughter fades into nothingness. Child Belle closes the door and looks longingly back at Hester and tries to hug her. Hester, however, does not return the affection. She simply places a hand on Child-Belle's shoulder and without saying a word, she leaves. Then, in the doorway, she turns, and starts to say something, but the words catch in her throat and only her eyes speak "I'm sorry." Then she's gone. And Child-Belle, left alone in the dimly lit room, gathers up her paper dolls and sitting on the floor, she opens the folded scrap of paper and reads Willie's poem.

"If kisses sweet you'll give to me
If dreams unsung you'll dream with me
Then I will fly with the Great Gray Hawk.
And give my heart to she
Who gave me first her kisses free."

Your friend, Willie Sutphin

Her voice breaks, "Please God, don't let Willie die. Please." The little girl buries her head in her lap, sobbing. Spirit Belle stands in the doorway, remembering the poem.

As the crooked house on West Main fades, Billy places a strong arm around Spirit Belle's waiste. "What happened to Willie Sutphin, Belle?"

"He died. Two days later."

"What happened to Willie's friend? His childhood playmate who hankered for play-pretend?"

Spirit Belle closes her eyes, "She died, too, Billy. Two days later." She pulls free from Billy's hold, "I'm tired, ya understand."

Billy takes Spirit Belle into his arms, and kisses her gently on her forehead.

From downstairs, Flora's voice sings out strong. It's a familiar spiritual, "Hush, hush, somebody's callin' my name."

Billy glances at the clock, "Flora's right about one thing. It sure is hot. Powerful hot."

CHAPTER FOURTEEN

Valentine's Day
February 14, 1874

As Flora's singing fades into a humming, Spirit Belle turns and looks at the Grandfather Clock. She looks at Billy, but his eyes betray nothing. Slowly, she tries once again to open the clock door. It's still locked. The hands quiver, but do not move. Behind her, Billy winds a Music Box. The tinny melody has a strong effect on Spirit Belle who whirls angrily, "Oh, something about that melody just irritates the living hell out of me." She starts to grab for the Music Box, then recognizes the fan held out in Billy's hands. "No, Billy – no."

With clear purpose of intention, he ignores Belle and reads the inscription on the Valentine, "Presented to Miss Belle Brezing by Dionesia Mucci, February 14th, 1879." He opens the card, "Look Kitten, the Valentine's a fan."

As if attached to some invisible string, the Valentine's opening triggers the chandelier. As it spins round, creating a strobe-light effect, Spirit Belle shuts the Music Box. But it's too late. The memory appears, at first, in shades of greys and charcoal – as if being colored by a child's hand. And then Belle's childhood home appears. Child-Belle, slightly older, flirts with an unseen admirer in a long petticoat glass mirror. Behind her, Mucci, a thin, black haired man with a shadowed beard, watches. As he comes towards Belle, she suddenly sees his reflection in the glass and turns, slightly surprised. Suddenly, he grabs her playfully and swings her off her feet. Her bare toes brush across the top of his dusty, thinly soled boots. He laughs, a deep, vulgar laugh.

"Mucci, stop. You'll make me dizzy."

He swings her up, one last time, then lets go; she falls to the floor, unhurt but dizzy.

"Come, baby doll, sit on Mucci's lap." He makes his way to a chair, filled with dirty laundry. He throws the laundry onto the dirt floor and wipes the sweat from his neck. He rolls up his shirt-sleeves, pushing a wad of chewing tobacco back behind his yellowed teeth. He tries to grab her; she pulls away – teasing him with her swaying skirt.

"Play nice, Mucci. How'd ya git in?" She smiles, teasing him.

"I waited until I saw your mama go out."

"Oh ya did?" She goes up on tip-toe, turns in circles.

"Ah, you are bewitching me."

"Am I a witch?

Mucci kicks through the unclean laundry, looking for something, "A beautiful bewitching witch." He suddenly folds a dirty handkerchief over something in his hand – baiting her. She comes down off of her tip-goes and walks towards him. He sweeps off the handkerchief, revealing the present, a hand mirror. "Take a look, Bella."

"My name's Belle." She holds the mirror up to her face and brushes wisps of hair out of her eyes. She stares at her reflection in the mirror, then hands the mirror back to Mucci.

"Ah – you are bella. But the eyes, they are always so sad. Why?" He reaches for her; she backs away, playfully. "Come. Come here. Don't be shy. Mucci has more presents. Surprises, yes?" He leans down, and opens a worn leather satchel. She's missed seeing this and watches, curious. He holds out the satchel to Belle. She leans down, and takes out a box. Inside, there is a Music Box. It is old, crudely carved and tied with a tired ribbon. Excited, Child-Belle slips off the ribbon and ties it in her hair.

"Open it." Mucci's voice is soft now, coaxing the little girl with a secret in his laugh.

Child Belle opens the box and a tinny-sounding waltz plays. Two tin figures rise up and spin round, dancing to the music. She is mesmerized. Mucci leans in closer; his breath warm on the child's flushed cheeks. "And for my sweet Bella Rose, a Valentine." She looks up into his brown eyes and sees a look she has never seen before. But he teases her, pulling a fancy Valentine out from behind her neck. Child-Belle grabs the Valentine and reads out-loud, "With fondest love for my sweet Belle, You friend, Mr. Mucci. February 14, 1874."

Teasing, Belle turns the fan upside down. "Oh look, Mucci, the valentine's a fan." She fans her face with the fan.

Mucci laughs, "No, no my sweet. That is not the way it is done. At the Moulin Rouge in Paris, the ladies must appear – only appear to be shy. They are really quite coquettish." He places a sweaty bare arm around her slender shoulder, showing her how to hold the fan.

Child Belle feels the coarse hair on Mucci's arms, and the shadowed beard across his face; she tries to move out of his strong grasp. He tightens his hold; her body tenses. Beneath her white bodice, her heart beats fast. But she tries not to show the fear – tries to ignore the pulsing heart-beat and the intense warning that something is wrong. She takes the fan from Mucci, "The girls, Mucci, at the Moulin Rouge are they very beautiful?"

Mucci strokes her hair, threading the thick curls between his dirt-encrusted fingers, "Oh yes, my Bella. They are so beautiful. So fair. Like you. So soft, like a sweet peach. And their skin is . . ." Child-Belle tries to release Mucci's hand from her hair, but he tightens his grasp. "Sh-sh . . . their skin, Bella, it is milky white and pure." He bends his head to kiss her bare arm. "Sweet like cream"

Child Belle sits very, very still. Mucci lifts the child's long hair off of her neck and ties a lavender ribbon around her hair. She stares at the figures dancing round on the open music box. He turns her face up towards him – forcing her to look into his eyes. Frightened, Child-Belle again struggles, and tries to break free from his strong hold. "Mucci, please, I need to wind the music box." She actually breaks free for a second but he reaches out and grabs her, pulling her back into his arms.

"No, the music box is magic. The dancers cast an enchanted spell. And the waltz, sh- sh listen . . ." He kicks the music box away with his boot, "Ah – it plays for a long time. Sh-sh, my sweet Bella." He loosens the white ribbon on her bodice, turning her towards him and kissing her naked shoulder. Then his hands find her small breasts.

"Mucci, please, you're hurting me."

"Sh-sh, Bella." His face reddens and a strange, wild hungering glazes over his dull eyes.

"Mucci, please." She tries to smile, trying to move his hand, "Don't. Please."

Suddenly, Mucci's voice deepens; a mask draws down over his weak features and whatever kindness might have once existed in his nature disappears into a darkness that consumes him; he tightens his hand around Child-Belle's throat, "Sh-sh..."

Child-Belle, terrified, tries to force his hand off of her throat; but it is no use. She struggles to breathe, then closes her eyes and waits . . . He releases his hold. "Sh-sh, we are friends, eh? Are we not good friends, Bella. Be still. Be a good girl for Mucci. I won't hurt you."

Mucci kisses Child-Belle on her neck, where his hands have left heavy red marks; he moves down her neck, breathing his hot breath into her face. Then he traces her mouth with his finger, "Ah beautiful Bella..." And he kisses the child full on her rosebud lips.

Child-Belle opens her eyes, staring in horror at the monster who holds her, and she makes a choice to let the dark magic swallow her up. She stops struggling. "Mucci, the ladies at the Moulin Rouge, are they . . . virgins?"

Mucci laughs, a low, almost demonic laugh. "No, my sweet. At Moulin Rouge, no virgins." He slips her bodice over her head, forcing her to hold up her arms and as she sits there, naked on his fat, naked belly, he looks at her. He looks at her breasts and her slender hips and he pulls her head down, laughing "No virgins, Bella, only painted ladies. Yes. Come. Come . . . Come to the Moulin Rouge, Bella! Come!"

He starts to grab for her.

She suddenly leans in and kisses him. Hard on the lips. She slips out of his rough hands and stares at him. "You are a buzzard. A black buzzard with a broken wing. But I am a goddess. A powerful goddess. Come, take your kisses."

She holds up her hair, loosening the ribbon. She is now the goddess and in her eyes (which he misses) there is a look of defiance and mastery.

As the music box slowly unwinds, the dancing figures stop turning. And then, the haunting tune fades into the cicadas, clattering their fragile wings – outside Spirit Belle's bedroom window. The dirt-floored room on West Main in Belle's childhood home becomes a shadow-box. And the figures of Mucci and Child-Belle grow less and less distinct until they too slip into memory.

CHAPTER FIFTEEN

Broken winged buzzard

Spirit Belle shuts the Music Box. Her fingers tremble slightly as she leans forward; it is as if her body remembers what her mind had forgotten. But before the fear can erupt into physical convulsions, Spirit Belle kicks the music box. "The music box is broken. It no longer plays. And the ladies at the Moulin Rouge aren't painted ladies . . . they are whores. Isn't that right, Billy?"

Billy takes the Music Box, "Why'd ya save the Valentine, Belle? Keepsake of a rape?"

"Mucci didn't rape me. " Spirit Belle rises, places the Valentine back in the scrapbook and moves to the chaise lounge which has suddenly appeared. A faded French chintz with roses, the chaise seems oddly out of place with the heavy walnut bed and bull-horn chair. She falls back into the chaise, staring boldly at Billy. "We used each other." She opens the scrapbook, smoothing out the crumpled pages. "He wanted sex. I needed love. Fair trade. Mucci did me a favor. I had no illusions about what men want out of romance." Spirit Belle runs her fingers over the chaise – "I love the feel of French chintz."

"Mucci was a . . ."

"Mucci was a lonely buzzard. He was in good company with the other buzzards of West Main. And I was a witch, a beautiful, bewitching witch."

"Belle, no fourteen year old girl asks to be raped. You didn't want Mucci to . .."

She sits up, closes the scrapbook, "To what? Touch me? Bring me pretty presents? A Music Box? I hadn't heard music since Willie died. Mucci was an escape from a hot cramped dirt floor room in a one-room house . . . an escape from suffocating heartache. I wanted Mucci to be my friend. That door – that grandfather clock with all its secrets and magic has nothing to do with the old buzzard. I forgave Mucci a long time ago."

Billy dangles a ribbon, "In exchange for a piece of candy and a scrap of advice."

He holds open his palm, offering the stick of candy. Somewhat surprised, she takes the candy. As she brings it to her lips, Billy takes her other hand and guides her off the chaise lounge. She steps down – not in the familiar bedroom – but onto a porch, wrapping around a white-washed house. A sign in the front yard reads "Boarding/Lodging Guests". The screen door opens and a younger Belle, in her late teens, comes out, holding a pot. She walks down the steps, trying not to unbalance the piss pot, and empties out the putrid smelling urine into some scraggly shrubs.

Wiping the sweat streaming down her bruised face out of her eyes, younger Belle walks over to a large copper wash tub, stirs the laundry; the water splashes out – staining her apron, purpling her bare hands with the indigo dye. Suddenly, she hears whistling; Mucci comes up behind her, whistling through his tobacco-stained teeth. He startles her. She shakes her apron at him – "Shew, go on. Mucci, ya remind me of a buzzard."

Mucci, still whistling, takes a ribbon out of his pocket and ties it around her hair. She pushes him away and walks over to another tub where she takes out a man's shirt and begins scrubbing it hard with a scrub brush. "I'm not a little girl anymore, Mucci."

"I know that. But even big girls, they like presents too, yes?" Mucci unwraps a hard stick of candy. He starts to take a lick, grins at Belle.

"You are a buzzard and you eat the worst candy."

"Who else but Dionesia Mucci eats the horehound candy, eh?" He comes up behind her; she's leaning over the scrub board with her legs slightly apart. He watches her hips move rhythmically with the brushing motion. She catches on and suddenly whirls – as if to slap him. He catches her hand, starts to kiss her and sees her badly bruised cheek and blackened eye. He lets out a soft whistle and lets go of her hand, "You got trouble, Bella."

She picks up the dropped scrub brush, "Nothin' I can't handle. Alone." She scrubs the shirt. "And my name's Belle not Bella."

Mucci softens his tone; there is something in his voice that hints of actual concern for Belle, "Why you let your boyfriends beat ya up, huh?" He offers the candy stick. She shakes her head – her wet hair sprays Mucci.

He backs up; sulking, he licks the candy. "This is my fault. I am a buzzard. A balding buzzard."

Young Belle stops scrubbing the shirt; she looks around – sees him sitting on the porch step, his belly hanging out over his trousers – licking the candy stick. And she feels sorry for him. A lost soul struggling with his own demons. She walks over and rubs her hands on his head.

"Careful, my sweet, even the hair is going."

"What hair?" She laughs.

Mucci breaks the candy stick; she takes the smaller piece and sits down beside him on the porch steps. They sit there, in silence, licking the horehound candy. Neither speaks – and then Mucci swallows the last bit of candy, "Bella, Bella, what are you doing emptying old men's piss pots?"

"I don't know, Mucci. Sometimes I can't think anymore. It's like when I was a little girl and Willie and I used to run off together down to the railroad tracks."

A curious wind blows back the leaves of a near-by catalpa tree, scattering the white blossoms. Young Belle glances up, closes her eyes. Sunlight feathers through the green leaves of the ancient tree – illumining the girl's fine features. In this light, she sees a boy, with freckles, smiling at her from another time. And in the wind, she hears the faint playing of an harmonica. "Willie?" For a second, she actually sees – or believes she sees – her beloved playmate. He waves to her, holding high the harmonica. "Willie!"

Mucci burps, "Who ya talkin' to Bella?" He blows his nose in a scrap of cloth, then wipes his face with the same kerchief. "So you – you and this Willie . . . you ran off to the railroad tracks?"

Belle glances back at Mucci, attacking his already reddened nose, "Yes." She picks up a shirt and begins again to scrub the dirt. Then, when she's sure the shirt is clean, she hangs it up on a line. She repeats this ritual with shirts, talking to Mucci – but also to the unseen Willie eavesdropping from beyond Time. "We'd take off and head up towards Sky Bridge and we'd walk along the tracks. Just like a tightrope."

Mucci, still perched on the porch steps, sticks out his arms, flapping comically. Belle ignores him.

"Pretty soon, my hands would clam up and I'd get kind of jittery feeling inside, as if part of me somewhere really believed I was balancing on a narrow slip of track. Maybe walking on a bridge trestle way up high and then, the track would lift down, real gentle, and I'd feel the wind blowing sweet and cool against my bare legs and carry me away."

Mucci places his fist beneath his scraggly bearded face, eyes closed. He snores.

But Belle is far away, on that distant railroad trestle of Sky Bridge. "Far from the dragons and demons. Far away from the river looking like a muddy brown watersnake below. Twisting and contorting, circling in the shadowed water. The wind would whisper to me and I'd no longer be afraid. Up there, on the train trestle, I couldn't hear my mama's drunken laugh or the bastard Dutchman shrieking. Or the sound of a gunshot. There was just the wind and the sunlight and me."

As Belle turns to face Mucci, the harmonica fades. She glances up into the branches of the catalpa tree – but Willie is no longer there. A single white blossom falls from the tree. She picks it up and holds it close to her heart, whispering, "Willie." She smiles up as a sea of catalpa blossoms fall magically out of the tree – "See, it's like that now, Mucci. Only I can't hear the wind anymore. I'm all alone balancing on a scrap of metal track, twisting and coiling, leading nowhere. And in the distance, I can hear the train with its angry whistle coming straight towards me. Faster and faster. And faster."

Mucci snores, then chokes on the wad of tobacco stuffed behind his teeth. The choking awakens him with a sudden jerking motion. He spits out the yellow wad of tobacco and stretches, yawning. But curiously, he has been listening – "Then, get off the track."

"What?"

"You heard me, get off the track."

Young Belle picks up another stack of laundry and starts pinning up freshly washed shirts. "I can't. It's too late."

"Then get on the train."

She throws a hard look over her shoulder, "It takes money to buy a ticket."

He stands, suddenly bored, or perhaps needing to find his own piss pot, "There's more ways to ride a train than buying a ticket. You're smart. And pretty. Your ribbon's faded but not too worn." He slaps her backside. She splashes out water; he retreats. "Ah, but Belle, once you get on that train, there's no getting off. So enjoy the hell out of that train ride." He sneaks over and grabs her backside; she whirls and he takes her face in his hands. "Easy, such a wild pony, Bella. Easy, Mucci deserves a kiss." He kisses her, passionately.

She pulls back, "Go on ya old buzzard. No more sweet kisses for the buzzard. I've got a train to catch." She winks, raises her skirt and gives him a peek at her bare thighs. Mucci takes out another stick of candy and tosses it to her – then takes off. Young Belle leans down and picks up the dirty stick of candy; she lifts it to her lips and then changes her mind and drops it. She rips off her apron, and kicks over the copper pot of dye. The water spills out of the tub, staining the ground, coloring the forgotten bloom of the catalpa a dark indigo. The wind blows hard; and the catalpa tree disappears.

The bedroom takes shape. Billy spits out the piece of horehound candy stick. "But you didn't get on that train, Kitten? Why not?"

Spirit Belle glances at the bed, aware of the little girl's presence, sitting now on the edge of the bed itself. She shivers. "Oh yes, I did."

"Nope, honey, you got married instead." Billy whistles "Here Comes the Bride".

CHAPTER SIXTEEN

Johnny

Spirit Belle glares at Billy, starts to challenge him but instead, changes her mind and curiously, walks over to the four-poster. Careful not to look directly at the little girl swaying the burlap bag back and forth, Spirit Belle leans down and pulls a trunk out from under the bed. She gingerly polishes the trunk brass label, "MBB" and begins to hum a lullabye. "Hush, little baby, don't say a word."

"Belle, what are ya doing?" Billy eyes her curiously. "Why are you dragging all that stuff out?"

Ignoring Billy, she finds the trunk's key, hidden beneath the plate and opens the trunk, lifting the lid. Dust rises from the heavy lid. Spirit Belle takes a breath, staring at the carefully folded layers of tissue. Then, she folds away the tissue paper and takes out a doll. Dressed in green velvet, with real eyelashes and real hair, the doll's china face bares a striking resemblance to Belle herself. But there is a crack in the doll's left cheek.

Billy breaks the spell, "Belle, honey, what are you doing?"

"You're not real, Billy. And you've made me feel sad. Sad about Willie and sad about Mucci. I want to remember Daisy May."

"Daisy May ain't born yet."

Spirit Belle curls up her legs beneath her kimono and cradles the baby doll, lovingly brushing her dusty hair out of her eyes. She hums, then sings the lullabye "Hush little baby, don't say a word. Mama's gonna buy you a mockingbird."

Billy kneels down in front of Belle, lifts her face towards him. "Belle".

She scoots away, hugging the doll tighter. Then she takes out a tattered baby blanket and a tarnished silver heart teething ring. Billy stands, gazing down at her. Letting her have a moment – a wisp of memory with the doll. Then he glances at the clock, and turns to her – "All right. What happened, Kitten? How'd ya end up with an illegitimate, imbecile . . ."

Furious, she whirls around, "Daisy May is not an imbecile. How dare you? And I was married."

"Belle, honey, who are you trying to fool? Ya can't just skip over the murder." Billy, with a curious sense of urgency, picks up a newspaper. Tattered and yellowed around its frayed edge, the paper slowly repairs itself until it looks surprisingly new. Belle stares at the newspaper. Undaunted, Billy opens the paper, "Lexington Daily Press: Suicide or Murder?'"

"Oh Billy, you are such a party-pooper. I don't want to think about murders when I'm remembering Daisy May . . ." She bites her lower lip, glaring up at him. "Or when I'm dying."

Billy ignores her, reading aloud "A young man was found shot to death in a Lexington alley yesterday afternoon. His brain penetrated by a pistol shot, and by his side a small derringer."

Spirit Belle sings louder, rising and moving towards the window, "If that mockingbird don't sing, Mama's gonna buy you a diamond ring."

Billy, suddenly quite passionate, slips into a vest and turns to dying Belle's figure on the bed . . . and the girl with the ribbon, dangling her legs over the edge. He takes on the role of a southern prosecutor, (not unlike a fiery southern preacher) and launches into his legal attack - "Who was Daisy May's father? Was it Mucci, or were you, Mary Belle Brezing . . ." He turns, facing Belle ". . . slipping off to the Lexington Cemetery so often, ya couldn't keep 'em all straight?"

Spirit Belle hurls the teething ring straight at Billy; she misses but she's close, "All right. His name was Johnny Cooke of Saint George Cooke, my mama's beau and Cooke's Saloon lineage and when he asked me to make love I knew nothing else but to say "Yes, yes, yes. A thousand yes's for his kisses."

As if waiting for her to cue the memory, the wind blows through the open window – pulling Spirit Belle and Billy towards the distant memory. The bedroom dissolves into moonlight and Spirit Belle stands, facing her younger self – in the shadow of stone angels at the Lexington Cemetery. A young Belle, about sixteen, and a handsome boy with shaggy dark hair kiss passionately.

Spirit Belle, drawn to the boy almost in spite of herself, whispers his name, "Johnny." She holds out her hand as if to touch him, to brush the dark curls out of his eyes, but her hand passes through moonlight. He is beyond her touch; beyond all but what is real in his own shadow-box of time. He turns, rolls a cigarette and blows smoke-rings up at the moon. He is irresistibly handsome, bold and confident. Belle is smitten with him. She rolls up her linen, peasant-style blouse and kisses him on the mouth and then, flirting, jumps up and curtsey's to a stone angel. The angel, moss-covered, has a half-broken wing. Rising playfully, she holds out her arms, mimicking wings and recites the grave's inscription, "Blessed are the pure in spirit, for they shall . . .

Johnny, blowing smoke-rings, says straight-faced, "Baby, damn you're pretty."

Belle smiles, reads another marker, "Miranda Ambrose. Born June 16th, 1834. Died: September 18th, 1864. Rejoice forever. May the trumpets of the Lord make a joyful noise and blow . . ."

"Blow Gabriel, blow." He reaches up, unties her hair ribbon. Young Belle jumps onto another grave, leans down and reads the marker. "Johnston, Graviss . . ."

"Dead-beat."

"Johnny Cooke, have you no respect for the dead?"

"I got no respect for the livin', Belle." Suddenly, he reaches up, grabs her bare legs and pulls her down to him. Then he stands, holding her close and twirls her around.

"Johnny! Johnny stop. You're making me dizzy." She breaks free, spins around on her own and then props up against the stone angel with the broken wing. "Mary Belle Brezing: Born June 11, 1860.' Me and the Great War Between the States. 'Died at the age of 104. She was a lover of . . .'"

Johnny cocks his head, grinning up at her, "That bastard Johnny Cooke." He tries to loosen her already open bodice. She slips one hand to cover her bare breasts, but then allows his hand to slip beneath her hand. "Hush Johnny, you're bad."

He leans down, as if to kiss her shoulder, slipping off the bodice, and whispers, "And you love it."

"I love you Johnny."

He tries to untie her skirt sash, but she's too high, "Hey, will ya git off that grave stone."

"No, I like it up here." She pulls back, spreading out her arms. "I'm an angel."

"Oh yeah?" He lies back down in the grass, staring up at her. She balances gracefully on toe and leans back her hair, letting the wind shake it free.

"Yes. My name good sir is Gabriel."

He plays along, rolling another cigarette, "How ya doin' Gabriel?"

"I have a message."

She stands still, as if listening to some unseen Winged Being, then she whispers, "Johnny."

"I'm listenin'."

Young Belle slowly climbs down off of the stone angel and takes Johnny's hand. He looks at her, curious. She holds her fingers to her lips, "Sh-sh-listen." As she places his hand over her heart, there is the sound of wind, folding back the giant leaves of the white-barked sycamore. Johnny sits up, "Hell it's jest the wind. Or a couple of old drunk grave-diggers."

"No, sh-sh" She is suddenly quite solemn. She holds his hand, pressing it firmly against her own heart, "Listen. Sometimes, I wait till the house is quiet, real quiet and I lie still. So still I can hear my heart beating. And I listen. I know she's out there in the night. Waiting. Only I can't see her and I feel so desperately alone . . ."

A curious hooting rises up out of the wind's stirring. Johnny, uncomfortable with the sudden change in Belle's mood, tosses a stick at the black beyond the grave stones -

"It's a damn hoot owl, Belle. Come on, git . . ."

"No." Her voice is strong, passionate. And something in her eyes silences Johnny's coarse laugh, ". . . No." Then she kisses the back of his hand and in a gentler tone, whispers ". . . so terribly alone. But then I hear her. Just before dawn. Singing. Sh-sh, Johnny listen." She stands still, listening. "The darkness can't silence her. Not even here. She's come to sing to you and me and to our little one."

Johnny suddenly pulls free his hand, he steps back. "What the hell are ya sayin'?"

She faces him, fearlessly "I'm gonna have a baby. Our baby, Johnny."

He doesn't quite understand. At first. And a strange, boyishly lost expression clouds his eyes. But that quickly disappears into another mask. A mask of fear, concealing a repulsion. The cockiness disappears into a cool aloofness. Young Belle, intuitive, senses the sudden change. Desperate, she tries to kiss him. He brushes her away, a little too hard. And she places her hands wildly around his neck. "Look at me. Say something"

Johnny removes her hands, and holds her wrists. "What the hell do ya want me to say? Ya want me to marry you?"

"Do you love me?" Her words are edged with a desperate fear of what she knows is his answer. "Johnny, do you . . ."

His answer surprises her, "Belle, it isn't that simple. The world isn't like ya think." He releases her wrists. She stands, visibly shaking, in front of him. Staring hard into his eyes, which lower away from her penetrating gaze. "Angels and mourning doves cooin' – hell, half the time I got no idea what you're babbling on about. You're so . . . complicated and so damn pretty."

She stands there before him, half-naked, shivering and forces him to look at her by taking hold of his face and turning him towards her, "Johnny, do you love me?"

He nods, "Yeah, yeah, Belle, I love ya, baby."

Relieved, she releases her hold. He seizes that moment to swing his jacket over his shoulder as if to leave. She catches on that he's not serious and grabs for his arm. He pulls away, quickly and she tears his shirt. She catches her breath, "I'm sorry."

He drops any pretense of being chivalrous and mocks her with a sickeningly sweet grin, "Don't ever grab me." He steps back, "I just need some time."

He moves away from the stone angel, into the shadows. As he opens a rusted iron gate, his footsteps rustle, echoing the stirring leaves. Young Belle follows him to the gate – "You want time, you have it. Only don't expect me to be waiting on West Main until you figure out whether you love me."

Johnny's eyes are hidden from her; his voice, lower now and strongly masculine, eases her fears, "Sh-sh, sweetheart. I just need some time to think. Don't worry, Bella, I ain't gonna leave ya."

"My name is Belle." She tries to push open the rusted gate; the latch falls, locking it shut. She leans over the iron spikes, "Johnny! Johnny!"

Johnny turns for a moment, shoots her his cocky grin, "I'll come by in the morning. Promise." Then, he turns around, unlocks the gate and lifts her up off the ground. He kisses her hard. Passionately. Then, he's gone. Disappearing through the gate, into the silence. Young Belle, standing barefoot, and half-dressed, wraps her arms around herself. She leans forward, as if about to weep. But she doesn't cry; slowly, she gathers a great strength from the core of her being and rises up – staring, dry-eyed into the darkness.

Spirit Belle watches, her own face a masque betraying no emotion.

CHAPTER SEVENTEEN

Mrs. James Kinney

Suddenly, Billy swings down from one of the stone angels, "Now about the murder."

The memory suddenly evaporates. The cemetery folds up like a child's cardboard game, disappearing behind Time. Spirit Belle, not as cavalier as Billy about the appearance and disappearance of other worlds – of memories and secrets – turns to face the one image that always remains: Billy. She glares at him, "I didn't murder anyone, Billy. I got married."

And suddenly, as if aware of her own power to create, to dictate what does and does not materialize, Spirit Belle calls up her childhood home. She closes her eyes, as if thinking – drawing from memory to picture what has been buried deep in the recesses of her own mind. Billy, impressed, watches.

"You're catching on, Belle. You decide. You have great power. You realize that now."

Ignoring him, Spirit Belle draws with her finger in the air - tracing what slowly becomes her younger self. Dressed in a wedding dress with a high neck and long sleeves, young Belle stares at her reflection in a shard of glass, then rips off the bridal veil. "Mama, I am not marrying James Kinney."

Sarah Brezing suddenly takes shape. She is older now, with grey wisps in her chestnut hair. And her figure is fuller but her scheming eyes narrow, blazing with fury –"Sixteen years old and expecting a baby and ya think ya ken be choosy about who ya'll marry. You're damaged goods, sweetie."

Spirit Belle steps closer to her younger self and starts to pick up the veil; Billy's hand is on her shoulder. She stands still and turns her gaze to Sarah. "I'd forgotten how old mama looked – even before the wedding. Before the horrible paper ..."

Sarah picks up the veil, brushes it off and picks at a loose thread in the netting, "You're lucky I talked James into marrying you."

"Oh am I, mama? Am I so lucky to be marrying some man I don't even know. Or love."

Sarah places the veil firmly in her daughter's hair, arranging the white violets in the head-piece, and smoothing out the creases. Then she takes Belle's face in her roughened hands, "Love's got nothin' to do with this. What do you think is going to happen to you?"

Young Belle tries to step back, away from her mother's stench. Sarah grabs her face harder. "What kind of future do ya think you have in this town? I'll tell ya, sweetheart, because your mama's already been there. None. You ain't got a future. There's no place in this town or any other for them that's poor and break the rules. Either ya march right down those stairs and marry James Kinney or . . ."

Young Belle whirls, facing Sarah, "Or what, Mama?"

"You'll end up just like your mama. A drunkard, in and out of court, a laundress cleaning out old men's piss pots and nothing but a wh . . ." Sarah's face contorts; she catches her own reflection behind Belle's in the mirror and she suddenly trembles, falling onto the dresser seat. Young Belle, frightened, hurries over to the vanity and pours some cologne into a metal cup. She holds this up to Sarah's lips. As Sarah drinks the liquor, a thin smile creases her lips and she smiles. "Your mama's pretty baby, Belle." Young Belle gives in; she pins on the ripped bridal veil, stoically staring into the mirror. Spirit Belle steps in front of the glass, but Young Belle sees through her and finishes pinning on the veil. Sarah, pleased with herself, holds out the cup to Belle who takes a sip, then wipes her lips. Sarah laughs, "Ah you'll git used to him. He's got a good job up at the factory."

"Where Johnny works?" Young Belle's voice catches with emotion.

Sarah stands, breathing the liquor into her daughter's face, "You forget about Johnny Cooke. He's no good. His father before him was no-good, the bastard Dutchman." She smoothes the veil down across Belle's touseled hair. "You've got a chance. Take it."

Young Belle takes the bottle out of Sarah's shaking hand and takes several quick drinks. Then she takes Sarah's arm, firmly and turns towards the bedroom door. As mother and daughter step through the doorway, wind from an open window blows back the muslin curtains.

A White Feather floats down onto the vanity. Spirit Belle, watching from the windowsill, slowly touches her bare toes to the bedroom floor. She walks over to the vanity and picks up the feather. Suddenly, a single gunshot shatters the vanity glass. Frightened, Spirit Belle cries out, "Billy! Billy! Get me out of here."

The memory vanishes.

CHAPTER EIGHTEEN

A Love Letter

Spirit Belle stands in her own familiar bedroom, near the four poster bed. For a moment, she sees the little girl with the ribbon, standing close to her dying body. She shivers, folds her arms around herself and drops the feather. Billy picks up the feather and places it in the scrapbook; he's whistling – a tune that sounds like a made-up rendition of *Dixie* and *Here Comes the Bride.*

"Billy, stop whistling."

Billy stretches out on the chaise lounge, looking through old newspapers suddenly appearing in the scrapbook. "Now the marriage didn't last real long. About nine days was all."

"You're wasting your time." Spirit Belle amuses herself with a bottle of perfume. She admires the glass, with painted flowers – holding it up to the light. "And mine."

Billy proceeds to unfold an entire yellowed and faded newspaper – tucked into the scrapbook. "Now this business, Kitten, about whether it was a suicide or murder." He shakes the scrapbook, turns it upside down. A letter slips out.

"Where did you get that?"

"It was in the scrapbook." Billy hands her the letter.

"That Door has no connection to Johnny Cooke. Trust me."

"A little love note. Kitten, how come you never wrote me one of these?" He opens the letter. "Dearest One . . ."

Spirit Belle turns, grabs for the letter, and almost drops the perfume bottle. Billy taunts her with the love letter, "Such passion and for a sixteen year old boy." He suddenly stands, reading the letter. ". . . I will be down at three o'clock. Look out for me." Spirit Belle grabs for the note; Billy releases his hold. It drops to the floor. She leans down, picks it up and tears it into shreds.

"It's not that easy, Kitten."

"It is. Watch." She rips up the last piece of paper and puts it her mouth and swallows it.

Billy looks at her, amused. "You never fail to surprise me. But about the murder – did he meet ya, Belle? Did Johnny tell you he didn't love you?"

Spirit Belle takes a sip of Billy's mint julep, shaking her head. Her face reddens. Furious, she throws down the drink and cradles the doll, lying forgotten on the vanity chair. Holding the doll close to her heart, she sits down, rocking the doll and singing the lullabye. "Hush little Daisy, don't say a word."

Billy leans over her shoulder, "Who shot Johnny, Kitten?"

Belle turns her back, singing to Daisy, drowning out Billy's voice. "If that mockingbird don't sing, mama's going buy you a diamond ring."

Billy rises, taking on an unemotional prosecutorial style, "Who shot Johnny? Was it your mama?" Spirit Belle covers her ears, letting the doll lie in her lap. The doll's green glass eyes open, then close beneath the real eyelashes. Billy opens the newspaper and addresses the doll as if it alone were the unseen jury, "When first seen, the pistol was some distance from the dead body. In a moment or so afterwards, it was lying upon his breast."

Spirit Belle suddenly stands, holding the doll and singing to her. She sways and turns, playfully singing to the doll. "If that diamond ring don't shine."

Billy, undaunted by Belle's behavior, continues, "Curious that your adoring husband of nine days mysteriously vanished the same day that Johnny got a bullet put through his brains."

Spirit Belle stops swinging the doll and stands still. "Leave this alone."

Billy presses on, "Now why would a good-looking young man like Johnny Cook commit suicide? Come on Kitten . . ."

"Why don't you just go ahead and say it? You think I murdered Johnny."

"Did you?" Billy's question is without judgment. A simple probing for truth. But she evades the direct path and turns back to the doll. Lovingly smoothing the hair, tying the ribbon.

"What if I did? Would that black sin keep the Door to Eternity locked? Would that mystical Clock never reveal its secret portal? Are there no murderers in Heaven, Billy?"

"A few."

Suddenly, Spirit Belle grabs a pistol, hidden beneath the doll's petticoat. She waves the gun wildly, her eyes blazing. Billy stares at her. "What the hell do you think you're doing?"

"Close your eyes, Daisy May." She shuts the doll's eyes.

"Put the pistol down, Belle. You don't want to shoot Daisy May." He slowly lowers the pistol, and takes out the one bullet. "What happened? Did you meet Johnny at three o'clock?"

Spirit Belle hands Daisy May to Billy, then turns to the open window. "No, I wrote him a note, asking him to meet me at Christ Church."

The bedroom shakes, slightly. From every direction comes the tolling of bells. Church bells. Spirit Belle closes her eyes; and the memory plays out. Her voice resonates with the powerful ringing of the church bells. "Johnny! Johnny! Johnny!" And suddenly, the bedroom vanishes and Spirit Belle stands outside the magnificent cathedral. Sunlight streams down from the massive stained glass windows. She sees her former self, sitting on the steps. Waiting. Covering her ears with her hands. Desperate. Anxious. Young-Belle stares up towards the distant Gratz Park. Behind her, unseen by Young-Belle, the door of the church swings open. Wide. Organ music reverberates across the marble floor.

Standing alone, in a hidden recess just inside the cathedral entrance, a younger Billy, in a white acolyte robe, lights white prayer candles. The organ music stops. Footsteps echo, coming closer to the boy. Billy tenses, staring at the candle's white flame, suspended just above the last candle. The man's voice whispers, "You forgot one."

Billy tries to light the last candle; his fingers shake uncontrollably. "Did you think I wouldn't notice." Suddenly, sweaty, pale hands grab the boy around the throat, silencing him. Then the man turns Billy's face towards him; he places a finger over the boy's trembling lips. Strong hands grasp the boy around his neck, then eagerly grope the boy's body.

A figure in black twists itself in grotesque movements tighter and tigher around the frightened boy. Slowly, the white acolyte robe slips to the floor. Satisfied, the man pushes the boy back against the wall. His heavy footsteps echo in retreat, back into the silent sanctuary. Billy pulls his robe around his shaking body; he spits at the burning candles. Then he turns, desperate for fresh air, for sweet sunlight, for the feel of rain. Outside on the steps, he sees Young-Belle. And hesitates.

Angry, Young Belle kicks her leg. Shooing pigeons who rise up, sweeping the air with their wings. Their cooing is sudden and startling. Young-Belle, furious, rips off her hair ribbon, and takes off. Running.

Billy watches, and comes out onto the steps. His robe is disheveled. And his eyes speak a thousand secrets. He sees the ribbon; picks it up and takes off the robe, discarding it on the stone steps.

And the memory fades. Spirit Belle is alone at her sunporch window. "I didn't see you, Billy."

"No, Kitten. But I was there. I was always there."

"I'm sorry."

"This isn't my 'dark night of the soul'. So what did you do?"

"I went home. And Johnny was there. He said he'd been thinking about it and he didn't want some bastard child ruining his life so if I tried to stop him, he'd swear the baby was Mucci's." She runs her fingers along the dusty curtains, tracing the faint outline of a hummingbird in the faded lace, "I watched him leave from the upstairs window. When he got to the wrought iron gate outside our house, he turned around and he . . . he laughed." The memory comes quickly, painfully. "I – I can't go there, Billy."

"Then just remember."

"He laughed. I don't know why. Maybe he saw someone or something outside in the road – I don't remember what happened next. I only remember the sound of the gunshot."

Billy goes to her, "What made that poor boy turn around and get the bullet in his belly?"

Spirit Belle shakes her head, "I – I told you. I don't remember."

Billy sighs, thinking aloud, "Where was your mama?"

"How dare you! My mama was exactly what being poor and an alcoholic made her?"

Billy places a strong arm over Belle's head, trapping her at the window, "You're still covering for her Belle? What's it going to take to pry the little girl's hands away from her eyes?"

Spirit Belle tries to duck, to escape his hold. He pins her with his gaze, a solemn, penetrating look that forces her to speak the truth. She slowly drops the pistol and places the doll in the cradle, rocking it faster and faster.

"Kitten, what the heck are ya doin'? You're going to make Daisy May dizzy."

Spirit Belle stops the cradle. "This isn't Daisy May. This is only a doll." She takes a breath – breathing in the courage needed to recall the memory. "I hated him."

"Enough to kill him."

Spirit Belle glances down, then slowly raises her eyes. They are no longer as wild and fearful; there is something else in her gaze. It is a letting go – a willingness to look back. And slowly, the bedroom fades. She stands by the steps of Christ Church. But she is not alone. A young Belle, in braids, carrying a trunk, waits on the steps. As the bells chime the hour, half-past four, the younger Belle slowly rises. Suddenly, as if nauseous, she bends forward and leans her head over the railing. She vomits into a bed of ivy. Wiping her face, Young Belle becomes strikingly clear. Not simply a vague, shadowed paperdoll figure – but Young Belle appears in the memory.

She takes her trunk and with resolution, turns and spits at the Church door. Then she makes her way back along the street, with its horse drawn carriages. One of the horses rears, throwing mud on Young Belle's lavender skirt. Furious, she glares at the carriage driver, crossing in between the carriages, risking the rearing hooves of other horses. As dusk gathers, storm clouds form on the horizon. Young Belle hurries down West Main towards her house. She kicks open the iron gate and sees her mother, hanging up laundry on a sagging clothes line.

Sarah, as if expecting the worse, takes a clothes pin out of her mouth and holds out her arms to Belle. The gesture of kindness is unexpected; the young girl throws herself into her mother's arms, crying out –

"Mama! Oh god, mama!"

Spirit Belle, standing in the shadows of the catalpa, leans back against a low-lying branch. She watches, calling the memory back. The sounds of the brewing storm heighten. Sarah brushes her hands through Young Belle's tangled hair, "Sh-sh baby."

"He's leaving. He's leaving me."

Young Belle feels her mother's body contort – with anguish and fury. Frightened, she lifts her eyes and sees Sarah's eyes glazed over with hatred. Sarah's voice sounds unfamiliar, scratchy and low. "Let him go."

"I cain't, mama. I'm havin' his baby. Oh god, I wish he was..."

Suddenly, Sarah pushes Belle back; she takes a pistol out from beneath her bodice. Sarah, perfectly calm now, stares straight into her daughter's eyes. "I should a'taken care of that bastard Dutchman a long time ago."

Young Belle wipes the tears from her cheeks; her fingers leave streaks of mud across her face. She catches on quickly that her mother has been drinking. Slowly, she reaches out for the pistol, "No, mama, not George."

Sarah, breathing in quick, shallow gasps of air, waves the pistol above her head. "George! I'm gonna kill you."

"Mama. no! Ya don't understand. I love him."

Young Belle feels the first heavy drops of rain; she gathers up her trunk and is halfway up the stone steps leading to the house. Then she senses, rather than hears something. A sound. A dove. Cooing. And then the brush of wind, against her face. She turns and sees a young man walking towards the gate. The rain pelts down in sudden, hard droplets. She looks at her mother, wildly waving the pistol and whipping down the sheets. And then there's a moment when the wind howls, and the sheets rise and fall, slapping the ground, swallowing up the shadows of Sarah and Young-Belle. And another shadow appears. Taller, lean and holding out something in his hands.

The gate hinges creak. Sarah hears the gate, opening. She points the pistol. The figure, coming through the gate, suddenly turns, as if to run. And Young Belle desperately grabs for her mother's out-stretched hand. "Johnny".

Young Belle's warning comes too late. A single gunshot penetrates through the eerie sound of the sheets flapping in the wind. Young Belle, terrified, screams and throws herself over Johnny's body. She lifts his head; blood, from his open mouth, stains her white bodice. "Johnny. Johnny, I love you. Please, please don't die."

The pistol drops by his lifeless body. Young-Belle leans down, crying hysterically. She cradles his lifeless body in her blood-stained hands. Then buries her face in her own blood-soaked hair.

A shadow falls across Young-Belle, holding the dead young boy. And two hands carefully slip the pistol onto Johnny's chest. Unseen, unnoticed, the stranger quietly steps back and retreats out of the yard.

And the memory stops. The images fade; the sounds grow distant.

CHAPTER NINETEEN

A suicide or murder?

Spirit Belle stands by the window in her familiar bedroom. Billy, sipping a fresh mint julep, sighs. "So what was it, honey. Suicide or murder?"

"Murder."

"But what made him turn around? Did Sarah . . ."

"She didn't do anything. I called out his name, that's all. I just called out . . . 'Johnny'."

"And then Sarah shot him?"

"Yes. Yes." Spirit Belle twists her hands into fists and pounds against the muslin curtain, "Yes. Yes. Yes."

Billy reads from the newspaper, pressing his point, "But in a moment or so afterwards, the pistol was lying upon his breast. Who had taken the pains to put it there? Why was not the mother of the girl examined? Why was not the girl herself forced to tell who was in the house at the time of the killing?"

Spirit Belle twists the cord of the muslin curtain, tighter and tighter. "Stop, Billy."

"Did you move the pistol, make it look like suicide?"

She shakes her head, "No".

"So it was murder."

Spirit Belle suddenly moves away from the curtain and laughs, "Ah, you're good. You would have made a brilliant prosecutor, Billy. But the paper got it wrong. And there never was any attempt to arrest me or my mama. Johnny Cooke tripped and fell, causing his own pistol to fire. Another tragic accident on West Main." She takes the newspaper out of Billy's hands. "I loved . . . I loved Johnny. And I forgave him a long, long time ago. Any portal leading out - beyond this – to a place of peace, a place of bliss –is not closed because of a boy who broke my heart in the shadow of stone angels."

Suddenly, she stops. Thinking. "Wait, rewind the memory, Billy."

"Why?"

"Someone else was there? Someone came into the yard. I saw a shadow. And hands, hands .. . Someone moved the pistol to make it look like an accident or suicide. Who was it?"

Billy shakes his head, "No, like I said, you missed things."

"It was that boy . . . . It was you, Billy."

He cracks his knuckles, almost too casually, "So, how's your adoring husband figure in all this?"

Spirit Belle, stunned by this revelation, stands by the window. Visibly shaking, she stares at Billy – painfully aware of the sound of the little girl, with the tired ribbon, now winding up a music box beside the bed. "He . . . James ran off when he found out I was expecting a baby. Mama hadn't told him about . . ."

"Sweet Daisy May." Billy, whistling to the same tune playing on the music box, picks up the doll.

"Yes. Daisy May."

"Destined to live all seventy-two years of idiocy in a Michigan Institution. A half-wit who inherited quite a sizeable estate before breaking her neck in some god-forsaken hospital in Detroit. What was the cost of not aborting Johnny's baby?"

Billy's words hit hard. Spirit Belle, tired of fighting, walks over to Billy and quietly takes the doll. Her voice has an edge hinting of an anger long repressed beneath the commanding powerful presence. "Daisy May was someone to hold, someone to talk to. Someone to fill in the silence. And by sixteen, I'd heard enough silence to last a life-time."

Billy stops whistling.

Spirit Belle faces him, holding the doll, "In a chill spring rain, I stood with Daisy May in my arms and watched as a couple of grave-diggers shoveled dirt into the silence of my mama's grave. Daisy May was the only reason I didn't put a bullet through my brains."

There is the sound of wind, rustling against leaves and suddenly, the room vanishes. Spirit Belle, with Billy, quickly ducks for cover beneath the naked branches of a sprawling sycamore – as heavy rain pelts down. Young-Belle, cradling a baby, leans down and places wild violets beside a freshly dug grave. The young baby in her arms cries softly, and Belle turns, making her way out of the cemetery. She walks stoically, numbed by feelings she cannot feel. A slight distance from the cemetery, she sees her familiar childhood house. The gate is locked; the windows are boarded up and lying in the muddy road there's a mattress. Young-Belle hurries to the gate, trying to open it. She takes off her thin jacket and holds it over the baby's head. Paralyzed, she stands beside the mattress. And then, rising above the rain, she hears Mucci's all too familiar laugh.

He is only a few feet away. Walking from his metal scrap yard, in the company of a young woman. She could easily be one of Mr. Megowan's "fancy girls" - with her hair piled high on her head; and her face painted with rouge and charcoal out-lining her large saucer like eyes. Mucci has his hand on her back, moving his fingers down, toying with her sash. They walk past the mattress, hurrying to get out of the rain. And neither Mucci or his prey seem to notice Young-Belle. But she notices him. Empowered by emotions she can no longer contain, she holds Daisy May close to her heart and starts walking, whispering, "Mucci, stop laughing. God-damn you Mucci, stop laughing." She covers her ears and sings the lullaby, "Hush little baby don't say a word, Mama's gonna buy you a mocking bird. If that mockingbird don't . . ." Finally, she looks up into the pouring rain, "I can't hear ya anymore, Mucci. I can't hear ya anymore, Mama. Are ya listening, God-- I can't hear ya anymore either." And she walks on, disappearing into the pelting rain and the mud.

Billy stands quietly beside Spirit-Belle. "What happened to Mucci, Belle?"

She sighs, "Mucci and I were both scavengers, Billy. He got what he thought he needed to survive; and I took what I needed to conquer."

They both watch Young Belle turn, with iron resolution, away from West Main; she wipes the dirt from her face, stands and starts walking up Main – towards town. She stops at the rusted gate and for a moment looks back. Laundry, now drenched, hangs on the clothes-line. The sheets rise in the sullen wind, then slap hard on the rain-christened grass. Young Belle stares at the sheets for a long time. A little girl's voice rises above the pain of the memory that now surges into her consciousness, "What ya doin', Mama?" Suddenly, Sarah appears. Smiling. Young and strong. Her voice speaks from a distant time, "Watchin', baby." And again, it is Child Belle's voice, "Watchin' what, mama?"

This time, Spirit Belle repeats her mother's words, "Watchin' the angel wings flappin' in the wind." And then she hears Sarah's laugh, a wild, raucous laugh that suddenly catches in the harsh firing of a pistol. And the shadows – of sheets and figures – disappear. Young Belle holds Daisy May closer and desperately afraid – afraid of the memory and the haunting sound of her mother's laugh, she pushes open the gate. Her boots slip in the mud; she leans down, balancing the baby on one hip and tries to pull the wet boots out of the mud. But they stick; the mud sucks the boots deeper and deeper into the quagmire. Exhausted, Young Belle leans down, slips her feet out of the worn leather shoes and hurries on. Behind her, like a pair of lost souls, the shoes lie, abandoned to the wild, untamed forces of wind and rain.

Spirit Belle follows Young Belle with her gaze; it is a look without regret. She starts to follow but Billy grasps hold of her arm. "So how long did it take ya to figure out that the only difference between a painted lady and a princess is the price?"

She turns, facing Billy, "Till I caught on nobody was going to rescue me." She takes a breath. The colors of the memory become paler; the sounds of the rain and the roaring near-by creek fade into a whisper. "We're all alone, aren't we, Billy? Was I really talking into silence?"

Billy's look holds her, "You've got to figure it out. Maybe it's just silence and maybe there's someone listening in the silence. But you don't just sit there. Sometimes, ya got to do something."

Spirit Belle throws back her head, letting the wind whip around her kimono. As the memory fades, the wind speaks with a different voice. The bells of Christ Church chime. "I did do something. I decided to get on the train."

Slowly, a new memory takes shape. Young Belle walks up Main, holding Daisy May. She crosses the now deserted street and stares into the window of Wolf Wiles department store. Something in the window display holds her attention. Spirit Belle watches, "I walked up West Main and stopped outside a shop. The bells of Christ Church were ringing. And inside the shop window, I saw a doll. The most beautiful doll I had ever seen. With real hair and real eyelashes. I pressed my face up against the glass and I could feel the warmth seeping through the pane, warmin' my bare skin. I stared at the doll. I wanted that doll so much. I wanted that doll for Daisy May. Then I saw a face reflected in the glass. A pale face with frightened eyes, full of longing. A longing to love – to be loved. To give love. It was my face. My eyes. My soul. Only it didn't belong to me anymore. Life wouldn't let me love . . . anyone. Ever."

Billy's voice is close, a whisper over her shoulder, "So you kept on walking."

"Yes".

"Up West Main to a large brick house."

"Yes."

"An historic house. Mary Todd Lincoln's grandmother's house."

"Yes. That's right."

"Who answered the door?"

Spirit Belle's voice is without emotion, "Jennie."

"No. She had another name . . ."

"Madam Jennie Hill. I was nineteen. I spent Christmas eve 1879 in a house of ill repute. And the day after Christmas I bought that doll for Daisy May."

"What about Mucci?"

"I never saw Mucci again. He sent me a postcard once. From Paris. With a picture of the Eiffel Tower. I wonder if perhaps the old buzzard finally got to dance with his 'la femme rouge' from the Moulin Rouge."

Spirit Belle turns, and gently places the doll back in the traveling trunk.

CHAPTER TWENTY

The Philadelphia boyfriend

"You paid an awful big price for that doll, Kitten. No one would ever be allowed to hurt or love you again."

Billy slips a strong arm around Spirit Belle. They are back in the bedroom with the peeling rose wallpaper, back in the present. She takes the feather out of her hair – "You're wrong, Billy. The door on that old Clock has nothing to do with Sarah Brezing or Mucci."

"Well, maybe it's another clock, Kitten." Billy winds up a Carriage Clock and places it near the bed.

"My old Carriage Clock." She blows dust off the clock, holding it up to the light. "I'd forgotten this clock."

Billy suddenly moves back towards the mantel. He opens the silver case and takes out the remaining cigars – putting them inside his jacket. Spirit Belle pounces – "I think you were jealous of my beau."

"Damn, Belle, ever' time your Philly boyfriend came to town, Ole Billy Boy had to move downstairs."

"Those Texas Longhorn chairs were a housewarming gift from the Senator. And you, sir," she brushes her hair up and pins it with pearls, "are re-coloring my memories. My Philadelphia beau was a southern gentleman."

"You've got a mighty convenient memory, Belle honey."

The clock rings, loudly. Billy glances back at the bed; as if cued by some unseen magic wand, the room darkens. And instantly, a candle appears, its flame flickering, then leaping high.

William Singerly, an over-powering, brusque man with thick hair kisses Young-Belle passionately. He caresses her body beneath her dress. Then,

87

impulsively, he pushes her back up against the mantel. A fire burns in the hearth behind her. He holds her face up to the light and looks at her.

Young-Belle, in her early twenties, meets his hungry gaze. "Mr. Singerly, what is your pleasure tonite, sir?"

"You. Undressing you is pure pleasure." His piercing blue eyes take in her eyes, her hair, face.

"Why, sir, you'll make me blush."

He slowly unties the ribbons on her dress and she stands in front of him, in a lace bodice and pantaloons. Singerly bursts out laughing, "We got to do something about the pantaloons. Get you a kimono - dress you like a lady." He grins, leans in, kissing her.

Young-Belle backs away from the scorching heat of the fire. "I'm all your's, sir. Dress me like your paper-doll."

Suddenly a clock rings.

Singerly backs away, "What the hell is that?"

"Carriage clock, Senator. Rings on the half hour." Belle smiles, coyly, as she reaches for the clock. She turns it off and looks back at the Senator.

"Damn Belle, is that all the time I'm supposed to get?"

Embers spark from the fire; she jumps back and he takes her two hands, guiding her over to a small trunk. "I brought you something. Take a look in that trunk." He watches her, then lights his cigar from the fire's flames.

She opens the trunk. And takes out a pair of sexy open-toe gold shoes. "I've never seen such beautiful slippers."

"They're from Paris. Latest fashion for the Moulin Rouge girls."

Young-Belle's eyes flash; but she covers her reaction, "Thank you." She starts to put the shoes back in the trunk. Singerly catches her hand and pulls her over towards him, down onto his lap.

"Here, sit, babe. I'll show you how to wear 'em. It's an art to wear these shoes."

She sits, allowing Singerly to lace up each shoe. He massages and kisses her legs.

"I wanted to bring you something that would dazzle you, Belle."

She gets up, easily finds her balance in the heels, and admires her reflection in the mirror." You mean, dazzle you, don't you, sir?"

She sees him looking at her reflection and laughs, kicking out her leg, "Well, maybe pantaloons and gold slippers aren't such a good match."

"I can fix that." Singerly grabs her and rips off the bodice, tearing down the pantaloons. Belle, suddenly cold and embarrassed, stands naked, in the open-toe shoes. "Git over here." He pulls her towards him, kissing her passionately. He slips off the shoes and pulls her up, carrying her over to the bed where he caresses her breasts, then tilts back her head, looking straight into her eyes.

"Damn Belle, you make me believe I'm a better man than I am." She reaches for a bottle of bourbon and pours it into his lips, "Damn, Lexington's got Philadelphia beat by a long shot. Fine whiskey. Fine fillies and . . .:" He catches Belle's hand; holds the bottle to her lips. She drinks. "Your mama did something right."

She looks at him, her green eyes flash, "My mama?" Then, impulsively, she laughs and begins to massage his thick neck. "Lean forward, sir."

He leans slightly forward and as she massages his back, the movement gives his voice a slight vibrato. "You feel good, babe. Ya know honey, I can talk to you. Really talk. Not just bullshit, ya know what I'm saying? You make me feel like a man. Not a publishing king pin or a man with power. Just a man who's got – I don't know. A soul. Damn, I said it. Something about me makes me feel god-like. Not religious. It's different; I can't explain it, baby. Something about your eyes. You're smart, Belle. Intelligent. See it in your eyes."

"I'm surprised you've ever noticed my eyes." She presses her fist into small circles and pushes her body into the massage. He turns, sitting up and holds her face, forcing her to look into his eyes. "I'm serious. I joke about a lot of nonsense, but this time I'm serious. I can count on you to listen and say what ya think; not just agree with me to publish editorials about getting' a tax lowered or women the right to vote or getting paid a decent wage."

She moves back, playfully – "Well, sir, I get paid for other sweet indulgences."

Singerly groans, "Hell yes, you get paid whether you agree with the troops in Cuba, the tariff on tobacco or women getting the right to vote. Damn females don't know their place." He waves his cigar – motions for a match. Young Belle strikes a match and lights his cigar. "These damn suffragettes . . . and they're all pug-faced ugly. They hit every branch fallin' down out of the ugly tree." He snorts, pleased with his analogy. "Ugly tree. Hell yes. They'll put you out of business, Belle. There's not too many women can be a lady in the day and a whore at night. But how in hell am I goin' stop women from getting the right to vote?" He kicks up his left leg, motioning for her to move down to his feet.

Young Belle firmly massages the bottom of his foot, "You can't. You might just as well surrender and pretend it was your idea."

"Surrender? Hell no. Surrender." She eases his leg down, kneels and smiles up at him. "Hell, you're smart. Too smart to be a woman."

Young Belle takes his hands and brings them close to her heart, allowing him to feel each naked breast. Then she kisses him, on his neck, his throat, his lips. He leans in to her, whispering, "Black Magic – damn, you're good. You've bewitched me Belle."

From outside a shrill train whistle blows. The train seems to be heading straight towards the bedroom. An intense whiteness suddenly illumines the room. The clicking of the wheels against the metal track roar. Black dust settles over the white curtains and bedcovers. "Damn, I feel like I'm swallowing coal dust." Impulsively, Singerly reaches for his trousers and takes out a check book. "Ya know what, Belle, I'm goin' buy you a house. Yes ma'am, the biggest, most lavish bordello south of the Mason-Dixie."

"Is that a promise, sir?" Young Belle stares into Singerly's eyes.

There is a second; he meets her gaze. "That's what I like about you. You're all business. Turn around." She turns. He writes the check, using her back. Then he reaches over and hands it to her. She takes it, gets out of bed and walks closer to the candlelight –

"Fifty thousand dollars!" She holds the check up the light – almost not believing her eyes.

"And I better not hear that damn Carriage Clock go off again."

"Mr. Singerly, sir, you just bought yourself that Carriage Clock."

"And you better build yourself a house, Madam." The kissing becomes more fierce. He lifts her up, "And buy yourself something besides these pantaloons." Singerly throws paper bills up over her; as she reaches for the money, he grabs her, slaps her on her backside, a little too hard. She winces.

"Damn darlin', you're too smart to be a whore."

He pulls her up onto his lap and lies back down on the bed. He forces her hands behind her back, holding her on top of his naked chest. "I got something different in mind tonite." He suddenly tilts back her head, holding her neck a little tight.

"I – I can't breathe."

He loosens his hold, just slightly, "Tonite, we're gonna try something different, babe." Suddenly, he pulls back his hand as if to hit her – but the room goes pitch black.

Spirit Belle abruptly blows out the candle on the nightstand. The memory dissolves into nothing more than puppet-figures, flickering in a shadowbox.

"Why didn't you rewind the Carriage Clock. Act like a business woman and get out of bed." Billy kicks Singerly's boot back into the memory; it too disappears.

Billy glances at the window; it rises – letting in the air. "What were you feeling when he rubbed his thick, calloused hands over your naked . . ."

"His hands weren't calloused, Billy. They were soft; fleshy. He was a . . ." her voice breaks slightly, "a gentleman. He was . . . Damn, I didn't feel anything. Singerly was a way out." She faces him, furious.

"Out? You didn't take that fifty grand and get out. You got in – in deep."

"So what if I did? I had one hell of a good time, didn't I? I went to New York – shopped in all the finest stores. I bought silk teddies that cost five dollars and twenty-five cents, more than a week's wage at the Lexington Water Company, Mr. Mabon."

Billy remains calm, "Belle, you could have moved to New York. Why couldn't ya leave his money alone?"

"I – I . . . you're such a horrible 'spirit guide'. You must be a fallen angel. An antagonist sent to bully me. I'm surprised I missed your Trojan horse – oh no, it's the Clock, isn't it?"

"Belle . . . calm down."

"I am not going to calm down. You're the bad guy, here."

"There are no bad guys. There are just choices."

"And I chose to be a painted lady. And I chose to learn how to do French manicures, and how to sweep my tangled mane up into a classy style, and how to wear the most seductive perfumes from the most lavish salons in Europe. And which lingerie is most alluring – white or black? I learned this from a timid Wolf Wiles store clerk." She laughs, a little too coarsely.

"Ah, my sweet Belle, you missed things."

The room vanishes. And Spirit Belle feels herself spinning, catching her reflection in a curious hall of mirrors that then lead to a street. Time flows backwards. And Spirit Belle stands beside Billy, outside a department store on Lexington's East Main Street. She observes the memory.

91

CHAPTER TWENTY-ONE

Shopping

A pretty face, framed with dark ringlets, stares out the second floor window of the Wolf Wiles Department Store, on East Main. Mary Elisabeth's eyes widen as she stares at a carriage, drawn by two plumed bay horses. As the carriage door opens, stylish white kid leather boots step down onto the bricked pavement. Spirit Belle, as if sensing the young woman's presence at the store's window, looks up. But all that she sees is the faint flicker of a window sash, fluttering.

Young-Belle, in a fashionable dress, turns gracefully and motions for the other passengers inside the carriage to follow her. One by one, the women, in dark, attractive gowns, make their way towards the store's impressive front entrance. The last lingering light of the summer dusk glints off the store's tall glass windows. Belle catches her own reflection in this glass and then sees the reflection of another girl – the last to emerge from the carriage. Slender, with her hair pulled back from a face with high cheek-bones, the young woman's skin glistens; she is exquisitely beautiful and also somewhat exotic. Only when she comes full into the light is it apparent that she is bi-racial. Belle turns and holds out her hand to the girl, "Beatrice, you'll walk with me."

Although the sign on the store says "Closed", Young-Belle pushes through the revolving glass door, trailed by her entourage. There are four girls, counting Beatrice. Each has a quiet demeanor – as if completely awed by the beauty and rich intoxicating aroma inside the elegant store. Although their hair is swept up under carefully pinned hats, and identical in style, their respective hair colors suggest a difference in possible ethnicity. Two are blonde, with the shortest girl also being most likely the youngest in age. The taller girl, with striking black hair, has sharp cheekbones and wide luminous eyes suggesting a background that hints of Cherokee.

The lighting inside the elegant department store is muted. Mannequins in stylish gowns take shape in the shadows. Young-Belle stares at a red-haired mannequin dressed in a chocolate brown satin gown with a plumed hat. Her eyes take in every detail of the gown; she studies the buttoned bodice, the curve of the sleeve, the lace-trimmed neckline. Then, Young Belle throws back her shoulders, lifts her skirt and strides up the wide stairway. Waiting at the top of the stairs is Mary Elizabeth, a terribly nervous clerk, even more agitated by the thought that she was caught spying out the window. She moves eagerly from behind a counter and nervously places lingerie on a tray lined with black velvet. Belle looks up and smiles.

"Please thank Mr. Wiles for closing the store. You're very kind to assist me."

"I'm not kind. It's my job."

Belle ignores the clerk's accusatory tone and carefully picks up two pieces of lingerie - one is black, laced with red bows; the other is pure white, tied with a white ribbon. "Yes, well then, which color do you think is the most alluring?"

Mary Elisabeth blushes. "White is usually the choice for brides." A smug smile tightens the corners of her thin lips and she bends down to lock the lingerie case with a key.

Young-Belle holds the lacey lingerie up to the light, musing "White? Yes, but no man can resist in a woman in red." Belle laughs and turns to show her girls the fancy lingerie. As she is turned towards the girls, a large woman in a peacock feathered hat, saunters out of the dressing room. She sees Belle, gasps and disappears back behind the curtain.

"I'll take twenty pairs in white. Save the red for my hair." Young-Belle smiles at Beatrice. "I never can quite make up my mind on color!" She glances back at the girls and actually winks. The lightness of Belle's manner seems to invite the girls to relax. They smile.

Mary Elizabeth does not.

Then, unexpectedly, the sound of a sneeze – a stifled, rather high-pitched sneeze, emanates from behind the dressing room curtain. Mary Elizabeth's eyebrow arches – in a quizzical expression of disbelief.

Young Belle turns back around, facing the counter. But all eyes – those of the girls and Belle – are fixed on the dressing room.

"Mr. Wiles assured me that the store would be closed." Her eyes hold on the curtain which seems to be breathing, pulsing in and out. Then, there is another sneeze followed by a quick short sneeze. Belle whispers, "God bless you" – as her gloved hand pulls back the curtain. Revealing a large woman, holding out a large white garment that resembles a horse's saddle.

Mary Elisabeth's lips quiver, "Gertrude Lawrence – what on earth?"

"Mary Elizabeth, never mind. Never mind. None of these ridiculous undergarments fit me now that I've lost some weight – due to my nerves." Without acknowledging the presence of Belle or her girls, Mrs. Lawrence plops the girdle down on the black velvet tray, next to the white lace lingerie and glaring at Mary Elizabeth, makes her way down the stairs. Her feathered hat bounces wildly on her head. Half-way down, she sneezes. "What on earth is that smell - Wretched odor. Some cheap cologne." She reaches the bottom of the stairway, and as she pushes her considerable weight against the revolving glass door, she sneezes. Again.

Young-Belle whispers, "Poor soul, must be allergic to peacocks."

Then, suddenly, the lights dim. The faces of all of the girls, Young Belle and Mary Elisabeth freeze. Time stops and the store's walls, and stairway fold in . . . as a cardboard doll house being carefully folded up to fit in a traveling case.

And the memory disappears.

CHAPTER TWENTY-TWO

A bicycle ride

Spirit Belle picks up one of the scraggly cats and blows softly on the velvety black fur. The cat meows. "I'm sorry if I wasn't nice to Mary Elizabeth – how could I possibly know she was your sister. You don't look alike. But I was always polite to her. She later taught me how to do a French manicure." She glances at her nails. "I could use one now. Where is she?"

"Locked up in an asylum. Her nerves finally got the best of her."

"What is it with all these fine genteel southern ladies and their nerves. Too many repressed secrets. Really, you should have told Mary Elisabeth to speak up if she didn't want to wait on me and my girls."

"She needed the money."

"And so did I." She meets his gaze. "What color are your eyes, Billy? I don't remember them being so blue. Or is it this light? Colors can be tricky."

A can of paint suddenly materializes on the sunporch windowsill and Billy very casually opens it, dips in a paint brush and paints a swatch of color on the wall. Then another; each brush swipe produces a different color. Pearl white. Then, crimson red. And a dapple of fresh mint green.

"Well now you're a circus pony with a can of paint."

And the bedroom blows away – into the past. Spirit Belle stands beside Billy outside the newly constructed house at 59 Megowan. She steps back, gazing at the curious mixture of different bricks. At first she doesn't see her younger self, and then, as the memory pulls her deeper into its powerful spell, Spirit Belle hears the swishing of a brush – a paint brush dancing on hard brick. And she sees Young-Belle swiping different paint colors against the multi-colored bricks. The Victorian house, two stories high with a second floor sun porch, towers behind the young girl. Dressed in a simple cotton frock with a white apron and pig-tails, Young-Belle swishes the paint with the concentration of a young artist trying out different colors on a canvas.

Young Billy, in his early twenties, circles close to the house on a bike too small for his legs. He hesitates, starts to throw a paper up onto the porch and then sees Young-Belle. He quietly walks the bike up closer to the porch and takes cover behind a giant catalpa. Suddenly, his hands slip; the bike falls- startling Belle who turns, accidentally swiping the paintbrush across her cheek.

Billy quickly picks up the bike, jumps on and starts to pedal. Fast. But she sees him. "Hey, Billy Mabon, when are you going to step out of the shadows and stop watching me."

Billy slows the bike, scuffing his shoes in the dust. His face reddens.

"Hey, I'm talkin' to you." She walks over to the edge of the porch, holding up her hands to shield the morning light. Looking straight at him. "Ain't you a little old to be a paperboy?" She places her hands firmly on her slender hips, baiting him with her smile. One pig-tail ribbon is loosely untied; her cotton dress falls simply around her figure.

"It--t-it's *aren't* -- not . . . ain't." Struggling hard to speak, he looks up.

"Well, aren't you?"

"M-my bro-brother broke his arm." Billy says this as if it took all of his courage – and strength just to utter the words.

She takes the paint brush and casually lifts her skirt, exposing her bare leg and then she sits down and begins painting her toenails. "You don't have to talk fast, Billy. Breathe before you speak. Got it." She smiles, "Aren't all the Mabons lawyers." She looks him straight in the eyes; and there is something very empowering about her gaze.

"Ain't you a Mabon?"

He finds his voice.

"Aren't you a little young . . . to be a . . . Madam?"

She lifts her skirt higher, wiggling her painted toes. "Ya want to find out?" He turns the bike around as if heading back down the hill. Then, suddenly, he stands and plays tricks on the bike. It goes up, flies air-borne, and then lands. She laughs. "Someone will have to put you in a circus!"

Billy grins, pushes back his cap, gazing up at the multi-colored bricks, "Ya . . . got a . . . funny looking house, Miss Brezing."

"The different bricks are cheaper; ya want to fix it?" She holds out the paintbrush.

"Nawh, unless – you want to – to deliver papers?"

Young-Belle tosses down the paintbrush and accepts the challenge. "I'd love to be a paper boy." He's shocked. She pulls up her skirt, folds it around her legs and gets on the bike.

He hands her his cap. "Tuck in your mane."

She pulls back her hair, pushing it up beneath the borrowed cap. Then she grabs hold of his waist. Young Billy stands, guiding the bike down the hill. He kicks up speed, letting the old tin bicycle find a second wind.

And the bike flies.(Almost.)

Billy takes the corner at Megowan and Main like a seasoned cowboy on a well-trained horse. He scuffs his shoes in the dust as he reins in the bike and then nods, "Toss it." Belle reaches back into the basket and throws the paper up onto the porch of a five and dime. Then they head west, gliding past the stores and the early morning risers, shoe shine boys and the Ice-man with his chunks of glistening hard ice in the back of his cart and the older milk man carrying the bottles of fresh cream, past stray dogs chasing squawking chickens. And suddenly, for Belle, this is no ordinary bicycle ride.

The bike has strange and wonderful powers. Lifting her up, off the ground – freeing her from fear. The bike's wheels spin at an incredible speed and she closes her eyes. Feeling the lilt, the lift over bricks and earth – she lets go. And in that moment, she realizes, unexpectedly, that she is flying. Up through the greens and lavenders of the spring morning – up through the sweetness of wild honeysuckle and lilac . . . then through the sun-drenched dew and clouds, feathering sunlight – up and up until she feels as if she and her paper boy are the only Beings. Alive. Exhilerated by the sheer joy of riding behind Billy, Belle opens her eyes to a world of colors and vibrancy she has never before witnessed.

She throws back her head, breathing in rhythm with the bike; feeling the rush of wind across her cheeks and the tingling warmth from holding on tight – oh so tight – to her paper boy.

At the corner of Limestone, they head up towards Gratz Park where the house belonging to Lexington's first millionaire (John Hunt) rises up across from a magnificent southern mansion. Billy slows the bike in front of this house, on the corner of Market and Mill, crossing over towards the stately mansion with a high brick wall. He does the honor with the newspaper and hurls it up across the wrought iron gate, intending to hit the porch but narrowly missing the front window. He gets off the bike, opens the gate and searches through the wild tangle of over-grown ivey for the newspaper. Then, he places it firmly down by the front door and turns back to Belle.

"You hungry?"

Belle remains on the bike, "Maybe a little."

"Ya up for a picnic."

"Isn't it a little early . . ."

"Breakfast." He hesitates then says quietly, "You don't always have to lead; sometimes it's all right to trust someone else to .. ."

"Lead on." She pushes her hair back up under the cap, then holds out her hand.

He takes out a small bag, "Come on."

She gets off the bike and curious, follows him around to the side of the house where a tall brick wall encloses a secret garden. The gate allows only a small view of the boxwood and flowering trees; there are several large grist mill stones placed around the garden, suggesting a path leading to a fountain. Billy offers his hands as a lift for Belle; she takes hold of his shoulder and climbs up onto the wall. He follows and they make their way along the wall to the shadow of a dogwood.

"All right now." Billy brushes off some petals and leaves, then lays out his cloth handkerchief. "My lady."

She sits. And leans back, looking up through the branches at the sky. "This is delicious."

"You ain't tried it yet." He holds out a hard cinnamon biscuit.

"Oh, I meant . . . Break it."

Billy carefully breaks the biscuit; and offers her the largest piece.

And there, beneath a canopy of white dogwood, they escape Time. The sunlight flickers across the garden, revealing what had only been glimpsed through the gate. There are roses in the space of rich green and intoxicating scents of bread baking – coming from the back kitchen of the house. Belle loosens her hair and lets it fall around her shoulders. She gets very quiet; and he gets even quieter. And in that Stillness, twenty-two years of waiting and watching from the shadows melts away.

The silhouettes of the young Billy and Belle fade into the shadow of the tree branch, brushing light across the wall.

And then disappear completely.

CHAPTER TWENTY-THREE

Sassafras tea

And Spirit Belle, who has been observing this with her guide Billy, catches her breath. "I'd forgotten that cinnamon biscuit. The taste of sugar and real lavender baked into the bread." She smiles, teasing him. But he is waiting, waiting for her to stay with the memory.

"Most of life – even memories – can either be sweet biscuits or hard cold dough."

"I think you missed your calling; you should have written greeting cards." She faces him, "Why are we here, Billy?"

Billy doesn't answer. Not quite. Instead, he gazes up.

A solitary white feather floats down. Billy catches the feather and uses it to stir a cup of tea, which has magically appeared – mid-air. He holds the cup out to Belle, "Sassafras tea? Sweetened with sugared violets?"

Billy walks casually up onto the porch of the mansion.

"Billy, what are you up to now? I was enjoying that cinnamon biscuit with a rather amusing, if shy, paper boy."

"Moving time forward, Kitten. The ladies of Gratz Park are playing bridge- on the porch of the historic Bodley House, rented out for Lexington's Finest Ladies to play bridge."

"I don't know these women, Billy. You're wasting time."

"Oh but Kitten, I didn't bring us here. You did."

Belle, still in her kimono, cocks her head, "I think I'm slightly under-dressed."

"They can't see you, Belle."

Belle takes this as a cue and sits down on a bench, near the bridge table. One of the women, Maude Lockard, a well-groomed, soft-spoken Bluegrass aristocrat, fastens her hat, pushing up loose strands of hair. The hat droops over her face, giving the impression of something rather canine – the long drooping ears of a Bassett Hound. Maude then glances at the card table, set for a game of bridge and covered with a starched and pressed ivory Irish linen. Maude, the hostess, smoothes a slight crease in the cloth and then places a silver dish of nuts over a stain. Isabel, younger and more delicate than Maude, slips out onto the porch, carrying a candy dish filled with sugared violets. She pops one of these in her mouth and relishes the sugary sweetness as if it is the most delicious delicacy she has ever let touch her thin lips.

"Do they dip real violets in sugar or are these fake?"

As if not hearing Isabel, Maude sits down across from Nellie, a bird-like creature in pink, shuffling the cards. Several cards fly out from the deck.

Maude looks up, "Why Mrs. Van Meter, whatever is the matter?"

Isabel flutters around the table, "Oh wasn't it the most beautiful ball Mrs. Lockard? Everyone looked so nice." She drawls out the *i* making it a long two-syllable sound. "And the flowers- oh so *nice*! And the orchestra – wasn't it *nice*!" She pops another sugared violet in her mouth. "Are these –" she swallows the sugar whole - "real?"

Nellie wrestles in the escapee cards, "Where for heaven's sake is Mrs. Lawrence?"

Maude looks at her, "Shuffle."

Nellie shuffles.

"Deal. She'll be here."

Nellie shuffles the cards, backwards, forwards, then deals. Maude eyes each card; then picks up her hand. She takes a quick look, then leans in, whispering, "Can you imagine 'her' trying to give sheets to those poor little orphan children. It's sad."

Isabel burps, covers her mouth with a gloved hand, "Oops, sorry. What's sad? What sheets?"

Maude rearranges her cards – eyes Isabel who is circling the table. "Miss Pinkston, it would be very *nice* if you would please sit down. This is not at all like Mrs. Lawrence."

Nellie muses over her cards, counting in her head (but mouthing spades, hearts, clubs, diamonds, etc.) "No, I can't understand it really."

Suddenly, Gertrude Lawrence, tiny eyes glittering with gossip, bursts through the garden gate. Her graying curls are piled up under a big hat with a drooping fake purple hydrangea. She comes in through the garden gate, waving an umbrella. "Oh my! Sorry, I'm late. Oh my, my, my!" Out of breath, she manages to just make it up onto the porch before a sudden clap of thunder sends her scurrying to the bridge table and taking her seat. Isabel, flustered, also sits.

"Mrs. Lawrence, where on earth have you been? We've been worried sick about you!" Nellie folds her cards.

Isabel picks up her cards, eyes wide – "We have?"

Nellie waves her finger at Maude, "Mrs. Lockard, do you mind, there's something sticky – here on the table. We'll need another napkin."

Slightly ruffled but not wanting to miss anything, Maude hands Nellie her own napkin. "Go on, Mrs. Lawrence."

"Well . . ." She sighs, releasing a great breath that also seems to loosen some of the tightness in her girdle for she sways for a second, side to side, before settling back into the seat. Satisfied that she is now in control, Gertrude sets her jaw and announces, with an accent chosen (and indeed practiced) for this very occasion, "I saw HER."

Maude's mouth quivers; she freshens her lipstick - "Who dear?"

"That woman." Gertrude holds her cards close to her large, palpitating bosom.

"What woman?" Maude arranges her cards.

"Who shuffled these cards?" Isabel turns her cards upside down, revealing her hand. All of the other women shield their eyes.

"Isabel!" Gertrude gestures for Isabel to pull her cards back. "I'm a Christian but I'm no saint. If you give me a flash, dear, I'll be obliged to take a peek."

"So, Mrs. Lawrence . . . what woman?"

"Belle Brezing." Gertrude clucks her tongue.

It is this tongue-clucking, rather than the actual mention of her name, that lures Spirit Belle up onto the porch. She eyes Gertrude's hand.

"Where were you, dear?" Maude snaps shut her gold lipstick.

"In the Wolf Wiles dressing room." Gertude lifts up her empty glass, intending to take a long sip of tea – but there is no tea. "Mrs. Lockard, is there any tea?"

Maude is on her feet, "Yes, Yes, of course, dear. I hope you'll like it. Sassafras tea with lemon and mint." Her sturdy, navy blue heels click across the porch as she makes her way towards a side-board and picks up the pitcher of tea. Then she opens the silver ice bucket and spoons out several ice cubes with the silver prongs and finally pours Gertrude a glass of ice tea. Spirit Belle stands over Gertrude's shoulder, eyeing her cards.

Maude turns and with an expression of hoping to please, to be the perfect hostess, she places the glass down in front of Gertrude, "I hope it's not too warm. There's more ice and lemon. Oh and here . . . I almost forgot." She pops in a sprig of mint. "Picked it from the garden this morning. Can't get any fresher."

Belle fingers the bowl of fresh mint by the tea, "I hope some bird . . ."

Billy shoots Belle a look, "Behave."

"Do you have something to eat, dear?" Gertrude glances over at Maude who instantly rises and disappears towards the house. "Of course, of course. Be right back."

Gertrude takes long, dramatic sips from the iced mint sassafras tea. Savoring, relishing the dramatic pause before the pounce.

Spirit Belle fans her face with Isabel's fan. Billy motions for her to put it down. She does and then reaches to try on Gertrude's hat. Billy gets up.

"Belle."

"I thought they couldn't see me."

"They can see the hat." She puts the hat back down.

Nellie sweeps up her cards, "So, Mrs. Lawrence, where were you?"

"I was in the Wolf Wiles dressing room trying on a . . ." She lowers her voice, "an . . . an undergarment."

Maude returns with a plate of lemon bars and gingersnaps. She is all a'flutter. "What? What? I couldn't hear. Start over."

Isabel scoops up a lemon meringue, "Mrs. Lawrence was in the dressing room trying on a girdle."

Spirit Belle spits out her sassafras tea, then mouths "*Sorry*" to Billy.

"Did anyone get rid of the jokers?" Nellie glances at Maude who quivers again.

Nellie puts down her cards, and carefully picks up the joker and sets it aside. "Well, we'll have to reshuffle. Gertrude, you deal this time."

"Oh, but I had such a nice hand." Isabel sighs.

Gertrude shuffles. Maude prompts her, "So, you were in the dressing room?"

Gertrude nods, "Well, of course, they didn't see me. Not at first. And I heard Millie's sweet voice . . ."

Nellie turns an ace right-side up; Maude pretends she didn't see the card. "Oh dear, poor Mary Elizabeth Butterworth. Such a sweet woman."

Maude finishes Nellie's thought, "Yes but poor as a church mouse. Her husband, Archie, left her penniless. He had the Life Insurance Policy right on his desk when he died. All he had to do was sign it . . . but instead, he had a heart attack and died. Can you imagine. If he had just picked up the pen and signed his name?"

All the women shake their heads simultaneously. Isabel licks a gingersnap, "Poor Mrs. Butterworth. She has no choice but to be a shop clerk."

Maude's eyes flash, "She has a choice, Miss Pinkston. She could always teach school or be a librarian."

Nellie studies her cards, "Well, I guess she could be a nurse. But now she's too old, isn't she? Practically too old to do anything really except be a clerk or . . ."

Isabel pipes in, "She could get married."

The other women look at Isabel. Maude says what they're all thinking, "She's too old, dear."

Isabel is quite fascinated by her cards, murmurs, "Perfectly dreadful."

Maude echoes, "Dreadful."

Spirit Belle whispers, "I guess poor Mary Elizabeth could always be a seamstress or a laundress." Billy motions for her to sit. She moves over to a porch swing.

Maude, ever the gracious hostess, whisks up Isabel's glass, "Shall I freshen it?"

Isabel nods, "Yes, but please, Mrs. Lawrence, do tell. Go on."

"Well, I peeked under the dressing room curtain and that was when I saw her."

Nellie's eyelashes flutter, "Show us. Where were you? How close, Mrs. Lawrence?"

"Oh very close, dear. Very close indeed. I got a whiff of her perfume. Roses. Yes definitely rose – very expensive. She came in first – in front of the other girls. She swished up that Wolf Wiles stairway like she was the grand dame, the Empress of Russia, all dolled up in black taffeta with her hair pulled up." Gertrude pulls up her own hair and the others gasp at the style.

Maude's nose twitches, as if holding back a sneeze, "Is it red, Mrs. Lawrence?"

"Oh yes, dear, it's very red. But not the kind of red I've ever seen on any decent woman's head."

Nellie reaches for a chocolate bon-bon, "Is she fat?"

Spirit Belle, sitting in the porch swing, kicks out her legs – and flies back. Billy catches the swing.

"No, she's not fat, Nellie. Sort of round. Curvy." She clears her voice, lowering her eyes, "Here." Blushing, she pats her chest.

Eyes roll.

"Go on, dear." Maude flicks a card, prompting Gertrude to continue.

"There's not much else. She's really a rather unremarkable creature. Not at all what you'd expect, really?"

Isabel eyes a plate of meringue kisses, "Is she a Negress, Mrs. Lawrence?"

The other ladies, appalled, stare at Isabel who punches one of the chocolates – considers whether she likes the particular sugar oozing out of the bon-bon and simply smiles, a rather demure smile. "Well, I just wondered."

Spirit Belle gets out of the swing and walks over to the bridge table. She leans over Isabel's shoulder, as if about to spit in her tea. Billy motions to her – "Get back." Reluctantly, she swallows her spit, and retreats back to the swing.

Nellie motions to her empty glass and Maude springs to her feet. "Thank you, Mrs. Lockard. Now then, what did you do?"

Maude freshens the ice tea glasses; as they lift their glasses, a curious gesture occurs – mirrored in each face of the women. They simultaneously do not take a sip; but rather wait – breathing in the moment of pure exhilaration as Gertrude, her hydrangea now tittering on her hat, continues her story. "So, I saw Mary Elizabeth . . Mrs. Butterworth, of course. Oh can you imagine how degrading it must be for Mrs. Butterworth to have to endure that sort of thing. She ushered those girls . . . there were about five or six, counting the colored girl . . . I think she's the maid or something . . . around to the back of the counter and then she brought out the silk, well, the silk . . ."—she gestures, drawing in the air the silhouette of negligees and pantaloons. Gertrude is a rather gifted artist with her finger brushing the air. She leans in closer, "Five dollars a pair for the silk . . . you know what. Five dollars a pair!"

The women sip their sassafras ice teas.

"Oh this is delicious, Mrs. Lockard." Isabel pops a violet in her mouth.

"Why it's a sin if you ask me – to wear undergarments that cost more than your husband makes in a week."

Amused, Spirit Belle lifts up her kimono, sensuously exposing her thigh, "Want a peek?"

"You should listen, Belle. You might learn something."

Gertrude rearranges her cards, "Now where was I? Oh yes . . . well, she . . ." She lowers her voice and bids, "Two diamonds. Miss Brezing, then chose the girls' dresses. And I must say, the woman has surprisingly good taste."

"Chose you, didn't I, Billy?"

Maude responds to the bid, "Diamond."

"How many, Mrs. Lockard. How many diamonds?"

Fluttered, Maude pats her nose, "Two. Two diamonds."

"It was all rather dignified." Gertrude pushes back her hat, fluffing up the drooping hydrangea.

"Oh Mrs. Lawrence, how could such a wicked concierge possibly be dignified. That woman is living in sin." Maude bites into an ice cube.

"Well, Mrs. Lockard, she was most polite. Nothing vulgar. Not at first."

Nellie's in, "I'll bid a spade. One spade. What do you mean 'not at first'"?

"Ah-a-choo!" Isabel sneezes – waving her small hand over her tilted nose – "Who's wearing all that . . . ah-ah-choo! Perfume?"

Billy glances over at Belle, whose spraying perfume around her head.

"It's the goldenrod, Miss Pinkston. Just eat some honey when you get home." Maude gently hands Isabel a handkerchief. Miss Pinkston, sneezing, smiles and takes the handkerchief. "I'll have Wilamenia wash it and bring it back to you."

"No, no, no! All very dignified. It was only later . . . " She pauses for effect and then lays down a card; others follow suit. "I saw one of the girls, the 'negress' undressing."

"What? What I missed something." Isabel puts down a club.

Maude swooshes up the card and hands it back – "Diamond, Miss Pinkston. A diamond was played. Follow suit, dear. Now, Gertrude, oh dear – Mrs. Lawrence was hiding in the . . ."

"I was not hiding." Gertrude takes the trick.

Nellie smiles demurely, "Go on, dear."

"I peeped through the curtains and I saw the girl in the mirror. She had a . . . a tattoo in the shape of a . . ." Her lips purse as if she cannot bring herself to say the hideous, foul word and then she hisses . . .

"A what?" Isabel holds a finger under her nose but sneezes nonetheless.

"Shaped like what?" Maude leans in.

"A snake."

The ladies are undone. And gasp in chorus.

Nellie's mouth opens but no sound escapes; only Maude can barely utter, "Ooh-ooh!"

Isabel, now in a sneezing fit, bursts out, "I don't . . . understand. There was a snake in the Wolf Wiles dressing room?" She sneezes, shaking the table. The women grab for their ice teas.

"Isabel, hush." Nellie is all a'twitter. "Mrs. Lawrence, where was the tattoo?"

"On her . . ." Gertrude fans her face.

"Speak up, dear." Maude leans in.

"On her . . ." Gertrude's cheeks flush; and in the sunlight, the rouge and powder suddenly begin to ooze down her face, melting. She fans her face, "On her . . . oh never mind. Never mind." Gertrude fans her face with her fan, painted with lilies. Maude, always the proper hostess, also fans her face.

"Where was it?" Isabel is now quite pink from the sneezing.

Finally able to gain her composure, Gertrude Lawrence gathers up her courage and leans forward. All the ladies, including Spirit Belle, on the swing, lean in. Gertrude whispers to Maude the location of the snake tattoo. It's rather like a child's game of telephone, with each woman passing the word on to the next. Only Spirit Belle is left out of the circle. She looks at Billy, "Where was it?"

Isabel whispers the word back to Gertrude who starts to whisper the word to Maude and then catches herself. "What? No, for goodness sake, not on her . . . oh never mind. Never mind. Nellie, it's your turn."

"No, dear. You took the last trick. Remember?"

Isabel isn't about to let the snake go. "Where was it?"

Spirit Belle gets up, whispers to Isabel, "On her sweet little ass."

Isabel, almost as if she has heard Spirit Belle, giggles, "On her ass?"

The other women's jaws drop; they stare at Isabel who says simply, "Was she a pretty lass then?" And she hiccoughs.

Spirit Belle bursts out laughing.

Maude puts down a card, sighs, "This is really sad, ladies."

"What's sad?" Nellie follows suit and lays down a Queen.

"Well, that house is a den of iniquity. I've always said so. This confirms my wildest suspicions." Gertrude trumps Nellie's ace. "Diamond, dear. The bid was diamonds not hearts."

Maude keeps score on the bridge pad, looking up over her sequined periwinkle blue glasses, "But what can we do? What are we going to do, Mrs. Lawrence? She's listed in the phone book. Yes, did you all know that? Listed. "Madam Belle Brezing."

"No!" A simultaneous utterance escapes from the ladies puckered lips.

"Well, I'm sending my Charles straight to the sheriff tomorrow morning." Gertrude's lips curl around her glass of iced sassafras tea.

Isabel, who is a little late catching on to the entire picture of the girl in the dressing room with her snake tattoo, smiles, then giggles.

"A snake tattooed on her . . ."

Maude puts a hand firmly on Isabel's hand, "Sh-sh, now not a word. No one is to breathe a word."

"Certainly not." Gertrude shuffles the cards.

"They've already been shuffled, Mrs. Lawrence." Nellie glances over at Maude for support.

But Maude is now catching Isabel's sense of humor and smiles, "Why, of course not. Who would believe it – our very own Gertrude Lawrence a peeping tom?"

Isabel starts to giggle; Maude giggles. Their laughter shakes the little card table. Gertrude grabs for her iced sassafras tea. "This is not funny in the least. I was trapped. Like a fly in a Venus Fly Trap. That woman and her circus gypsies will give us all dreaded diseases."

"And she's probably a Yankee." Nellie tightens her hold on her cards.

Maude picks up the silver dish of candies and offers a violet to Gertrude, "Oh Gertie, take off your girdle, I mean gloves, and shuffle. This is bridge club. No one will breathe a word of what's said here; you know that!" Maude winks at Nellie who smiles and then they all take out their gold compacts, and freshen their lipsticks. All except Isabel who is lost in her own reverie –

"A little green snake tattooed on her ..." And in a fit of giggles, Isabel plunges her fingers into the sugared violets and pops several in her mouth.

Gertrude glares, "Maude, shuffle. Nellie move. Switch chairs. You're my partner now. And Isabel, you just sit there and be dummy."

Isabel considers the candy, "Do they dip real violets in sugar or are these fake?"

As Isabel pops the last sugared violet into her puckered lips, a feather floats down and lands in Isabel's tea. She sees it. "Oh my, there's a feather – in my tea."

CHAPTER TWENTY-FOUR

Mixed bricks

Young Belle hands the handkerchief back to Billy, then quietly slips down off the wall. "I better go home now, Billy."

She is subdued; she climbs up behind Billy and he turns the bike back around. This time, he takes back alleys, avoiding the busy Main Street, turning in and out of less traveled side streets until finally reaching Megowan Street. As he guides the bicycle up the hill, Billy breathes faster. Sweat shows through his shirt and his hands grip the bike handles unsteadily. He slows the bike in front of the steps leading up to 59 Megowan. Belle slips off the bicycle.

Without looking back at him, Belle says quietly, "Thank you for the ride."

"Hey, hold up a'bit. I'm ready. Just get me a paintbrush and I'll help ya fix those crazy, mixed-up bricks!" Billy tilts the bike onto its side and takes off after her.

She turns but doesn't stop walking, "No, Billy. I had a good time."

"I'm sorry about those . . ."

"I could care less."

"Belle . . . you're not like them."

"No, I'm not. I'm better." She allows herself to breathe; she kicks out her dress, stepping back into the familiar. "You want to see my house? It's not finished but . . ."

Billy jumps up onto the porch. She smiles, leading him into the partially constructed 59 Megowan. Curious, he gazes up at the high ceiling, the long windows.

He whistles softly.

"How do you like my stairway?" She steps in closer to the grand stairway, watching Billy's reaction. Suddenly, he takes the stairs two at a time, then grabs hold of the banister.

"Hey, Billy - it's not safe."

He climbs up and slides down the banister. She shakes her head, "If you get hurt, Billy Mabon, I'm not to blame. Ya got that?"

Billy jumps off, "Got it." He winks at her.

"I liked you better when you stt-tt-uttered."

He follows her into an adjacent room, off the entrance hall. Young Belle steps through a doorway and in the yellow light streaming into the parlor, she seems to grow taller, bolder. "This is the parlor. I'm going to have my portrait painted. And hang it right over the mantel."

Billy doesn't miss a beat, "Nude?"

She turns, "Absolutely."

He ducks under a ladder, then turns – holds out his hand in a dare, "You supers-superstitious?" He struggles slightly with the word. She stares at him.

"No. I'm not afraid of anyone or anything."

"How's that?"

"Fierceness in my soul."

"You read too much poetry."

Suddenly, she grabs his hand and pulls him out from under the ladder. He holds her, whirling around. Spinning her. "Dance with me, Kitten."

"I'm not your kitten, Billy Mabon."

She lets him spin her, but slows the turns. He leans in closer, "Dance with me." She dances with him. But her eyes flash; he misreads the signal and steals a kiss on her lips. She slaps him. Hard.

"Get out. There are no free kisses in 59 Megowan."

Suddenly, she takes off his cap; her long hair falls wildly over her shoulders. She holds out his cap. "Here. Take it and get out."

Surprised, both by the slap and the strange fierceness in her voice, he takes his cap, starts to leave. He reaches the door and turns around, "Then I'll pay for the kisses. Where do I buy my ticket?"

Young Belle is looking in the mirror; her girlish innocence gone, she speaks firmly. She's all business, "I'll send you an Invitation, Mr. Mabon, to the Opening of 59 Megowan Street. Go on now."

Billy, grateful for the slight hint of kindness in her voice, grins and makes his way back out onto the porch. She lets him go, and faces the mirror. She carefully pins up her unruly hair and then, impulsively turns and walks to the window. She watches Billy pick up the bike and take off. Only once does he dare a glance back; and then he is gone.

Vanishing – back into the shadows.

Behind Young-Belle, reflected in the long mirror, Spirit Belle watches as the room transforms into a parlor with elegant curtains, decorated in the plush Victorian fashion. She recites the poem she wrote as a young girl, "Kisses. Well I remember. Memories linger. School boys in pantalets romping, Boys that now are growing to be young lads, Boys that liked to be Kissed; and like to give kisses. Kisses. I remember them. Smokey memories . . . surround me."

Young-Belle's reflection changes; she stares into the mirror, pinning up her hair – now a deep auburn shade with combs. Her hands smooth her long dress. From outside, a crusty voice calls out, "Miss Belle, you got another present from that admirer."

As Belle turns, Pearl, older and spindly, enters the room, carrying a package.

Young Belle casts a quizzical look at the package, "Open it, Pearl."

"No ma'am. I ain't opening that package; that ain't my name on the mailing label. You open it. You're the Madam of this house. Aren't ya. Now!" She rolls her eyes.

Curious, Young Belle opens the package and takes out several Godey Fashion Magazines; beneath the stylish drawings is a red turban, with a card. Young Belle reads the card, "This is for you, Pearl."

"Now." Pearls eyes widen.

"You can wear that when we open 59 Megowan."

"I ain't waiting for my invitation." Pearl puts on the red turban, grinning.

Young Belle takes out more tissue paper and catches her breath . . .

But suddenly, the memory evaporates into thin air.

CHAPTER TWENTY-FIVE

Little Black book

Billy twirls a dusty, faded red turban on his finger, "What was in the box, Kitten."

Spirit Belle, startled by the sudden disappearance of the memory, grabs the turban, "Give me that, Billy." She stuffs it back in a hat box. "I'd forgotten what a carnival gypsy Pearl could be." She slips the hat box back under the bed, careful not to glance at her old body – scarcely breathing. Then, she turns and begins to dust off the mantel, straightening the glass perfume bottles.

"What the hell are you doing?"

"59 Megowan may be turned into some sort of museum. Placed on the Historical Register – like those other mansions in Gratz Park."

Billy simply looks at her. "Dust away, babe." He casually turns to the windowsill where he has placed a Little Black book. "You sold your life for a little Black Book. It's too bad I'm dead- a fellow could make a fortune with . . ."

She grabs for the book; he taunts her with the prize possession – keeping it just out of reach. "Give me that, Billy. I don't want some man pissin' in a john, oogle-eying one of my girls."

"Your girls." He tosses it up, catches it.

"What – you're an acrobat now?" She almost grabs it; he backs up. "I was a damn good madam."

Billy retreats back towards the bed, "You made money off these girls."

Belle glances at her former self, a thin shape breathing in shallow gasps beneath the covers and stands still, thinking. When she speaks, her own voice is calm, convincing. "So what? Is making money the unpardonable sin? I taught my girls to be 'tres charming'. Because that's all men want, isn't it, Billy? The sole purpose of the female sex is to charm and be charming. Well, the only difference between my girls and the Sunday school teachers was the cost of the charm."

Billy holds out the Black Book, palm-flat, "What about love?"

She takes the book, "Love is a luxury my girls couldn't afford." She curls up in the chaise lounge and slowly, deliberately begins to rip out each page in the book.

Billy suddenly opens a large armoire, rummaging through the moth-eaten gowns. Belle looks up, eyeing him suspiciously but continues her systematic ripping of the pages. Billy turns, holds out a faded dress. The gown is thick with dust; there are holes in the once-sequined shoulders. The gown catches Belle by surprise; she starts to rise. Billy slips the gown over her head. "Get up."

"Get that moth-eaten .. ." She sneezes, protesting. But as the gown slips over Belle' head, it suddenly transforms into a gorgeous bronze gown with a gold sheen. "Do you know what this is?" She smoothes the dress, puffing the sleeves, "This is a Charles Worth gown." Turning to the mirror, she admires her reflection. Then she sees Billy's reflection, staring at her. "What are you up to now?"

"You're going to remember the night you opened 59 Megowan?"

"Why? That was a happy memory."

"Because there's something you're forgetting."

Spirit Belle instinctively pulls up her hair; Billy pins white rosebuds in her thick hair – and slowly, the color of her curls deepens into a rich auburn. She smiles, turns slightly, admiring the back which cuts quite low. Billy gives a soft whistle of approval – "Will ya look at her?"

She touches the rosebuds – as if not quite believing they're real. Her voice softens, "No, you look Mister Mabon."

"Do you think it's too early for a Mint Julep?" Billy, with great charm, holds out a silver cup and bows. She takes the empty cup, laughing. And suddenly, a sprig of mint appears inside the glass, and then the sugary drink takes shape. Wide-eyed, Spirit Belle holds the mint julep glass – staring at her own reflection in the silver. "I remember the night we opened Megowan." She walks towards the window, "I threw open the doors to all three parlors and there was a long banquet table. Oh, an orchestra played beneath real palm trees."

Billy eats the mint out of Belle's glass, "I didn't think Kentucky had any palm trees, Kitten."

As if waiting for Billy's cue the palm trees appear. Quite large; with feathery fronds that shiver from a fan blowing cool air across the parlor.

"Don't do this, Billy."

"Do what?" He chews the mint; some sticks in his teeth.

"This. Calling up a happy memory to taunt me; you have something green stuck in your teeth." She points; he smiles, then grins and steals the mint out of her julep.

Spirit Belle takes hold of her glass; she turns, slightly. Waiting as the present dissolves and the past takes shape. At first, the room is seen as if through a lens, slightly blurred and sepia in tone. But then, as Spirit Belle steps into the memory, the lines of the table and over-stuffed chairs sharpen; the colors deepen in hue. Spirit Belle is transfixed by the power of this memory. She sees her own reflection in the gold-gilt parlor mirror; and then behind her, she catches another reflection: This is Belle, younger, in her early thirties. Wearing the same Charles Worth gown. Spirit Belle turns, staring at her younger self. Sunlight streams through an amber colored stain glass window just above the front entrance. Young Belle, with her hair pulled up off her neck, glistens. Spirit Belle steps back-

"How is this possible?"

"Just watch."

"But she's . . . I'm wearing her dress."

"Things can be in two places at one time. Gold gowns. White roses. Memories."

"It's magic."

"It is magic . .. different times pressing against one another. Invisible. Until suddenly a portal appears and then we glimpse what we believed was behind us. But it's not. It's right in front of us. Waiting for us to step through the glass, or ripple the pond or find the secret door in the garden. It's all magic. And it's all good . . ."

She looks at him, suspicious.

"No... it's not all good."

"It's good because it lets us see the Truth."

The chandelier glistens; and Spirit Belle closes her eyes. Billy gently places his arm around her – whispering, "It's all good. Remember, you're the magician."

CHAPTER TWENTY-SIX

The Dandyman and Painted Ladies

The front door opens, and Billy, younger, dripping rainwater, enters, holding a bouquet of white roses. He shakes his hair – spraying more water – and laughs. "Damn, someone must a'delivered a monsoon in with the palm trees." He suddenly sees Belle, dressed in the gold gown. And he smiles, "Will ya look at her."

Young Belle turns in the gold dress, showing all sides of the gown and then lifts her leg, exposing gold silk hose and a gold slipper. "No, Mr. Mabon, you look" He grins; the sexual attraction is magnetic. But she quickly becomes all business. "Billy Mabon, what are you doin' here?"

"I got my invitation." He holds out the Invitation.

"You printed that invitation yourself." She sees the water dripping from his wet feet. "Damn Billy, you're making a puddle."

Billy steps back towards the door and wipes his boots, holding up a bouquet of white roses. "Belle, these are . . .? Ouch, pricklish little she-devils!"

Belle takes the roses.

The beads leading into the back hall jangle and Pearl, wearing the red turban enters with a silver tray filled with bourbon balls. "Where'd those roses come from?"

Billy grins at Pearl, "Guilty as charged." He recognizes Pearl but doesn't let on. At first. He lets her take the lead.

Pearl clucks her tongue, "Hello Mr. Billy."

Belle looks up from arranging the roses, "You two know each other?"

Neither Billy or Pearl speaks.

Belle straightens a silver dish filled with mints. "Billy! Where did you find these - fresh roses in the winter? Oh, never mind, don't tell me. I'm sure I'll find out from the sheriff or the undertaker tomorrow. Roses!!"

Billy tries to help himself to a bourbon ball; Pearl sways, holding the tray just out of Billy's reach. Young Belle, ignoring the banter and game-playing between Pearl and Billy, fingers a crease in the starched white eyelet table cloth, "The scent of a rose is like a woman's perfume. Sweet. Sensuous and seductive. The secret lies in what is invisible to the eye, but inviting to the soul."

Pearl clears her throat. Billy swallows his bourbon ball, "Well you always were the poet, Belle. I just smoke the cigars. Good. Bad or ugly. Once you git them out of their fancy wrappers, they all taste – smoke – pretty much the same."

Young Belle isn't listening. She arranges the roses as a center piece, places them in a silver champagne cooler. "We'll give our guests the finest bourbon, music and white roses. It's all an illusion. A very expensive illusion."

Billy moves onto the bourbon; he opens a bottle – "Someone should name a bourbon for you Belle – considerin' all the Mint Juleps . . ."

". . . and they'll tell their sons and grandsons. And the very finest houses in Europe will whisper 59 Megowan. Like the Taj Maja, the Crystal Palace in St. Petersburg, even Versailles . . . They're coming for the roses."

"No ma'am, they ain't." Pearl sets the tray of bourbon balls down on the table; the tray hits the glass hurricane and causes the flame to leap. "No ma'am. They ain't comin' for the roses."

"They're comin' for the roses." Without looking at Pearl, Young Belle re-arranges the bourbon balls, placing small white rose buds in and among the chocolates.

"No they ain't." Pearl's eyes sizzle.

Young Belle whirls and stares straight into Pearl's black eyes; Pearl stares back.

"They ain't."

"They is ... . are." Young Belle arches her perfectly framed eyebrow.

"Humph." Pearl, as if remembering her position, picks up the tray of bourbon balls and balances them mid-air. "Where you want me to put these bourbon balls, Miss Belle?"

"Just keep them away from Billy." Young Belle glances at her reflection in a long, gold mirror. A stately grandfather clock chimes the hour. "Eight already. I hope the girls are all dressed."

Billy wipes his chocolate fingers on a linen napkin, "Want me to go see?" He grins.

Young-Belle takes the linen napkin out of his hand, "Yes, why don't you do just that. Billy, you can be 59 Megowan Street's dandyman." Go on upstairs and make sure everyone's ready. Oh and here." (Tosses a necklace.) "Give this to Lottie."

Billy catches the necklace. "How will I know which one is Lottie."

Young-Belle shoots him a look, "Ask her." The beads dangle behind her as she disappears into the back hallway. Billy suddenly swirls Pearl around - dancing with her as she balances the bourbon balls. "What the hell is a dandy-man?"

Pearl rolls her eyes; she puts the bourbon balls on the table. "You ain't fixin' to find out with me, Mr. Billy. Go on upstairs and make sure those girls look jest the way Miss Belle done told them to look."

Pearl picks up a silver case of cigars, shines the lid. Billy suddenly steals a couple of cigars. Before Pearl can protest, Billy is up the stairs. He turns – "Oh, I like that turban. Looks good on you. No man can resist a woman in red." He comes back down a few steps and places a rose in the turban. She takes it out – meeting his gaze.

"Mr. Billy, go on. Git." Then she lowers her voice, "It's good to see you. It sure is good to see you. How's your mama?"

"I don't see my family very often. They... didn't like it when I left the church."

"Um-hmm. I knows, Mr. Billy. I knows more than you may think I know. And I know you are the one's been putting them presents on the porch. You got a mighty fine eye for fashion."

"Belle doesn't know it's me though, does she, Pearl?"

"Now!!" She rolls her eyes. "She ain't seein' what she thinks she's seeing. Now – git!"

Billy gives a mock salute, "What's a dandyman for?"

Pearl smiles, a wry, half smile, "Other things. Now go. Git upstairs and get them down here. Now."

"My pleasure, your Ladyship."

He sneaks a bourbon ball; Pearls sees this and shews him up the stairs.

Spirit Belle, curious, follows Billy up the stairs which have materialized in the room. "You know, I always wondered exactly what Billy did with my girls. They all adored him." She slips off her shoes, walking barefoot, behind the younger Billy. He stops on the landing, glances back – down at Young

Belle (as if making sure she's not watching) and then slips a small flask out of his pocket. He steals several sips of the bourbon. Spirit Belle, surprised by this, stands back. She hears voices – coming from further down the hall and passes Billy. He remains behind.

Spirit Belle reaches the first closed door and stares – curiously, she sees through the wood door. Several young, beautiful women are in various stages of dressing. Lace slips lie on the bed and chaise lounge; there is a pile of fancy shoes. She moves on, to another door. And as she stares at the door, again it becomes transparent. The room is small, but finely furnished. The bed is neatly made-up and a gold cherub on a seat, swings down, suspended from the ceiling. A young girl, a dark-eyed brunette with curls pulled back from a chiseled white face, is tying ribbons on her shoes. Spirit Belle recognizing her, reaches out her hand, as if to touch her gently, "Molly? Oh, I'd forgotten how graceful . . . I'd forgotten how very young Molly . . ."

Suddenly, a side-door to the bedroom bursts open and a curvy, red-haired young woman, carrying a sign *"Women's Right to Vote"* enters. Molly glances over her shoulder – "Lottie, where have you been?"

"Out." Lottie throws off her brown cape and quickly slips into a dress, laid out on the bed. The gown catches on her hair; from within the folds of the taffeta dress, Lottie's voice calls out – "Molly, help me."

Molly finishes tying up the slipper, then gently tugs the dress down over Lottie's head. "I know what you're doing, Lottie."

Lottie's hair, now completely disheveled, falls around her face; she turns her back to Molly. "Help me. Hurry."

Somewhat reluctantly, Molly fastens the gown around Lottie's curvy hips, "Suck in."

"I can't suck in my hips."

"Well, stand there." Molly moves in closer, trying to squeeze the dress around Lottie. "But you shouldn't be out in the streets. What if someone recognizes you?"

Lottie laughs a short, almost cynical laugh, "Like who? And who cares?"

"Like one of our clients – that's who. It could be bad for business."

"Oh my god, tell me you're not saying this." She whirls, and struggles to fasten the remainder of the dress, pulling the fabric forward. She gets stuck. And her firey-temper finds a release in her hands, fighting with the dress.

"You've got to stop . . . Stop marching for . . ."

"Us. I'm marching for us, Molly. For women to have a voice. To vote."

"If Miss Belle finds out . . . she'll . . . Oh, I don't know what she'll do."

Molly steps forward and again tries to fasten the dress. It is now turned completely backwards on Lottie who is feeling trapped – the color rises in her freckled cheeks.

"God, I can't breathe. Get me out of this."

"Just stand still."

There's a moment. Molly, with calm hands, gently maneuvers the dress until it relaxes over Lottie's fuller chest. She seizes her chance – a small victory with the recalcitrant gown – "If Miss Belle finds out, she'll kick you out, Lottie. You'll have no where to go. You'll have to go be a Nun or something."

Lottie looks straight into Molly's innocent eyes, "Molly, listen to me, sweetie. You're such a darlin' but you don't know anything. Miss Belle is one of us."

Molly shakes her head, stepping back. Lottie grabs her hands and holds them, a little too tight. "She may not be out there marching on Main Street or throwing rocks through Wolf Wiles' windows – but she's a suffragette more than anyone I know. She only does this – this charade of pleasing gentlemen – because she couldn't do anything else. She has more power than any other woman in this town. Maybe in the state."

Molly frees her hands and walks over to the door. "You're late. Brush your hair and paint your pretty face. March on your own time. But this is Miss Belle's grand opening. I'm not going to let you spoil it for her . . . put that sign under the bed."

Suddenly, they hear whistling from outside the bedroom door.

Molly hushes Lottie with a look, "Hide that sign under the bed."

There's a knock at the door, "Are ya decent?" And again, whistling.

The two girls scramble to hide the sign and turn as the door opens. They quickly put their hands up to their bodices, trying to cover the low-necklines.

"Whoa - easy ladies. I'm Billy. Miss Belle sent me up to make sure you've got everything ya need. Which one of you is Lottie?"

Lottie smiles, "Hello."

"Got something for you from Miss Belle."

She turns around, lowering her head, in a shy, submissive gesture. Billy fastens the necklace around her neck. She is breathing in quick breaths.

"Hey, ya nervous?"

Lottie blushes. "A little."

Hearing Billy's voice, several of the other girls appear in the doorway. Billy turns Lottie back around, and brushes a stray curl out of her eyes, then he faces the on-lookers, "Hello ladies, I'm Billy. And I think I've got something to take a little edge off your nerves. Shut the door."

The ladies edge in closer to Billy. He slips out one of the Cuban cigars, lights it, takes a puff. "It's kinda like smokin' a peace-pipe."

He offers the cigar to Lottie and winks.

From downstairs, there is the sound of knocking. Tentative at first, the knocking gets louder.

Young Belle's voice rises over the knocking, "Pearl. It's too early for the guests. Just see who it is. No one's supposed to use that entrance."

"Yes ma'am, Miss Belle. Family Entrance is only for the family." She rolls her eyes and heads towards the door. Out of the corner of her eye, Pearl catches Billy, half-sliding down the banister. Pearl shoots him a look. He grins, nodding at the girls, gorgeous, lining up behind him on the stairs. He lets out a soft whistle of approval.

Young Belle glances up at "her girls" – looking breathtakingly beautiful, lined-up. Waiting for Belle's approval; she leans in closer, adjusting a strap on Lottie's dress and suddenly, fans her face, "Has one of you been smoking cigars?"

Billy ducks in behind Charlotte, a petite blonde with a bow in her long hair.

She giggles. Young-Belle, not amused, turns to Pearl, "Spray some rose water on each girl and keep Billy away from the cigars." She slips a small bottle of rose water out of her pocket and hands it to Pearl who comes up to the first girl and sprays the rose water. Then she sprays Billy who protests by lighting another cigar. Young-Belle arches her eye brows, and blowing the smoke away, whispers, "They're coming for the roses."

CHAPTER TWENTY-SEVEN

Musicians/magicians

Pearl sprays Billy again. And again. He taunts her, licking the rose water with his tongue and she threatens to spray him again – "Mr. Billy, you behave. This is Miss Belle's night. And they ain't comin' for the roses." She straightens her shoulders, makes her way to the front door. Pearl turns the knob. Suddenly, the front-door opens wide, letting in a rush of winter wind. Pearl ushers in a timid-looking young man with a fiddle case strapped to his back. His hair, long and snow-covered, falls over his face. He looks up – with kind light blue eyes – and then bows slightly to Young Belle, "Good evening, ma'am. I'm Miles Townsend. I was told you might be looking for some musical entertainment tonight?"

Young Belle sizes up the musician in an instant – noting his weathered navy coat and worn shoes, "Oh yes, come in, Mr. Townsend. And get that fiddle out of the cold. Where are the others?" She glances towards the still open door. Pearl follows her gaze, shakes her head as if to say "Ain't no others." She shuts the door.

Miles, suddenly quite shy glances at the nude above the fireplace. Titled "Venus". It depicts a red-haired woman lounging on a chaise lounge; her fingers touch a near-by black cat. Miles stares at the painting, then at the woman before him. Seeing the striking resemblance, he blushes. Pearl, who doesn't miss a trick, catches on that Miles has mistaken Belle for the "Nude" and snorts. Belle shoots Pearl a look; the snort vaporizes into a sort of deep-throated coughing fit. Pearl steps back, towards the kitchen door.

Young Belle steps closer to the musician. "The others?"

"Sorry, I was just . . .", he sneezes – trying not to look at the painting but seemingly unable to redirect his gaze, "I'm allergic to cats."

"We don't have any cats here." Young Belle seizes the moment and leans in closer to Miles, offering him her handkerchief and allowing him to catch the scent of her perfume. The trick works. He takes the handkerchief and stares straight into Belle's bewitching green eyes.

"Well ma'am, the truth is that the others aren't comin' . . . It's just me and Baxter." He casts a side-ways, almost errant gaze out the front window. And for the first time, Young Belle and Pearl see another young man. Standing under a yellow pool of light shining out onto the porch.

Young Belle immediately walks over and opens the door, "Mr. Baxter?"

"His name's uh . . . Teddy. Teddy Baxter." Miles shifts his weight, which isn't much, back and forth from one leg to another.

Young Belle waits, shivering in the cold wind blowing in from the outside. The other musician hesitates and then saunters towards the door. As he steps inside, Belle closes the door. Teddy Baxter, blonde, and good-looking in a boyish sort of way, stuffs his reddened hands into his pockets. He smiles, somewhat awkwardly which elicits a laugh from several of the girls standing, staring from the stairway.

Young Belle ushers Teddy over towards the fire, burning with a great warmth. She looks at the two young musicians, both wearing bow-ties and slightly wrinkled dress shirts. Miles breaks the silence.

"But I play fiddle like a one man band. And Baxter, - Teddy – well he uh . . ."

"Yes, Mr. Baxter, come closer to the fire. What instrument do you play, sir?"

"Well, ma'am.. . I . . ."

"Teddy, uh, Mr. Baxter plays the harmonica, ma'am."

Molly, from the stairwell, leans in, "Like I play the spoons."

The other girls giggle.

Young Belle turns her back to the girls on the stairs, and graciously holds out her purse, exposing several large bills. "Really? Well, I've always had a soft spot in my heart for the harmonica." She takes out several bills and holds them out, palm flat, as an offering of sweet grass to wild colts. "Take off your coats, gentleman. Come in. I thought you'd come for the roses."

Baxter bursts in, "Oh no, ma'am."

Young Belle teases him, "No?"

Baxter stutters, "Well, yes."

She turns to Miles, "Well, what do you think, Mr. Townsend. Will they do?"

Baxter steals a peek at the girls, wearing white and red roses in their hair. Standing on the curved stairs, leaning slightly in towards the candlelight from the parlor, they are ravishingly beautiful. Elegant. Stylishly attired southern belles – poised as delicate debutantes waiting to be announced at their own coming-out ball. Baxter sucks in air through his frozen lips; his teeth slightly chatter as he exhales, "Yes ma'am, they're the most beautiful roses I have ever seen." Molly winks at him.

Pearl re-entering from the back kitchen hears this; holding high a silver tray, she rolls her eyes. "What should I do with these beaten biscuits and ham, Miss Belle?"

Young Belle places one beautifully powdered arm around Miles and the other around the shivering Baxter, "Just place the biscuits on the table, Pearl. Thank you." Her voice oozes charm. "Now, gentleman, I was wondering about something, I bet two well-mannered southern boys like you – from nice Lexington families – two handsome musicians who play the fiddle and the harmonica . . . I'll bet you both attended Miss Hall's School of Ballroom Dancing."

Slipping easily into the web, Miles and Baxter nod their heads, "Yes ma'am."

"Well, Mr. Townsend, I was hoping that you might play that fiddle and Mr. Baxter might be kind enough to lead . . . to show some of the ladies a few dance moves."

This catches the girls by surprise; Lottie whispers to Billy, "This ain't what I signed up for."

Billy slips her his flask.

Miles nudges Baxter; then he takes out his fiddle and tunes it.

Baxter, trying to follow Miles' unspoken lead, stutters again, "It'd be a pleasure."

Delighted, Young Belle turns and gazes at the girls. Almost coyly, she eyes each girl – then decides on her choice for his dancing partner. Suddenly, Molly pushes a sweet looking, somewhat plump girl with long blonde curls tied up with a bow, forward.

"Nickki dances."

Nickki whirls, glaring at Molly; her voice has the hint of a slightly foreign accent. "Oh non. No, Miss Belle."

"She does." Molly speaks with absolute resolve.

Young Belle, curious, looks up at the youngest and shortest of her girls, "Nicholette?"

Billy, as if on cue, turns and gently coaxes Nicholette away from the banister and down the stairs.

"No ma'am, I couldn't. I don't really have any formal training."

Young Belle smiles, "Well Mr. Baxter will teach you, won't you?"

Baxter clears his throat, "Well, it'd be a . . . a pleasure."

"And the other ladies will watch. And learn."

Shyly, Nickki walks down the stairs, past the other girls – staring with amusement and some awe. As Nickki reaches the last step, she almost trips – catches herself and then, with natural grace makes her way across the parlor to Belle.

"Please show us." Belle steps back.

Miles raises his fiddle, nods his head to Baxter and places his bow on the strings. There is a slight scratching sound at first and then as the resin releases the natural sound, the melody of a waltz escapes from the old violin. It is a Strauss waltz; and Miles plays with strength and passion.

Baxter stands frozen, "Uh hello . . ."

Nickki goes up on tip-toe and whispers, "You just . . . uh . . . you put your left hand here." He places his hand on her bare shoulder; she reacts. "Sorry."

"No, it's all right. Just cold, yes. That's right." She takes his hand and places it firmly on her shoulder. "Then, the other hand – here." Again, she places his trembling fingers around her waiste." She winces. "Not so hard please."

Baxter starts to back away; Nickki pulls him gently towards her. "No, it's all right. What's your name?"

He can't look into her eyes, "Teddy."

"You're sweet, Teddy. I will show you how this is done. Just follow my cues. Yes?" Then she speaks louder, "Shall we?"

He puts his hand around her small waiste and tentatively, at first, they begin to dance. Then, as the fiddle gains intensity, Nickki leads the shy Teddy into a beautiful and graceful waltz. Baxter catches on quickly; as if intoxicated by the fire, the burning candles, the fiddle and Nickki- he lifts her up off the floor, turns her out and then catches her, letting her fall back gracefully in his arms. Behind them, the other girls watch, mesmerized.

Spirit Belle slips closer to the girls. In silhouettes of gold and burnished brown taffeta, they stand. Breathlessly waiting. Their eyes remain frozen in time. In faces that seem to be chiseled from white marble. The make-up is flawless. The powder blends evenly into their soft skin. Spirit Belle gazes lovingly, almost hungrily into the faces of these girls whose names she no longer remembers. Billy touches her shoulder, turning her towards the young couple dancing. Breathless, Miles glances at Teddy as if to say "Hold up."

Then one of the taller girls, with a long, curved neck and artistic hands, steps forward and whispers to Nichollete. "Dance like you do upstairs." Nikki, suddenly shy, shakes her head, silencing the others who are now pressing forward. "Come on – show Miss Belle that dance you do when ya think no one's watching." Charlotte, the smallest of the girls applauds her from the top of the stairs. As the other girls begin to clap, Nikki turns and glances at Young Belle who nods her permission.

Nikki smiles, showing the dimples in her cheeks. There is a quick turn to Miles, as she leans in and whispers the requested song. He grins and instantly, the bow hits the fiddle and bounces off the string. Nikki instantly lifts her skirt and bursts into a much more spirited dance – the CanCan. She kicks her legs high, swaying her small hips and blows a kiss to Billy who calls out, "Where the hell did she learn to dance the Can-Can?"

Charlotte's voice, soft and edged with a southern drawl, rises over the fiddle, "Her mama danced in the Moulin Rouge in Paris."

The words sting the air. Suddenly, Young Belle steps forward and takes Miles' arm, a little too hard. The bow hits the fiddle with a loud clang. Belle glares at Nicholette who lowers her leg, "I'm sorry, I thought – I thought you'd like the Can Can."

Billy holds out a mint julep to Belle "The Moulin Rouge, darlin'. Nothin' wrong with showing a few feathers behind swishing fans." He smiles, weakly, catching on that something has hit Belle wrong. Terribly wrong. Nikki still with her legs kicking high, whirls from Belle's strong grip on her shoulder. Nickki, confused, turns towards the other girls but they step-back, staring at Belle. She grabs hold of Niccki's wrist, "The girls in the Moulin Rouge are cheap and vulgar. Go upstairs and change. I don't want other gentlemen seeing what only one customer will be paying for upstairs in a private room. Is that clear, Nicholette?" She holds her wrist tighter. "And wipe that rouge off your cheeks. It makes you look like a common showgirl."

Billy hands Nickki his handkerchief; her eyes, filled with tears, look up at him – not understanding. Billy steps in closer to Belle, "What the hell is wrong with you, Belle? If I didn't know any better I'd think that you're jealous of that poor girl. And the Moulin Rouge is . . ."

Belle's eyes harden, "Stay out of this, Billy. If it weren't for me you'd be nothing more than a lousy paperboy."

Billy hurt, glances at Charlotte who quickly slips her arm around the now visibly shaking Nikki and moves her towards the stairs. The other girls step back; some stare stoically at Belle. The energy in the parlor seems to darken; as if a stone was thrown into idyllic water and now ripples out in ever deepening, somber colors. The two musicians glance at one another. And there is a moment when it seems that Miles is about to unwind his bow and pack up his fiddle; but then Young Belle, with grace and unexpected change of temperament, offers a mint julep. The silver cup glistens.

"You play brilliantly." She hands the cup to Baxter. He takes the bait, sips the drink. Playfully, almost as if bewitching him with her eyes and alluring voice, Young Belle turns to Miles. "And where did you learn to dance like that? Certainly not at any Charm School? Now, kindly move over there – by the palm trees. And I'll let you know when we'll want to have the orchestra play."

Baxter starts to object, "Uh, Miss Belle, there ain't goin' be any . . ."

"Illusion, Mr. Baxter. It is all just a beautiful illusion. Yes?" She nods to Charlotte to come over. "Charlotte, please show our musicians where they may put their coats." Then she turns to Baxter, "I will pay you well. A hundred dollars for the first hour. Is that acceptable?"

She doesn't wait for a response, but turns to the other girls, "Beautiful. You all look beautiful." For a second, she sees Billy and motions quickly, "See if Pearl has those beaten biscuits ready – with the ham."

Billy nods, and does a half-hearted mock salute. There's knocking on the Family Entrance Door. Billy heads towards the kitchen, "Looks like you got some guests comin' to the Resort." Billy leans in and kisses Young-Belle on the cheek, "Save me the last dance, Kitten."

Young-Belle dismisses him, wiping her cheek with a handkerchief and turns to the musicians. "A hundred dollars if you'll stay till midnight? Yes – oh, thank you, gentlemen. Set up over by those palm trees."

As Baxter and Townsend turn towards the palms, they narrowly miss Pearl, entering with a tray of fresh fruit –pineapple and strawberries. She hands Billy the tray- "Humph, they ain't comin' for the fiddle or spoons neither. Now!"

Young Belle takes full control, "Ladies, our guests are just outside that door." The young women take their places in the parlor. Billy fixes a drink.

As the door opens, a chill wind sweeps up Pearl's apron. She steps back, allowing several gentlemen to enter. Shaking off snow, Singerly hands his coat to Pearl; his eyes find Belle. She goes to him, "Mr. Singerly, sir, how lovely to see you. You're the first here. Welcome to 59 Megowan." She kisses him lightly on his roughened cheek.

He laughs, "Well I bought the damn resort didn't I?"

As Singerly grabs Belle's arm and pulls her in towards him, she winces. Billy sees this; he stares angrily. Belle, however, handles Singerly with a quick gesture; playfully laughing, she teases the Senator and slips in under his arm. He kisses her on her neck, "How's it feel to finally be the belle of the ball?"

"Intoxicatingly delicious."

"I like that dress, babe."

"You always have good taste, sir."

Singerly looks at her, not understanding. "Hell, I didn't buy the dress – just the damn house. I like what's underneath that dress better." He twists her neck towards him; she winces but covers any discomfort with a smile. Billy, watching from behind the musician's stands, sees this and starts to step forward. Pearl's strong arm is on his shoulder, "You know how to fix a Mint Julep, Mr. Billy?" She doesn't let go; Billy allows Pearl to lead him over to the bar where bottles of bourbon are in silver trophy urns. Billy pours a drink, then another. Then, he helps himself to a bottle of bourbon and quietly disappears into the back kitchen.

Townsend and Baxter, the two musicians, ignite the social event of the season with popular music. The door bell rings, again and again. And as Pearl opens the door - the "gentlemen" of Megowan Street enter. Among the evening's guests are racehorse kings, governors and senators, publishers – the landed gentry and the established old guard. A white-haired man in his late seventies, motions to Belle and discreetly moves her towards a far corner of the parlor.

"Miss Brezing . . . may I ask you something Madam?"

"Why Governor, what a pleasure."

Singerly suddenly breaks in, "Evening sir."

The governor lowers his voice, "How's the newspaper publishing business? I hope you're off-duty tonite."

Singerly waves his cigar, "I run a respectable newspaper, governor."

"Grand. I brought my grandson, Chandler. Come over here, son."

Chandler, dressed in a military uniform, looks up from a glass of bourbon.

Young-Belle smiles, demurely, "Chandler?"

The young man's face reddens. He finds a sudden interest in lighting a cigar.

"Mr. Singerly, if you'll excuse us, I have something I'd like to discuss with Madam Brezing."

Singerly slaps the Governor on his back. "Ah governor, you're acting like a skinned rabbit. Tell Belle what it is you're looking for. She's got 'em all shapes and sizes, hoop skirts, no hoops, all the way from Sweetwater Mississippi, as far south as Baton Rouge."

"Chandler is, well, he's never rightly been with a girl." The governor's cigar smoulders.

"Tell him he can have any girl but the Madam. I paid for her dance card in advance." Singerly kisses Belle – hard, on the lips.

Young Belle tightens, then turns towards a young woman standing alone by the fireplace, "Oh Charlotte, come over here please. I want to introduce you to the Governor's grandson, Chandler."

Charlotte, hair pulled up with a lavender ribbon, smiles demurely at Chandler. She straightens his bow-tie; he places an unsure arm around her waiste and they walk towards the bar.

Singerly watches this, amused, then turns to Belle, "There's talk of a coal strike; coal and politics make strange bedfellows. And those damn suffragettes! Three things a woman can be. A wife, a whore or a damn ugly suffragette." He cracks his jaw; his eyes narrow into pinpoints of steele.

She rubs his neck, gently. "Can you stay the night?"

"No Belle, I only came to kiss the Madam good luck. But I'll be back."

"I'll see you out." Belle smiles over at Charlotte, dancing a slow dance in Chandler's awkward embrace; then, with the grace of a seasoned southern hostess, she gazes into Singerly's eyes, "Give me a moment, sir." She takes in the servants, the musicians, the clients and their possible dates, and only when assured that all is well does she turn and walk Singerly to the front entrance. Once in the quiet of the front hallway, Singerly takes Belle into his arms and kisses her. Passionately. His hands over-power what he owns; his mouth finds her mouth and forces his desire into her willing lips. Singerly pushes her slim body up against the wall and takes with pleasure and power all that he has bought – with the price of a Carriage Clock.

There are footsteps, but neither Singerly or Belle hears Billy as he comes down the stairs. He starts to say something – but suddenly his voice goes mute. The familiar fear that he might stutter comes in a black wave. The stutter that he lost that moment Belle first looked into his eyes and dared him to speak his truth – now threatens to return. An ugly, painful reminder that he is, despite his deep feelings, but a "dandyman" at Megowan Street. Trapped on the stairs, he sees Belle in Singerly's arms and sinks slowly down. Hurt, jealous, he tightens his hold on the bottle of expensive bourbon and stares. Unseen. Invisible. As silent as the gold cherubs watching from their swings, suspended from the ceiling.

Alone on the stairs, Billy drinks the bourbon. Taking in the wisps of smoke, puffed from the expensive cigars and listening to the clinking of glasses, silver mint julep glasses raised in toasts to the "Opening of the most lavish bordello south of the Mason-Dixie" - this from the Governor. And with each sip of bourbon, the palm fronds wave more sensuously; the fiddle bow bounces more vigorously, striking the strings. And the ebony hands of servants move even more smoothly, elegantly, pouring the amber elixir into goblets of the finest crystal.

Billy watches, staring through the banister spools as the ladies of Megowan take their respective dates. Long satin dresses turn round, effortlessly, as the les femmes rouge dance, melting into their gentlemen's arms. Sometime before midnight, Billy makes his way down the stairs and retreats back to the musicians – where he opens another bottle. And then another. The dancing slows and as the couples move upstairs, Billy drowns out the sound of doors opening, shutting, footsteps and laughter with the bittersweet bourbon.

Spirit Belle observes the opening with a curious sense of excitement – thrilled with the absolute elegance of the party. She never actually looks directly at the younger Billy – as if he remains apart from her memories.

Billy's voice – as her spirit guide – catches her by surprise. "Did you ever wonder what went on behind those closed doors?"

Spirit Belle smacks him, lightly, "Those doors were closed for a reason." She pushes through the dangling gold beads, into the parlor. But there is no one there. The room is cold, and still.

Suddenly, white rose petals fall down, and Spirit Belle stands in the center of the parlor. Alone. A brilliant white light projects against the wall;

images – like giant dancing puppet figures – cast against the wall and she watches- the girls, her girls, in their private rooms. With their respective customers. But the light is blinding, allowing only a glimpse. She sees Charlotte leaning down to kiss a very nervous Chandler. He unties her ribbon; her long hair falls down over his bare chest and he takes her into his arms.

White roses fall around Belle and the next bedroom takes shape against the wall. Lottie slips off her gold beaded dress, allowing an older gentleman to gaze at her bare shoulders; she slowly unbuttons her bodice. And then Molly appears, kneeling beside a bed; she is massaging the feet of a middle-aged bearded man. And still, the white rose petals fall. Until the image fades into Caroline, a strikingly beautiful, somewhat older, woman lying in bed. She stares up at a Cherub, flying from an invisible cord; rings of cigar smoke float down over her white skin. The images play, appear dream-like, surreal, and then disappear into the falling rose petals.

The last rose petal falls to the floor; and the bedrooms – the girls and their gentlemen – disappear into a light more familiar. Candlelight, flickering across the velvet folds of curtains, and the painted walls. Young-Belle picks up this petal and turns, looking for Billy, her spirit guide. "Why did you show me those girls? They knew what was expected."

"And they were safe."

She glares at him. Suddenly, the parlor takes shape. There are empty bottles and crystal glasses with the stain of rouged lips and the violin bow races up the E string with a burst of wild abandon. Then, both musicians hold up their instruments and take their bows. Young-Belle claps, thrilled with the success of the evening. She pops open a bottle of champagne, and offers the bottle to the young, if now exhausted musicians. "Don't put up that fiddle. I want to dance till the sun comes up all fiery red and hung-over in the sky."

Teddy Baxter shakes his head; he's done. But Miles stands and plays a violin concerto – with great passion. Showing that he is a real musician. Spirit Belle moves towards the center of the room, and as he plays the piece, she dances. Alone. Young-Billy, watching from behind the palm trees, takes several more drinks of bourbon before finding his nerve. He slips up behind Belle –"Is this dance taken?"

Surprised, Young-Belle drops her arms to her side, "Why I don't know. Let me check my dance card."

He doesn't wait but suddenly places his arm around her waist and they dance. Baxter takes a cue from Townsend and the two musicians quickly find the tempo and romance of a waltz. She closes her eyes, leaning into him. He holds her close. And there is a moment when he almost finds the courage to kiss her. But she opens her eyes and smiles up at him. Then he says, what she knows he will say – what he has said before so often in his own fantasies – what he has imagined and hoped for – he speaks, finding his voice, "Belle, promise me something."

She smiles, "What?"

"That no matter what happens - you'll always save the last dance for me."

She laughs, "I promise."

And they dance. The waltz slows, then ends. The weary musicians pack up their instruments and quietly go out – using the front Family Entrance. And in the stillness, the scent of roses is powerful. There is the sound of knocking. Coming from the back of the house. Young Belle glances towards the kitchen, "Pearl?"

The knocking grows louder. More insistent. And the sound has a chilling effect on Young-Belle, as if she senses something is wrong. "Pearl! Pearl." Her voice catches.

Billy holds her close, then kisses her hair lightly, whispering, "You gave Pearl the night off."

She glances up, not quite sure if she remembers doing this, "Oh, did I?"

Billy holds her closer, "Belle . . ."

The knocking is intensely loud. Echoing throughout the parlor. Young-Belle steps back, her shoulders straighten, "I have to go see. Good-night, Billy." She turns, disappears through the dangling beads and for a moment, turns, looks back – "I'll save you that last dance – another time." And smiling, she is gone.

Billy, left alone in the company of empty bourbon bottles and empty silver trays, takes a rose out of the vase, smells its sweetness, then holds it to his lips.

Spirit Belle sees this for the first time and starts to follow him, "Billy." But the past closes. The parlor fades; the colors once deep in hue now melt into more somber shades of charcoal and smoky gray. And the music that once swirled round slows – like a music box unwinding. She turns to Billy, now her guide and demands an explanation "What are you doing?"

From somewhere behind the thin veil of time, there is the sound of knocking. At first faint, the sound grows more distinct. Belle shivers. Billy's voice catches her by surprise, "Who's at the door?"

"I . . . I don't remember." She slips out of the ball gown; it falls to the floor and suddenly, fades into the moth-eaten dress she had first found in the trunk. Billy moves towards her, "There's something else. Who was at the door, Belle?"

CHAPTER TWENTY-EIGHT

Alice Elly

The knocking grows louder. And louder. And suddenly, there is movement in the parlor. And Young Belle appears. Clearly. Her face is flushed from the dancing; she looks radiant. She brushes her fingers through her hair and smiling at the musicians, calls out "Oh don't stop. Don't put up that fiddle. I want to dance till the sun comes up all rose colored in the mornin' sky."

The knocking grows louder. She calls out, "Pearl. Pearl, someone's at the door."

The young musicians fade; the fiddle stops playing. Belle, curious, walks towards the kitchen, "Pearl!"

Billy, as a spirit-guide, says simply, "You gave Pearl the night off. Remember?"

Spirit Belle backs away from the memory. "No, no Billy, I don't remember."

"Who was at the door, Belle?"

"I told you I can't remember."

"What was her name?" He gently touches her shoulder; she whirls – furious.

"Let go of me. You're no angel."

"It was so pretty. It was such a glamorous life up here on the Hill."

Spirit Belle reaches down and slowly steps out of the dress, holding the faded fabric in folds around her body. "Yes. Yes. All I remember is the scent of the roses. And the feel of satin sheets from Paris. And the taste of champagne."

The sound of knocking grows louder. Billy takes Belle's face in his hands and gently turns her back towards the memory, "Open the door."

Protesting, she closes her eyes. "No. No."

"Belle, listen. Was there one girl you should have turned away from 59 Megowan?" He stares into her eyes. And there is a curious light in his eyes – a powerful strength goes out to her. "You remember, Kitten. She's been standing at that kitchen door a long time now. What was her name?"

The knocking grows louder and louder. Spirit Belle walks over to the mantel; she turns over a silver-framed photograph lying face down. And she stares at the photograph. "Alice. Pretty Alice Elly with hair the color of sunburnt poppies and eyes you could get lost in. I heard a knock. Only Pearl didn't come . . . so I . . . I opened the door." Slowly, Spirit Belle faces the door that has suddenly materialized. The parlor disappears and the old kitchen takes shape. The oak table, the black stove, and the door – leading out into the back garden. As young Belle opens the kitchen door, Spirit Belle faces the memory.

As the door opens, a chill wind blows across the kitchen table and the glass vase of roses spills. The white roses fall, as if in slow motion, onto the floor. Belle turns to catch the vase before it shatters – hitting the floor and splintering into glass shards. She leans down and picks up the roses. When she looks up, she sees a young girl, about seventeen. The girl's long flaxen hair is covered with snow. She looks almost other-worldly.

"Oh, you startled me. I was expecting the colored girl."

Surprised, Belle shivers from the rush of wind, "I gave Pearl the night off." She starts to close the door.

The girl, frozen, leans in towards the door, catching it before it closes, "Please ma'am, I've walked a long way."

"Barefoot?" Belle stares at her feet, swollen and bleeding at the heels. "Where are you from?"

"My name's Alice. Alice Elly. I'm from Tazwell. I been walking pretty near three days."

"Barefoot? You walked from Tazwell? Do you know what kind of house this is?"

Belle, drawn to the young girl despite her impulse to close the door, leans forward, whispering over the howling wind, "Do you have any idea who I am?"

Alice Elly nods "Yes ma'am." Her words come quickly, breathlessly – as if she might at any moment lose this moment that she has spun over and over in her mind. "My daddy's a preacher, ma'am, and he talked about you in one of his sermons."

"Well I guess that's one way to get to Church." Belle, pulling her shimmering wrap closer about her open bodice, starts to laugh – catches herself, "Alice, honey, you go on now. Nobody's here who can help you. Go on."

Alice Elly turns, then glances back up at Belle, "I'm sorry to have bothered you ma'am."

As the young girl walks back down the porch steps, Belle watches her. Held there by some invisible force that seems to attract her to the girl. Suddenly, Alice Elly slips; she grabs hold of the iron banister but it's too late. The strong wind whips around her, pulling her into its grip. Belle opens the door and takes hold of the girl. "Alice, here . . ." As she touches her skin, Belle reacts. "My god, child, you're freezing. Come inside."

Alice Elly follows Belle into the house. Spirit Belle, watching from a distance of time and heart, moves towards the oak table. She is drawn to the young girl – and also repulsed by the memory. Belle turns and takes the coffee pot off the stove. She pours a cup of coffee in a white porcelain cup. "I'm not much of a coffee maker. Pearl always makes the coffee but . . ."

Alice Elly touches Belle's hand, "I heard you was a lady, ma'am."

Belle hands her the cup of steaming hot coffee, "I doubt if you heard that from your preacher daddy."

"No ma'am." Alice folds her frozen hands around the cup; she is trembling.

"Go on now, just sip that coffee. It'll do the trick. Get you warmed up."

"I got to tell someone." Alice's voice is edged with fear, she lifts the cup, not drinking.

"You don't need to talk, Alice. Pearl will find you some fresh clothes, and you can . . ."

Alice, wild-eyed, sets down the cup, spilling the hot black coffee. "No! No! You ain't listening. You don't understand. You're my only hope."

Belle impulsively starts to clean up the coffee, soaking up the chicory with a fresh linen napkin. "All right." She speaks slower, calmer, "You're safe here. You can tell me anything you want. I'll listen." She leaves the stained napkin on the table.

"I'm . . . I'm sorry." Alice Elly smoothes her rough fingers over the cloth, trying to smooth out the stain. And as she speaks, her voice lowers; it is as if she has rehearsed this so often – in her mind – for three days walking barefoot from the mountains to this House – that the words spill out, like the coffee, without emotion. "See, my mama's been real sick. And my step-daddy, he's a preacher man. Me and him been raisin' the young 'uns. Till Sunday." Alice rubs at the stain in the napkin, a curious gesture. Pressing her fingers deep into the blush of coffee that has now discolored the cloth. "Sunday, 'bout six weeks ago. I was out in the shed gathering eggs like I always done and he's watching me. And I said, 'Papa, what ya want?' And he says, 'Alice, honey, I ain't a'gonna hurt ya. Your mama won't never know.' Then he laid me down in the straw and he put his big, calloused hands on me and he made me . . ." She lowers her eyes and digs at the coffee stain with her dirty fingernails. "He made me."

Belle, visibly uncomfortable, reaches over and touches Alice's wrist. "It's all right. No one is going to hurt you." She brushes Alice's wild hair out of her eyes. "I'll just get you another cup of . . ."

Alice Elly shakes her head, "No. I ain't finished."

Belle sits back down, "Go on then."

"Later, I got dressed in my frilly cotton dress and I come up to the porch and he was a'sittin' at the supper table like nothin' had happened. Only it had happened and it kept on a'happening. Every day or so. Then something must a'snapped inside a'him or something cuz one day I come up the steps and I hear him hollerin' at my mama, 'She's no good. She's a common harlot.' And my mama's crying. Then he come out onto the porch and the little ones, shy-like huddle around him and he says to me, 'Alice Elly, you git. Go on. Git on out of here.' And I held out my arms to little Tabitha who come a'runnin' and she dropped her rag doll ..." Alice's voice catches, ". . . only he caught her and slapped her hard across the face and she started to cry. Then, mama come to the window. I can still see her eyes. Eyes that don't belong to the living. And I knowed I'd never see my mama again. Then, he come at me with a belt – hollerin', 'Git thee behind me Satan.' And his black eyes was a'burning. Eyes that got no soul."

Belle realizes that she should say something but she remains silent. Staring at Alice Elly, sitting in the chair, staring hard at the coffee stain, Belle turns slightly and then picks up the coffee pot; she freshens Alice Elly's cup of coffee.

"Pearl will be comin' round soon. She'll fix you up with some clothes and shoes . . . and she can make you breakfast. Pearl makes the most delicious apple-cinnamon flapjacks."

CHAPTER TWENTY-NINE

Cyrus

Spirit Belle, watching, stands still. From outside, there is the faint whispering of a mourning dove and then the clatter, the ceaseless clattering of the cicada wings. Billy closes the window. The room is silent. The light fades into darkness, as if Belle had suddenly shut out the memory and retreated far from the shadowy figure of Alice Elly, frozen at the oak table, forever rubbing out the stain with her slender, frozen fingers. Billy doesn't let Spirit Belle retreat too far – "You made Alice Elly into a . . ."

"A whore? So what if I did? At least I saw her. Did you, did anyone else in this god-forsaken town ever see Alice Elly?"

"Did you, Belle? Did you really see Alice Elly?" Billy dangles a gold locket in front of her.

"Give me that locket." As Belle grabs for the locket, Billy suddenly lets go and the locket slips off its thin gold chain, falling onto the floor. Spirit Belle picks up the locket, holding it in her hands.

"What happened to Alice Elly?"

"He killed her." Her voice betrays no emotion.

"Who?"

She threads the thin chain into the locket's clasp, not looking at Billy. "What does it matter now. He was just another customer." She places the locket beside Alice Elly's photograph and turns the picture face-down. "Cyrus. His name was Cyrus."

As if the name alone held dark magic, the room blackens. Spirit Belle stares into the vanity mirror where the now all too familiar face of Alice Elly appears behind the reflection of a younger Belle.

Flora's soulful singing fades into music of a lighter tone – Christmas bells ring. And suddenly, the bedroom disappears into a magical light. A light that illumines a towering Christmas tree, lit with burning white candles. Spirit Belle, delighted with her power to create such a magnificent tree, claps her hands. She gazes with intense longing at the tree, touching the lace hearts, and various painted wood and tin ornaments. Then she turns to the gifts, stacked high around the tree. Freshly cut pine and holly decorate the parlor mantel and stairway banister. Spirit Belle glances at Billy; the look in his eyes is a warning. She steps back from the tree, catching on too late.

"Christmas was a happy time at Megowan, Billy."

Suddenly, she sees her younger self, sitting on a chaise, placing lemons and apples in a wreath. Only occasionally does the younger Belle steal a glance at the well-dressed, rather short man with the goatee, Sam Rosenberg. He is decorating a much more slender, radiant Alice Elly with expensive jewelry.

Spirit Belle turns her back to the jeweler, facing Billy, "Don't do this."

Billy gets up and steals an apple from the mantel – "Too bad I'm dead, an apple a day keeps ole doc away." He starts to take a bite, then places it back in the ribboned pine. Young Belle looks up, "So Mr. Rosenberg – Sam – have you decided whether to join us for Christmas dinner?"

The younger Belle's voice catches Spirit Belle by surprise; she turns, facing the memory she alone has manifested.

Sam grins, fingering a pair of emerald and pearl droplet earrings, "What else is a Russian Jew going to do on Christmas eve in a small southern town, eh?" He holds the earrings up to the candlelight, "It would be my pleasure." He places the earrings in Alice Elly's hands and motions for her to put them on. Then, he fastens a glistening diamond bracelet tied with a black ribbon around Alice Elly's petite wrist.

Alice Elly, who has been standing very still, almost mesmerized by the jeweler's careful adornment of his model, whispers, "Miss Belle, I wonder if I could maybe talk to you sometime."

Young Belle fastens a lemon into the wreath, "I'm listening, Alice."

"In private, ma'am."

Sam steps back, as if to leave but Young Belle shakes her head, "Stay. Mr. Rosenberg is part of our family. What is this about, Alice?"

Nervous, Alice Elly fidgets with the bracelet's clasp, not looking up, "It's about Cyrus. Cyrus Cutler, ma'am." Her voice shakes, seeming almost to disappear into the higher tones. Sam turns his head, sifting through several gold, jangling bracelets, trying not to intrude or eavesdrop on what is clearly a very painful moment for Alice Elly. He drops a gold ring and leans down, pretending to look for it among the presents.

Young Belle, slightly annoyed, kicks out her leg, stretching her arms over her head and turns her full attention on Alice Elly. "Yes, go on. What about Cyrus?"

"Mr. Cutler thinks I belong to him, ma'am. Only to him. He gets real jealous and when I have other customers . . ."

Sam blows his nose. It is a rather loud, obnoxious blowing. Then he carefully folds his linen handkerchief and places it in his pocket.

Young Belle casts an annoyed look at the jeweler, "Did you find the ring, Sam?"

"Sorry, yes. Yes. Here it is." He places the ring back in the box.

Alice Elly blushes; her heart-shaped lips partially close. "Ma'am?"

"Cyrus will have to book you. It's strictly business."

Sam blows his nose again. Irritated, Young Belle raises an eyebrow.

"Yes ma'am, I told him but . . ." Alice Elly's soft voice seems to grow softer.

"For god's sake, Alice Elly, speak up. No one can read your mind. And Sam can't hear you." She laughs.

Alice Elly looks up, meets Sam's kind eyes, "Cyrus gets kind'a fiery when he's been drinking and . . ."

"She doesn't want to be with him, Belle." Sam holds out a diamond brooch, star-shaped. Considers it for Alice Elly, then changes his mind.

Both Alice Elly and Young Belle stare at the small Russian, wiping his nose. Young Belle stands, letting the lemon wreath drop to the chaise, "Fine. Alice Elly tell Mr. Cutler that you're booked through the holidays. And if he has a problem, to see me."

"Thank you, ma'am." Alice Elly turns to leave, then remembers the tear-drop pearl earrings. She hands them back to Sam. He takes them but then, for a second his hand closes over her smaller hand.

"Please, keep the earrings. A small present yes, for an angel." He smiles. It is a kind, fatherly smile. Alice Elly blushes and quietly leaves the parlor; her footsteps resound on the stairs.

Sam steps in close to Belle, "Forgive the foolish fears of an old Russian Jew. But that one – she is different from the others. When I first saw her, there was a light all around her. I thought she must be an angel."

His words have a strong effect on Young Belle. She gets up, "Take what I owe you out of the cash on the table. See yourself out, Mr. Rosenberg." As Belle goes out, Sam folds the pieces of jewelry into the black velvet cases.

Pearl enters, balancing boxes of tinsel and mutters under her breath. "My mama always says that 'pearls bring tears.'" She opens the box and furiously throws the tinsel up onto the Christmas tree.

Sam turns and glances back at Pearl; there is a strange look of foreboding in her eyes.

Suddenly, a curious wind blows out every candle on the towering Christmas tree. The room grows eerily quiet and dark. And both the younger Pearl and Sam disappear. A different scene unfolds in the parlor. Spirit Belle watches as time moves forward. She sees herself, in a white gown, sinking down onto the chaise. The candles on the tree have burnt down to stubs; and the tree's branches are lower, shedding their needles. The parlor shows the remains of a party -- with half-full mint juleps and smoldering cigars. From upstairs, Young-Belle hears footsteps. Her eyes open. Wide. As if she has a premonition of what is about to take place. She listens. Slowly, she rises and walks to the bottom of the stairs. Gazing up at light streaming in through the stained glass window above the second floor landing, Young Belle shivers. She stares at the glass, now tinted blood red. And she whispers, "Alice? Alice Elly?" She waits, paralyzed by fear. Listening.

Billy, standing beside Spirit Belle, ushers her up the wide Victorian stairway. And there, on the second floor landing, they see a man, crouching in the shadows. He makes his way along the hallway. The doors to the girls' bedrooms are closed. And silent. He reaches a bedroom near the back stairs and slips a knife out from beneath his shirt. Without warning, he kicks open the door -- revealing Alice Elly, half-naked, making love to her client. Cyrus lunges towards the man, pulling him out of the bed. Terrified, Alice Elly screams. The client, also naked, gathers up his shirt and trousers and retreats out the door.

Young Belle, hearing the scream, hurries up the stairs. Terrified, Young-Belle rushes down the hall to Alice Elly's room. She hears footsteps behind her and turns -- catching a fleeting glimpse of Cyrus, disappearing down the back stairs. He has a blood-stained knife and petticoat. Young Belle opens the door, and screams. But no sound escapes her lips.

The memory scene vanishes. Spirit Belle stands very still. Staring at the pearl earrings in her fingers. Suddenly, there is a scream. It splinters the heavy silence. Spirit Belle glances towards the bed and for a moment, she sees the little girl with the ribbon – sitting in the windowsill. Belle throws the pearl earrings down onto the vanity table.

"Stop. Stop, Billy."

"What happened to Alice Elly, Kitten?"

Spirit Belle whirls, staring at the girl in the window, staring at Billy. Then she remembers, letting the pain of the memory take hold and over-power any resistance. "By the time I got to her room, Cyrus had carved a heart into Alice's naked breast. He had gouged her throat so she could hardly speak. Her eyes were wild, frightened, like a dying animal. She took hold of my hand and whispered, 'Please ma'am, hold me. I'm one of your girls, aren't I, Miss Belle? I'm one of your girls.'"

As she remembers, Billy gently picks up the photograph of Alice Elly, dressed in a white gown with roses in her hair. Spirit Belle turns and for the first time, faces the photograph. "Cyrus got away. They found him down by the railroad tracks. He still had her bloody petticoat and the locket. They arrested him; put him on trial. It all caused quite a sensation. But then, he escaped and nobody made any effort to look for him. There's no great sin, Billy, in killing a whore."

Spirit Belle gently places the locket beside a glass angel, "Did I see Alice Elly? I don't know." She takes a breath. "No, probably not. But I've seen her every time I close my eyes . . . every time I go to sleep for the last twenty years. Billy, I'm tired. Ya understand, I'm tired."

Billy holds her with his eyes, "Miss Flora's right about one thing. It sure is hot. Powerful hot."

From outside the bedroom door, Miss Flora's heavy footsteps resound against the floorboards. She opens the door, glancing in at the frail figure lying in the bed. She pulls up the sheet around dying Belle's painfully thin shoulders and touches her forehead. Slowly, she kneels down and hums a spiritual. The girl with the ribbon, sitting in the window, swings the bag back and forth – staring at Belle's body. Then Flora bows her head and prays.

And the hands of the ancient grandfather clock tick . . . moving Time forward. The bells of Christ Church chime. And a single white feather floats down onto the four poster bed where the body of dying Belle lies still, faintly breathing.

CHAPTER THIRTY

The Kentucky Association Track

A burnished gold light settles around the Grandfather's Clock – streaming in from some unseen portal beyond the shadowed bedroom. As Flora's voice fades into the sound of her footsteps on the stair-landing, the Clock's hands slow. Billy, undaunted by shadows or light or Time, and seemingly detached from Belle's emotional journey, opens wide the window, allowing in birdsong. He then rummages through an old armoire – magically hovering just beyond the clock – brings it down and disappears inside. Seconds later, he comes out, sneezing – holding a large dust-covered painting. As he blows gently across the face of the painting, dust flies and reveals a scene of ladies at a race course. Center-front is a woman with red hair, dressed in a becoming white dress. She smiles up at a jockey, seated on a handsome cold black horse. In her hand, she holds a bouquet of white roses.

Spirit Belle sits on the floor, lost in the past. Billy's whistling takes her by surprise. She looks up – sees the painting.

"Oh my ... well where did you steal ...?"

"Borrowed. I borrowed this from The Kentucky Association Track's historic collection."

"The Kentucky Association Track, really? I thought that race track closed."

"Yep – hangs just above the fireplace. Attracts quite a crowd of admirers every year. Course the old track over on Race is gone, darlin'. They got a new track, called Keeneland."

She's not listening, muses "So that young artist – oh I can't remember his name – from Ireland? He kept his promise." She gets up, curious despite herself.

"What promise is that?"

"He said if I let him paint me – he'd make sure I got in the Club House."

Billy studies the painting, "So – which of these fine fillies is Miss Belle Brezing?"

She slaps his wrist playfully, "Oh Billy, I'm the main attraction next to the horse." She stands up close to the painting. The light streams through the window, illuminating the tiniest details in the horse scene; the other ladies in the crowd now become quite clear. They are standing slightly behind "Belle" who clearly has caught the eye of several gentlemen pictured as well as the handsome jockey smiling at Belle. The ladies are also well-dressed in lavender and shades of green. But Belle is by far the most refined and elegant of the women.

"Well no use dawdling on the past." Billy opens the armoire and disappears inside.

Spirit Belle remains in front of the painting, seemingly unaware that it is hanging magically suspended mid-air. "Harry was kind. He gave me a small waiste and slim hips. I never really was a small hipped woman." She laughs. "But he took some other indulgences." She winks.

Billy steps out of the armoire, sneezing. "But you went to the races darlin'."

"Yes. There was another course. The Kentucky Association Track. It ran down Broadway . . ." She turns slightly, and sees the wicker basket in Billy's hand.

"I don't know where you think you're heading with this but I loved the horses. That door has nothing to do with . . ."

"You keep saying that, but honey, I'm not calling up these memories." He twirls a white parasol over her head. She grabs it. He glances at the painting, "Now, lets see, after you flirted with the jockey . . ."

"I never flirted with . . ."

"You must have found the box that the Senator had reserved in his name and enjoyed a picnic." He opens the picnic basket, munches on several carrot sticks and considers the sandwiches, "Cucumber or olive nut, Kitten?"

"I'm not hungry."

"Nonsense, you've never not been hungry in your life. You're like Scarlet ..." He bites into the olive nut sandwich, chewing with relish and swallows, washing it down with the mint julep.

"Who?"

"Scarlet. The belle in *Gone With the Wind*."

"Oh her."

"Scatlet plucks a carrot ..." Billy holds up a baby carrot, grinning "And vows to never go hungry again."

"I'm not hungry."

"Well suit yourself, darlin'. But come on down here." He holds out his arm, twirling the frills on the parasol. "We're having a picnic. Some fresh air will do you good."

"Fresh air?"

Billy gently offers the parasol; she ducks under its frills and they step into the painting. Belle slips in close to Billy. The bedroom fades. "Who was that filly – won the Bluegrass Stakes that first year?"

"Racing Fool."

"No Belle, that horse doesn't win for another twenty years." From somewhere close – in that place where the skin between the worlds is thin – the clanging bell of a street car resounds. Billy suddenly grabs her hand. "Whoa, sweetheart. Don't want to miss the street car."

There's the deafening roar of a streetcar's clattering against metal. Then the scene takes shape. Billy and Belle slip through time, and find themselves riding the Street Car. They step off at the corner of Fifth and Race Streets and emerge in the middle of a well-dressed crowd. All headed for the Kentucky Association Track – which rises up somewhat unexpectedly. The ramshackle, wooden grandstand looms large over the track. Street vendors call out "Peanuts" and "Ice cold Cocoa-Cola." Billy guides Spirit Belle past the noisy vendors and around large blackboards (with the names of previous race winners) towards a grassy section, with rows of open-air boxes.

Billy gently leads Spirit Belle towards one of the boxes right on the finish line. She glimpses her younger self, in a stylish white dress, gazing at the parade of horses. A much younger Billy, looking very handsome, presses in close to the box and whispers to Belle, "Hello, Kitten. Got a tip in the first race. Pink Star." Billy drops a small piece of folded paper into her lap and steals the mint out of her glass. She smiles but doesn't look up.

"Thank you, Mr. Mabon. For the tip."

A jockey, in colorful red and white silks, tips his cap to Belle, then rides on. Other jockeys ride past Belle's box. She smiles, discreetly. All the jockeys seem to know her. She glances up, surprised that Billy is still hovering around her box. "Yes?"

Billy grins, then a more serious expression clouds his light blue eyes, "Oh and you might consider passing this tip on to Mrs. Lockard."

Belle looks down; her jaw tightens. "Now why would I want to do that, Mr. Mabon?"

Billy cracks his knuckles, a habit that obviously annoys Belle and he drops his voice even lower, "Her husband's having an affair with a Hungarian countess; the countess says she's expecting his baby and he's paying her half his pay-check from his bank wages. It would just be a nice gesture of kindness. One southern belle to another." He waits, then adds, "They have children, Belle."

Belle unfolds the scrap of paper and reads the tip, "Number 4?"

Billy nods.

Belle pushes back the veil on her hat and gazes straight into Billy's eyes, "I may run a house of pleasure, but I never broke up a man's marriage or tried to steal a husband away from a married man with children."

"Thanks, Belle." He hands her two tickets.

She takes the tickets, and quietly waves him on with her gloved hand.

Billy takes off, whistles, then turns, "I bet the tickets across the board."

Belle quietly motions a waiter with a tray of drinks over to her box. She leans in, whispers something to the young man and hands him one of the tickets, gesturing towards a near-by box and pointing out a middle-aged woman in a blue hat. Seconds later, the waiter makes his way towards the woman whom Spirit Belle recognizes as Maude Lockard. Dressed in a tasteful blue hat with a yellow rose, Maude sits in a box close to the railing. Gertrude is eating a chicken leg; she turns her binoculars towards the crowd, as if searching for someone. Also in the box are Isabel and Nellie, rummaging through a picnic basket.

The waiter appears with a tray of silver mint juleps; he offers a glass to Maude who waves him away, politely.

"Ma'am, I was told to give you this Mint Julep."

Maude glances at the waiter, "Really?"

Gertrude lowers the binoculars, "Who? Who sent it? Be careful, Maude."

The waiter offers a white napkin, "It's from a lady in the Clubhouse section."

"Oh. Well, I suppose . . ." Maude takes the glass and sees the ticket in the napkin. She glances up at the waiter.

The young waiter smiles, "I'd take the tip if I were you."

Gertrude, who isn't accustomed to being left out and doesn't usually miss a trick, misses seeing the ticket discreetly delivered to Maude. She is suddenly distracted by the playing of *My Old Kentucky Home*. "Stand up, Mrs. Lockard. Up. Up. Up!"

Maude, a'flutter, tucks the ticket into her beaded hand bag and rises, singing out.

Spirit Belle sits up on the railing, kicking out her legs in rhythm with the patriotic song. Billy motions for her to "Please, get down. Get down."

Spirit Belle obliges and moves in closer to Maude's box.

Women in stylish gowns lean over the boxes, holding out fresh bouquets of flowers – waving to the jockeys on horses parading past. Billy hands Spirit Belle a pair of binoculars. "Might as well sit back down and enjoy the race."

Slightly behind Belle's box, Maude Lockard's box decorated with patriotic flags sharpens into clearer focus. Gertrude, Maude, Isabel and Nellie simultaneously open their white parasols, click open their fans. Nellie, in a lavender dress with a matching, drooping hat, arranges fresh cut flowers, opens a picnic basket and smiles. She takes out four box lunches with fried chicken legs and wings, finger sandwiches and cheese balls stuffed with pimentos.

Gertrude, in a fitted yellow dress with a large brooch, peers through diamond edged binoculars. Her voice quivers with emotion, "Why I declare. Imagine her coming to the races!"

Maude freshens her lipstick, pinches her cheeks and chooses a pimento cheese sandwich, "Who dear?"

Gertrude's lips quiver, "That woman." She hands the binoculars to Maude who is dabbing a napkin at her lips. Maude takes a look and gasps. "Oh and after last night."

Isabel, twirling her parasol with practiced grace, sputters "What happened last night?"

"No Mrs. Lockard, not last night. It was a week ago Saturday."

Isabel leans forward, her nose twitching rather rabbit-like, "What was?"

Oblivious to this exchange, Nellie, in a sporting green suit reminiscent of something equestrian, pipes in, "Has anyone seen George Van de Vere?

He just lost his wife. Poor thing." She bites into a cheese puff; the pimento oozes out onto her lips.

"They say she tried to save the girl." Maude squeezes lemon into a cup of ice.

"Humph, save the girl my foot." Gertrude attacks a second olive nut. "Why the way any decent human being sees it, she's responsible for the murder."

"Murder? Who?" Isabel fingers the sweets – licking the powdered sugar off of a wedding cookie.

"Taking innocent young girls – ruining their lives." Gertrude pounces on the sweet pickles.

Nellie, oblivious to the other ladies, sees someone waving and waves back, "Yew-hew."

"Yew-hew!" Spirit Belle repeats.

Nellie smiles, batting her eyelashes – "George Van de Vere was coming with his cousin Tallie. Has anyone seen Tallie Tucker? Yew-hew!" She gracefully tucks a linen napkin into her sleeve and waves desperately, "Yew-hew!"

Maude squirts in melted sugar, "You know Mrs. Morgan's brother, Billy, is seeing her."

"Yes, I'd heard that." Gertrude nods, "They are heart-sick about Billy. Heart-sick about his life."

Nellie parrots, "Heart-sick."

Gertrude takes the lead, "My Charles said he saw Billy at the Family Entrance."

"Billy who?" Isabel turns quickly, narrowly missing Gertrude with her bobbing parasol.

"What was your Charles doing up at the …" Maude lowers her voice ".. . Family Entrance?"

"Well I don't think my Charles actually saw Billy. He saw someone who said they saw Billy."

Maude's light blue eyes squint above her periwinkle glasses, "Oh I see."

"Who? See who?" Isabel quivers with excitement, punching a cucumber sandwich squarely in the middle of the thinly sliced white bread. A cucumber pops out onto her chin. Gertrude points her finger and Isabel blushes, licking off the cucumber slice.

Gertrude very matter-of-factly rummages through the picnic basket, "It's disgraceful if you ask me. Her out parading around. Why next thing, they'll be letting her in the Club House." She seizes the last ham and biscuit and chews with relish, "It's just like the Emperor's New Clothes."

Isabel blows bubbles with her straw, "The Emperor. Is he here? I heard the Queen might be coming. She loves horses but where is he?" Isabel goes up on tip-toe, twirling with her parasol.

Gertrude ignores the dizzying Isabel, "Everyone knows who she is and what she does and nobody has nerve enough to shut her down. It'll take the U.S. Army to close that brothel. I am not afraid to say it, 'The Emperor is wearing his underwear.'"

Isabel giggles, "He is? Where is he?"

Maude leans down, just missing Isabel's parasol, now a weapon in perpetual motion, "Who keeps biting into the pimento cheese and putting them back. That makes me so mad."

Nellie sinks down onto the bench, deflated in spirit, "Oh this is not at all like Mr. Van de Vere." She takes a bite of a sweet pickle, licks the sugary juice.

Maude smoothes a napkin across the bench and readjusts her seat, Well, Mrs. Lawrence as far as I know there's just been the one murder."

Isabel looks down, "Whose murder?"

Gertrude pours herself some fresh lemonade, with lemons drowning in the sugary liquid. She tastes it, approves and drinks a glass. She eyes Isabel, signaling that she will answer once she's quenched her thirst.

Nellie holds out her glass, "Mr. Van de Vere is never late."

"Whose murder?" This from parasol-twirling Isabel.

Maude sips her lemonade, "Have there been any more murders, Mrs. Lawrence? There's just been that one girl murdered as far as I know."

"Well I can only imagine." Gertrude's eyes flutter and disappear backwards, then reappear. She's like an owl.

"What? Imagine what?" Isabel stares at Gertrude, fascinated by the trick with her eyes.

Gertrude does not disappoint her and rolls her eyes back into her head again. Then she leans in, whispering "Wild dancing. They say she has a juke box."

The women gasp in union. Isabel's mouth hangs open., "Oh my! . . . What's that?"

Nellie, oblivious to all but missing George, considers a powdered-sugar brownie, "Oh my, my, my . . . George is going to miss the race."

"Well, if you ask me, we're responsible. If we allow Sodom and Gamorah in our own backyard – if we allow our husbands and sons to participate and look the other way, then we're responsible for the murder." Gertrude folds her hands in her lap.

Maude rises slightly, "What on earth are you saying?"

Isabel interrupts, "Whose murder?"

Gertrude's back straightens, her jaw sets. "What I think is that this woman will ruin our chance to vote. As long as we continue to tolerate women of her kind – sordid, trashy women, then what chance is there for decent, intelligent women to take positions of leadership and influence? No, what she is doing is wrong. Very, very wrong. And we're wrong for tolerating her wrongness. I'm tired of mealy mouthed women. The Emperor is wearing his undershorts." She bites into an olive nut sandwich, spits out the pit. "Mrs. Lockard, you put pits in the olives. Who took a bite out of this and put it back in the basket?"

Nellie's light almost white lashes are about to take off, "Oh, my, my, my has anyone seen Mr. Van de Vere?"

Gertrude wipes her tongue around her front teeth, then curls her tongue, "Nellie, sit down. For heaven's sake you're acting like a silly school girl. I saw Tallie and she said George is not coming."

Isabel squeals, "Sally who?"

Gertrude grabs the twirling parasol, "Tally."

"Oh is Tally here?" Isabel flutters on tip-toe, ignoring Gertrude's hand on her no longer twirling parasol.

"Miss Pinkston, drink your sarsaparilla." Gertrude clicks the parasol shut.

"Hush, they're in the gate. I bet on the horse with the jockey in pink silks. Pink Star. Isn't that a lovely name for a gelding?"

Isabel gazes at the flying silks as the horses break from the gate, "Is a gelding a horse without a tail?" Her words are lost in the sound of pounding hooves.

A grey horse pulls to the lead. He runs neck to neck with a strong bay; the jockeys lean in, tight to their horses. The grey pulls ahead. A majestic red horse out-distances the bay and the gray. Only Maude sees the small filly, Number Four, suddenly come up from dead last; the little filly whips around the other horses and thunders her way towards the lead.

Maude stares at the horses, sweeping closer and closer towards the finish line. "Is that – is that Number Four?"

The other ladies turn, staring at Maude who is now undone with excitement. The filly, covered in sweat and mud, nostrils flaring, ears flat against her silken head, gains the lead.

Maude suddenly catches on that the filly is Number 4. Ecstatic, she rises to her feet. Cheered on by Maude, Number Four pulls a length ahead of the other two leading horses. The jockey rises up out of the saddle urging the filly on, faster and faster. Maude waves her hand, at first just a small wave. Then, as the horse races past the box, Maude claps louder. "Pink Star . . . go go . . . you go sugar baby!"

Gertrude glares at Maude; but Maude is oblivious to anyone but the winning filly. She takes off her white glove and whistles. In that instant, the filly races across the finish line.

Maude bursts out, "Oh my! Oh my, my, my! I WON!!" Maude hugs Isabel, then throws her arms around Nellie and kisses a mortified Gertrude on her cheek. Tickets fly through the air. The filly, enjoying the spotlight, preens for the crowd, walks past the boxes and seems to almost dance. Impulsively, the jockey on Number Four blows a kiss to a woman in white, sitting in the box directly beside Gertrude's box. In that moment, Gertrude turns her binoculars and stares at Belle. She suddenly gasps. Speechless, Gertrude hands the binoculars to Maude who looks straight at Belle.

Young Belle smiles at Maude and mouths the words, "We won!"

Maude, stunned, drops the binoculars down onto her lap. She turns, slightly, and then glances back at Belle. Then, she very purposely drops the ticket and turns her back. All four ladies open their parasols, turning their backs to Belle.

Wind picks up the winning ticket, blowing it up and out of the box. A man's hand suddenly reaches up, catches the ticket. There is the sound of whistling and the race track, the winning filly and the ladies at the race track freeze. As if swept away by the painter's brush, the horses and ladies then simply vanish. All that remains is a blank canvas with a single red rose. And then, slowly, the original painting begins to reappear.

And Spirit Belle is again alone - staring at the painted Lady in White offering a rose to a jockey in brilliant red silks. Billy snaps his fingers and the painting, covered in dust, disappears back into the armoire which then just as magically, rises and disappears.

CHAPTER THIRTY-ONE

Young Billy

"Pink Star! Sounds more like a drink than a horse." Billy pops some mint in a sterling silver cup and then sips the drink. "Nobody makes a mint julep like ole Billy boy." He hands Belle the glass, then pulls a ticket out from behind her ear.

She grabs his wrist, "I'm tired of tricks, Billy." She sees the ticket and lets go of his hand, "Let this go."

"You had a winning ticket but never cashed it, sugar-belle. Why not?"

"Gertrude Lawrence is not fat."

"No." His tone changes; he sets down the glass, actually filled with nothing but ice and mint.

"She's actually one smart southern lady, isn't she? I was responsible for what happened to Alice Elly." She suddenly takes the ticket. "So that's it. I get it." She walks over to the grandfather clock.

Billy doesn't follow. He cracks the ice with his teeth, "Wonder if it's too late to cash this ticket."

Belle hesitates before trying the clock's door, "Is . . . is it time?"

"Well most folk live about as long as they make up their minds to . . . ah whoa- hey Kitten."

She turns, "Yes, angel darlin'."

"You can't take the Mint Julep."

"Really? No Mint Juleps in heaven? Are you sure?"

He nods. She takes a quick sip, then sets down the drink and tries the Clock's door. It doesn't open. "Billy, it's still locked." She looks up at the Clock's hands. "I think it's broken." She starts to give the Clock a kick.

"Belle! No sense in kickin' the clock. The right time will chime when ya figure out who you need to forgive. Wonder whatever happened to your Philadelphia beau?"

Slightly annoyed, Belle glances out the window, as if remembering something she long ago tucked away in that worn scrapbook. "He introduced me to some very influential men – some of the great men of our time."

"You're dodging the question, darlin'? Where was he? Years later, after you closed the House? Did he ever come to see you?"

She turns to the window, caresses the velvet, smiling, "You're still jealous of my Philadelphia beau? Oh Singerly still came to see me. After the United States Army shut me down, I never heard from him again but sometimes late at night, I would wake up. Suddenly. And I'd go to the window and see it. His carriage. With the black horses. And all the gawdy tassels on their manes and tails. He was like a show pony himself. He'd sit there in that carriage – sometimes for hours – and then he'd be gone. But once, I remember Pearl saying that she'd gone to pay my electric bill and the clerk told her that it'd already been paid. Singerly always said touching me was like makin' love in a lightning storm." She winks at Billy. "That Door isn't closed because of my Philadelphia beau."

He doesn't smile, "Ya sure about that, honey?"

She bites her lower lip, "I was a Madam. A very successful Madam. Oh, don't look so serious, Billy. He forgot me. In his own way, Mr. Singerly moved on."

"You didn't just close your heart to Singerly, Belle. Not even ole Billy was ever really allowed to love you. Or have you forgotten Kitten?"

Spirit Belle drops the mint julep glass. And suddenly turns. It is as if for a terrified moment she remembered something – a memory that cuts deep. A white feather falls slowly down, landing at her feet. She leans down, picks up the feather, "Billy?" The bedroom disappears. Spirit Belle stands, alone, in the old familiar kitchen.

A younger Billy, in his late-thirties, with a ponytail and handlebar moustache is in the midst of a hot poker game -- up against Pearl and two other girls. Billy lights his cigar and is about to blow a smoke ring when suddenly, from outside there's the sound of a carriage, hitting loose gravel. Billy swings his legs over the chair, grinning and throws down his cards. "Damn, train must have been early. Stall her, Pearl." Billy folds his cards, slaps Pearl on the backside and heads up the back stairs. Pearl rolls her eyes, then takes a quick peek at Billy's cards. "I knew it. I knew it. Humph – you was bluffing Mr. Billy!"

Pearl puts down the hand of cards and quickly makes her way to the front door. Seconds later she opens the door. Young Belle, looking absolutely exquisite, dressed in the latest fashion, with pointed white leather boots steps out of the carriage. Belle motions to the driver who starts unloading trunks and more packages. She looks up, "Oh, hello Pearl. Where's Billy?"

"Welcome home, Miss Belle. Uh, Mr. Billy's around here somewhere's. You're early ain't ya?"

"Here, this is for you." Belle hands Pearl a parasol with lace and elegant jewels. "I found this in a boutique. The lace is from Belgium. Oh, and there are some chocolate liquors in . . . Where's Billy? Joey can't unload all the trunks."

Pearl starts down the stairs, "Here, I got two strong arms . . ."

Young Belle catches her arm, "Leave it. That's not your job."

Pearl steps back, holding open the door, shaking her red turban, "You look tired, Miss Belle. Don't be foolin' with them trunks now. Git on in out of this air."

"What's wrong with this air? Pearl, I was raised breathin' air sweet with the scent of honeysuckle and . . . what is that? Pearl, have you been smoking cigars?"

Pearl waves the air. Her eyes roll. "Licorice. I told Mr. Billy to cut that grass. Done growed up to the railing. Licorice grass--smells like . . ."

Young-Belle has her hand on the railing, for a second she turns. "Horehound candy. I want it cut down first thing in the morning." Pearl takes one of the trunks out of Belle's hands. "Thank you, Pearl. Where in heaven's name is Billy?"

Pearl closes the door behind Belle. They both enter the parlor. Spirit Belle, watching from the stairs, suddenly gasps – remembering in vivid detail the rich colors, the elegance of 59 Megowan. The parlor is draped in heavy gold and red fabrics --covering the sofa, the chaise lounge, the chairs. Pearl fusses with the muslin coverings; Young Belle motions her towards the stairs, "Oh, don't fuss with that now, Pearl. I'm tired."

Pearl fluffs a pillow with a good swift fist, then places it back on the chaise, "Yes ma'am. Good to have you back. Megowan ain't the same without you and . . . Come on in here and let me fix you some iced chicory coffee."

Young Belle glances at Pearl, as if suspicious that she is up to something but she dismisses the thought, "Thank you but I'll have some tea upstairs."

Under her breath, Pearl whistles softly, muttering "Tea? Well, if that ain't the jack rabbit eatin' hisself some turnip greens. She hums softly to herself as she disappears down the hall, into the kitchen. Young-Belle climbs the stairs, turns on the landing. She hears whistling. She turns the knob on her bedroom door and starts to enter. Billy sits on the stair railing, whistling. He turns and for a moment, we see Billy, as the spirit guide, start up the stairs. Spirit Belle, watching from the landing, calls out "Billy! Wait."

Billy, the wise spirit guide, turns, "I'll take it from here."

"What do you mean? Are you just going to . . ."

"I know this memory by heart."

Spirit Belle watches as the younger Billy comes up the stairs, whistling. Billy salutes Belle and then slips into his former younger self. Spirit Belle steps back. Billy comes up behind young Belle, standing outside the bedroom door. He places his hands over her eyes "No. Not yet. No peeking."

"Oh Billy, I'm tired." Young Belle sighs; playing along reluctantly.

"Close your eyes. Don't peek. Give me your hand." Billy gently kicks open the bedroom door.

Young Belle starts to enter the bedroom, "My hand. Why?"

Billy blocks her, "Your hand, my ladyship."

She holds out her hand.

"No gloves, please."

She takes off the glove, but protests, "Billy, I've had a long train ride. New York was hot and . . ."

Not listening, Billy slips his handkerchief over her eyes; then takes her hand and gently leads her into the bedroom.

"All right. You can open your eyes now."

She slips the handkerchief off of her eyes and stares at the bedroom. There are flowers everywhere. Roses are tucked into vases lining the mantel; daffodils peek out from the chandelier and rose petals line a path from the door to the bed. Young Belle, touched by his kindness, smiles and goes up on tip-toe to kiss him. But Billy goes down on one knee and suddenly holds out a box. "Open it."

Curious, Young Belle slips the lid off of the box. Inside, a small, black and white kitten looks up out of tissue paper. "Billy Mabon- what are you up to?"

Belle glances at the kitten; slowly, she pushes aside the tissue and holds the kitten up to the light. Tied to the kitten's collar is a ring. She puts the kitten back in the box. "Billy, I hardly need a kitten."

"How about a ring? He picks up the kitten, holding her up so that Belle is forced to see the engagement ring, "How about being Mrs. Mabon? No mystery. No more secrets. Just be my wife." He unties the ring and tries to slip it on her finger. The kitten purrs softly. Billy gently puts the kitten on the chaise.

Young Belle's eyes glint angrily, "Billy! Pearl, oh my god, she hates cats."

"Belle, I'm asking you to marry me." He tries to hide his disappointment, trying to smile and slowly rises. "Belle, I'm asking you . . ."

She twists the ring off of her slender finger, "It doesn't fit. It's too loose."

"I can fix it."

"No. No Billy, you can't fix it." She hands him the ring and pours herself a drink. "I love the flowers. I'll have Pearl send some to the Short Street Orphanage." She walks over to a vase filled with white roses. He reaches for her; she escapes from his desperate hold and he suddenly kicks the silver vase. It rolls, hitting the floor with a jarring clang.

"Damn, I'm asking you to marry me. Could you please, would it pain you too much to look at me. Just look me in the eyes and tell me . . . Belle, don't do this. I'm in love with you. I'm asking you to be my wife."

Young Belle pours a fresh drink. Billy tries to touch her shoulder; she moves away. "What is it? Am I not good enough for you? A lowly employee of the Water Company, is that it?"

She ignores him and walks over to the vanity. She glances in the mirror and removes a slight smudge of lipstick on the edge of her lips. "Oh Billy, we've been over all of this before."

"What? Are you waiting for the Senator to make you an honest woman?" He laughs; a short laugh edged with irony.

She stares into the mirror at Billy's reflection, "Don't you ever talk to me like that? Who do you think buys your fancy dress shirts and your Cuban cigars and liquor?"

"I buy my own damn liquor, honey."

"You're nothing more than a lackey-boy."

The remark stings. Billy steps back, away from the vanity. He cracks his jaw, starts to walk away, then regains control, "If I thought you meant that, I'd walk straight out that door and never come back."

"Believe whatever you want, Billy. I really don't give a damn what you think. Right now I want to be left alone." She steps behind a dressing curtain.

Billy picks up the cloak, holding it in his hands lovingly. "Belle, I'm asking you to marry me."

Young Belle senses that she may have pushed Billy a little too far; she turns, her voice gentle, almost as if talking down to a child, "Billy, dear sweet Billy, I can't marry you because I'm already married. I married James Kinney."

"And just where is this Mr. Kinney? That's crazy. You were sixteen. You call some damn arrangement your mama made with a nineteen year old boy that lasted all of nine days a marriage? Did you even sleep with Mr. Kinney."

Young Belle unties the ribbons of her bonnet, dismissing Billy with her hands, "I am married."

"Then get a divorce."

"I can't. I'm Catholic. Divorce is a sin." She smoothes the ribbons, placing the bonnet on the vanity and loosens her hair.

Billy suddenly walks over to the vanity; he stares into the mirror "You ever stop to think about how you make a living?"

Refusing to be drawn into the argument, Young Belle stands, remaining coldly aloof, almost taunting Billy with her lack of engagement in the conversation, "I've seen plenty of wives who get paid with pretty doll houses filled with pretty paper dolls doing just what I do."

"What? Playing the Madam? Why don't you just say it straight honey, playing a . . ."

Suddenly, Young Belle releases her fury; she attacks Billy with the full force of her rage. Trying not to be drawn into a fight, she now lashes out with uncontrolled power and fury, "All right. Is this the wife you want, Billy?" She strips off her jeweled cape, unbuttoning her bodice, "Playing a whore." She throws her petticoat and skirt on the bed and turns, facing Billy. Standing naked in the burnished gold light streaming in from the bedroom window, Young Belle stares coldly into Billy's frightened eyes.

He turns his eyes away from her naked body, holding out her kimono, "No. I'm sorry."

She takes the kimono and sips the drink. There is a chilling silence. Finally Billy finds the courage to speak his truth; his words, however, are spoken in defeat. There is a faintness of energy in his voice; he is a weak man painfully aware of his own weakness, "I'm sorry. I'm sorry for me. But mainly sorry for you because you'll never know . . . never be capable of knowing any real happiness. And you know why? It's not because of any Catholic religion – not because you can't or won't get a divorce. No, the truth is you can't let go of self long enough to trust . . ." He coughs; it's a horase, raspy cough. And the coughing fit lasts for several seconds. Then, he raises himself up, facing Belle, "... to find out if maybe, just maybe someone might love you long enough to want to love you – to want to take care of you the rest of your life."

Young Belle, without any emotion in her eyes, listens. She watches him pour a drink. He swallows the liquor; pours another drink and continues, "You're a wonderful actress, Kitten" He lets the whiskey dampen his parched lips, and almost smiles, "But you're one of life's wounded. There's a shield around that heart of your's that no one will ever..." Suddenly, Billy leans forward; a coughing fit over-whelms him.

Frightened, Young Belle turns from the vanity, reaching out her hand to him, "Billy!"

He breathes in quick, shallow gasps but finally finds his voice, "I'll be all right. The Billy Mabons are just ordinary guys. I'll keep waiting at the corner of Megowan and Wilson to open your carriage and welcome Mrs. James Kinney home from New York. I'll bring white roses and Mint Juleps . . . because, ya see, Belle, for some god-damn reason I love you."

Young Belle remains stoic. She sits still, holding her sterling silver hair brush in her hands. Billy opens the door as if to go out and suddenly, she calls out after him, "Billy! Where are you going?"

He turns, a tired smile creases his face. The dimples show in his unshaved cheeks, "Downstairs to help Pearl unload the carriage. Don't worry, Belle. I'll be right here for as long as you need me. I won't leave you. Promise. I'm your paperboy."

Billy walks out the bedroom door. The chandelier glistens; then the lights dim. A single feather falls onto the vanity where Spirit Belle stands, behind her former self. She doesn't pick up the feather. Instead, she lets the memory wash over her – closing her eyes. She is painfully aware, even though she doesn't actually see her former self – that Young Belle is materializing in front of that same vanity. Slowly, Young Belle puts on a black mourning hat with a veil, gloves and a black riding jacket.

Spirit Belle opens her eyes, "You didn't keep that promise, Billy. Neither did Mama or Willie. Or Johnny or Mr. Singerly. Not even Hester. Within six months, everyone I ever cared about would be dead."

Billy, standing by the window in the dusk light, appears. He comes gently, as if recalled by Spirit Belle's higher self. His fingers are closed; as he opens his hands- a lightning bug shimmers its yellow light. Billy speaks lovingly, "It's not your fault I died, Belle."

Spirit Belle, grateful for his appearance in her "dream", stares out at the sea of lightning bugs. "I let you die, Billy, just as if I'd put that whiskey bottle in your hands and forced you to take every drink of poison." She traps a firefly with her cupped fingers.

"Is that what you think, Belle?" He lets the lightning bug go free. It shimmers its magic, up along the peeling wall paper and then disappears into the chandelier's luminous glow. "Belle, is that what you've believed all these years - that I died because what – you wouldn't marry me?"

"No, because I didn't love you." Spirit Belle looks into his eyes.

"My poor Kitten, you did love me. Much more than you knew."

Church bells chime. They ring at first from a distance and then the somber tone becomes more clear. Closer. Spirit Belle stares at her younger self, dressed in the black over-coat and veil. Slowly, she allows the memory to play in her mind. But she doesn't actually step into the memory. She stands at the windowsill, letting the haunting images lure her deeper into the sepulcher of fear. "I remember now. I had to wait until late in the afternoon. I'd gone alone to your sister's. I closed the door to the parlor and sat in the dying light. Looking at you. Your eyes closed in death's sleep. It was a long time before I came out of that room. Then, I climbed into my carriage and Joey brought me back here. To 59 Megowan."

From downstairs – in present time – beyond the dream state – Flora Hudson's voice sings a powerful spiritual. It is a haunting melody. And the words sweep around Belle's mind, "Hush. Hush. Somebody's calling my name."

There's the sound of footsteps on the stairs and then on the landing. Spirit Belle places her hands over her ears, "No. No – not yet. It's too soon." She stares for one agonizingly painful moment back at the four poster bed. And she sees the little girl, with the tired white ribbon, holding the soggy bag. The little girl stares straight at Spirit Belle. Suddenly, she turns to Billy. "I – I came back here. But you . . . you were gone. There were too many lies, Billy. Too many deaths. I came home and I started looking for . . . kitten."

The lights suddenly go out. The room goes pitch black. Again, there's the sound of footsteps on the stairs, then on the landing and then the bedroom door opens. But it is not Flora. The present slips into the shadow-box of memories.

CHAPTER THIRTY-TWO

Kitten

Spirit Belle remains by the window. Billy lights a candle and holds it out to her. As she takes the candle holder from his hands, a haunting wind blows across the candle flame. It leaps high. Smoke curls around her fingers and suddenly, she sees her former self. A figure in black standing in the bedroom doorway. The bells of Christ Church ring loudly. Young Belle pushes back the veil from her face, "Kitten? Here, kitty, kitty. Come here." She calls softly, "Where are you?" Then her voice breaks into a shrill, piercing "Where's the god-damn cat?"

Young Belle, desperately afraid of the dark room and the demons lurking in the shadows of its empty walls, rushes to the vanity and opens a drawer. She takes out a needle and shoots morphine into her veins. "Kitten? Kitten. Be a good kitty, come to mama. Come here, Kitten."

Willie, in his cap and holding his harmonica, slowly takes shape in the eerie light streaming in from the window. He stares at her. An apparition in a ghostly pale blue light. She sees him. "Willie?" The morphine starts to take effect. She pulls a scrapbook out from a trunk, and flips the pages, looking for the poem which she curiously begins to recite by heart "I've often wished to have a friend with whom my choice hours to spend. I'd wish that friend to be my wife." She holds the poem in her shaking hands, looking up. But Willie has vanished. "Willie?"

Slowly, stumbling, she rises off the floor, "Mama? Oh why Mama, I didn't hear ya come in!" She looks frantically towards the door, "Mama! Oh God, mama, please, don't let Willie die!" She sinks down onto the bed, holding open the scrapbook, and rips out a poem which she recites "Kisses, well I remember." And in the pale light, Johnny appears. She sees him. He stands, with his cocky grin, undressing her with his eyes. She drops the poem, and goes towards him, "Oh Johnny. Yes, yes! You didn't forget. Oh listen, it's the mourning dove. She's come to say good-night to you and me and our little one. I'm gonna have a baby, Johnny." Suddenly, the light around Johnny deepens into a crimson red. "Blood on the moon, Johnny. No, no . . ." There's the sound of a pistol firing. Young Belle leans forward, terrified. "No, don't turn around." She backs away "Oh Mama, oh god Mama! Is he dead? Why mama? Why?" She stumbles, hitting the baby cradle. Leaning down, she picks up the doll. "Look Daisy May." Turning to the scrapbook, she shakes it violently – spilling out the ribbons and letters. A valentine slips out into her trembling hands. "Look Daisy May. See the pretty Valentine. 'Presented by Mr. Dionesia Mucci, February 14th, 1874.' Your mama was fourteen, Daisy May. Fourteen." Her voice rises; then she bursts into a lullabye sung with wild fierce passion and anger, "If that mockingbird don't sing, mama's going to buy you a diamond ring. If that diamond ring don't shine . . ."

Cradling the doll, young Belle sinks onto the hard floor. She hears the ringing of a Carriage Clock. Slowly, she lifts her eyes and sees the Senator, naked, standing above her, smoking his thick cigar and blowing smoke in her face. "Why Senator, you've just bought . . . you've just bought yourself that Carriage Clock."

A kitten purrs, close. The sounds jars young Belle back to reality. She throws the doll down. Hard. Then reaches for her, loving her, "I'm sorry, baby. Kitten! Kitten, don't be a shy kitty-cat. Come to mama." She stands, walks to the vanity and pours bourbon into a sliver mint julep glass. As she drinks the liquor, her hand shakes uncontrollably. She again reaches for a needle and shoots in more morphine. "Kitten?!" Suddenly, Alice Elly appears, reflected in the vanity mirror. "Alice? Pretty Alice Elly? Oh god, he's got a knife. He's slitting her throat. He's killing her. Billy! Billy!"

Frantic, young Belle throws down the mint julep and grabs the shot. Shooting in the morphine, "It's not enough. It's not enough. Got to make the demons go away." Young Belle pushes the needle into her now bleeding vein. The needle breaks off in her wrist. Repulsed, terrified, she tries to loosen the needle. First with her hands but her fingers are shaking so she leans down and tries to bite the needle. "Sweet Jesus, Billy- call Dr. Nevitt. The needle's broken off in my . . . Billy?" She looks up as if expecting to see Billy. But then her mind races and she catches on that he's dead. "Billy! No, no . ."

She stands, waving her arm with the needle sticking up out of her raw skin, shrieking, "NO! Oh god, I got to have more morphine. I can't make it. I can't . . ."

Young Belle turns, dizzily, spinning across the room, shaking her arm – and then she catches her own reflection in the mirror. Her reflection stops her. "Whore. You god-damn whore. I hate you." She stares at her face, grotesquely distorted through her own drug-induced glazed eyes. Slowly, she leans over the vanity and takes a red lipstick; she writes in large, wild handwriting the word WHORE.

Young Belle, her bodice now torn open, leans down her mouth and tries to bite off the needle, stuck in her bleeding vein. Her words erupt, hissing out in poisoned anger, "I hate me. Hate me!" Desperately, she tries to pull the broken needle out of her bruised arm. Finally, she sinks down, folding her half-naked body into the heavy folds of the black skirt. Then suddenly, she bursts out laughing, hysterically. She lifts her eyes, and stares at all the ghostly visitors now reflected in the vanity glass.

"God-damn you, don't ya talk? Look at me. Look at me! See this gold-gilded mansion for men where for five bucks, a gentleman and a whore can make-believe all night long that life is just one big party!"

She rises, holding up the black taffeta folds of the skirt and curtsies to the ghosts. "How lovely for all of you to come. Is it a party? Hush now, Kitten's gonna make a wish."

Mucci, winding a music box, appears in the vanity mirror. She greets him, looking straight into the glass. "Why Mucci, sh-sh! Aren't we friends. Best friends, eh? Mucci laugh. Laugh damn you. Laugh." Mucci stares. A lifeless wisp of memory. Suddenly, Young Belle whirls – but he is not behind her. She smiles, weakly. "Bella, sweet Bella, laugh so no one sees. Laugh so no one dimly suspects that you're dead inside." Then she hears whistling; frightened, she faces the mirror where Billy appears. "Oh Billy, don't you know, whores don't have souls. Just feel up their dresses, touch the lace, breathe the intoxicatingly sweet scent of their perfumed skin. Five dollars for the French lace teddy. See?" She turns, throws open her drawer and rummages madly through her lingerie, tossing out the moth-eaten silk teddies and dust-covered bodices and petticoats. "Make love to them in the dark. Kiss their naked breasts or look, damn it Senator, look at the whore's naked body. See. She's not real. She can't feel or cry. She's only a paper doll men will use and abuse and defile and color black."

Suddenly, she pulls out the drawer and dumps all of the remaining contents onto the floor. A silver mint cup falls out of a box, tied with a Tiffany blue ribbon. She stares, paralyzed by the demons of memory that now rush over her. Slowly, she unties the ribbon and takes out the silver mint julep cup. It is unpolished and dusty; but she remembers. Remembers what is now waiting inside that mint julep cup. Holding the glass up to the light, she reads the engraved name "Kitten" and slowly, almost in a holy, ritualistic act of repentance, she slips her small, shaking fingers into the mint julep and takes out the ring.

The diamond glistens – almost unnaturally. Taunting her, teasing her. She slips the ring on her finger and then cries out, "Billy! Oh god, why did ya take my Billy? My Billy!" She holds the mint julep cup close to her heart and grows very still. Standing in a stream of moonlight, she seems to almost disappear – becoming herself one with the ghostly apparitions that haunt her pain-infused mind. Slowly, she whispers to the woman in the glass, the woman whose image is also painted on the wallpaper above the four poster bed and whose face now takes shape as a blurred image in the julep cup, "I hate … Hate you. Hate me!" She grabs the lit candle and holds the flame close to the wallpaper, igniting a fire. The paper curls into brilliant orange ribbons; the fire spreads rapidly. Belle's voice rises, "Billy, how could I marry you . . . how could I love you, when I so despise me?"

Young Belle, exhausted, sinks down onto the floor, grasping the mint julep in her trembling, cold fingers. From outside the bedroom door, there's the sound of footsteps. The door opens and Pearl, in her red turban, rushes in. As the bedroom folds into itself, like cardboard rooms in a child's game, Billy takes Spirit Belle into his arms.

"Love is the process of leading one gently back to self." He holds her; whispering "You're safe, Kitten."

Spirit Belle closes her eyes, as if closing the past from her heart, "No, Billy, no one is ever safe from their past."

CHAPTER THIRTY-THREE

The last memory

"There's one more memory." Billy holds out the storybook.

Spirit Belle shakes her head, "No, I'm tired. Can't ya understand, I'm tired."

"We're running out of time. Here." He places her hands around the worn edges of the storybook. "Now, close your eyes and read from your heart."

Spirit Belle looks at Billy, then quietly takes the storybook and reads from memory. "Once upon a time, there was a duckling."

Billy steps back towards the window, glancing out at the yard where the first light of dawn now caresses the shadowed grass. "Keep reading the story."

A feather falls onto the open storybook, illuminating the last memory that Spirit Belle now draws to consciousness. As the familiar bedroom disappears, a different memory plays out in the shadow box. Spirit Belle gasps, re-creating her childhood home on West Main. Child Belle, much younger than in the earlier memories, takes shape. This little Belle, about four, kneels in front of a box.

Billy stands at the edge of the memory, guiding Belle back along this forgotten path, "Now listen to me, Belle. It's late in the afternoon. You come home from Sunday school; you put down your little Bible and walk over to the stove. Coal black. Breathing warmth. And there they are. There's Tabby and her kittens. You touch the little kittens, timidly. Careful, don't hurt the kittens. Their eyes are closed. They're so small. Helpless. Safe."

Spirit Belle starts to close the storybook, "Please, stop this."

Billy's voice is without judgment, "But the kittens aren't safe, are they? Life on West Main is no place for newborn kittens. You leave them alone – just for a moment."

Spirit Belle watches as the little Belle gently puts the kitten back in the box; she walks over to a cupboard, puts down her book satchel and goes up on tip-toe to take down a favorite storybook, "The Ugly Duckling" by Hans Christian Anderson. She smiles, secretly, and begins to whisper the story aloud, reading from memory to the newborn kittens. Suddenly, a rush of wind disturbs the fairytale. Sarah Brezing's shadow looms large across the hard dirt floor.

"You leave them alone – just for a moment. You go put your little Bible in the cupboard and when you turn back around, your mama is by the stove. What's she doing?"

Sarah, drunk, glares at the kittens. She walks over and picks up the box and then goes outside. Terrified, Child Belle rushes out the door, following her mother.

Spirit Belle tries to close the storybook, "Please Billy. No."

"She puts the kittens into a bag and walks out back to the trough and she lowers the bag under the water. Did you try to save the kittens? Did you cry out?"

"No, mama was right."

"You just watched. Silently. Then, you waited till she took the bag out of the trough and went back into the kitchen. And you took the bag to a grassy hillside behind the house and one by one, you lifted the drowned kittens out of the bag and buried them. And you never said a word. You never cried."

"No." Spirit Belle stares as the memory replays. The little girl caresses each dead kitten, kisses them on their closed eyes and places them in the freshly turned earth. Then, suddenly, she stops, staring at a small kitten, held in her hands.

"There was one kitten – still alive."

Spirit Belle turns away from the childhood memory, "No, Billy. All the kittens were dead."

Billy takes her shoulders and turns her back to look at the little girl, cradling the last kitten. "It was so small. You could feel its little heart beating."

Spirit Belle stares at the kitten, grasped in the child's hands, "It was alone."

"So you put the kitten back into the bag and you held the bag under the water . . ."

Spirit Belle whispers, "She would have died."

Billy closes the storybook, gently, and holds Spirit Belle with a powerful gaze of absolute love, "What was the kitten's name?" He takes the storybook and curiously, the white feather transforms into a rose. Billy holds the rose out to Spirit Belle, "What was the kitten's name?"

Spirit Belle stares at the rose, "She didn't have a name. I called her 'kitten.'"

"You never said a word."

"No."

"You never cried."

"No." Suddenly, Spirit Belle's heart opens, spontaneously. And she cries. The tears flow down her cheeks and the white rose held out in Billy's hand unfolds its luminous petals. Billy presses these petals into Spirit Belle's palms, and says quietly, "The execution of innocence is silent, on so very silent, isn't it, Kitten?"

Spirit Belle watches as the little girl takes the last kitten, now drowned and still, out of the bag. She holds it in her hand and kisses the kitten on her closed eyes.

Billy's voice is filled with strength, "There's a child waiting, Belle. She's waited a life-time for you to forgive her."

Spirit Belle steps into the memory; she walks over to the small child and for a moment hesitates, as if she might turn back. But Billy is now beside her. His presence is empowering. She looks back at him, then faces the little girl and sees clearly the memory as it plays forward in the present moment. Released from the anguish of that bitter memory, Spirit Belle now embraces her past. She feels the essence of the child's being. And the colors sharpen; the sounds roar. The water pump is loud, deafening. The cicadas sting the air with an intense, unnerving clattering of wings. Almost in slow motion, the little girl unties the ribbon, shaking free her wild tangled hair. Then she kisses the last drowned kitten and carefully places it in the bag with the other dead kittens. She wipes her eyes with her muddied fingers, but does not cry. And she ties her dirty white ribbon around the bag and places it in the shallow grave.

Repulsed, Spirit Belle calls out to Billy, "I can't. I'm afraid."

Billy's voice is strong, "Don't you want to love that child?"

"Yes."

"Then, forgive her."

Slowly, Spirit Belle again faces the child. This time, she kneels down beside Child Belle and watches as little Belle sprinkles dirt onto the grave and then turns and gathers some wild violets; gently, she presses the wildflowers onto the freshly mounded dirt. Her tears flow freely. Silently, Spirit Belle weeps with the little girl. Alone, beside that grave, she forgives the child whose heart closed to love so many years ago. A strong wind blows. It blows across the grass; blows fresh and free across the landscape of memory and frees Belle's imprisoned soul. In that instant, the little Belle beside that grave draws back into her self the other little girl with the tired white ribbon, holding a burlap bag. And as the two child-Belles become one, the little girl who has haunted dying Belle disappears.

Spirit Belle watches as an intense Light illumines the house on West Main – casting the wrought iron fence, the clothes line, the water pump and the grave in a splendorous iridescence. Then, all that once was held in memory simply vanishes and Spirit Belle stands in her familiar bedroom.

Church bells chime. They are the bells of Christ Church. And their ringing is no longer from a distant time. But the present. The light of dawn steals into the bedroom. And around the brass pendulum that hangs down in the grandfather clock a curious light emanates. The pendulum begins to swing.

"Belle, it's time."

As the childhood memory disappears, Spirit Belle hears the whisper of rain. It comes freely. She goes to the window and opens wide the shutters, "Listen, Billy. It's begun to rain. Sweet summer rain. Come, quench earth's dying thirst. Oh, I have waited – waited so long through all the hot nights. Waited on tip-toe to hear the gentle whisper of the rain. Come rain. Come, bless this child."

Billy holds out his arms, "Come, Kitten, awaken to dance."

Spirit Belle smiles, "Is this the last dance, Billy?"

"Yes, you always promised this one to me. Remember?"

Spirit Belle takes Billy's hands, "So I did."

Billy leads Spirit Belle across the room to the grandfather clock. Slowly, the pendulum swings; the clock chimes the hour. And magically, the door to the clock opens and a brilliant light streams into the bedroom. Spirit Belle hears footsteps and turns.

Gil Mabon opens the door and steps into the bedroom. He stares at the unnatural light streaming into the room. Then Gil looks up at the grandfather clock and there is a moment when he actually senses Spirit Belle's presence.

Impatient, Billy looks over his shoulder, "Belle, ya want to stay for the auction?"

"No, I'm ready. I just want to blow a kiss good-bye to my last paper boy." Spirit Belle blows a kiss to Gil and in that instant, the paper boy sees her and grins. Billy takes Belle's hand and they slip into the Grandfather's clock, disappearing into a portal leading to a place of Peace and Splendor and Light.

And then Belle's last paper boy delivers the newspaper. As he places it down on her bedside table, he sees her Bible, lying open. The inscription reads, "Blessed are the pure in heart; for they shall see God."

A white feather falls down into the paperboy's open hand.

Acknowledgements

I am grateful to Joe Ed Mainous, whose insightful editorial guidance was a *lighthouse* in the process of writing and re-writing this book. His generosity is boundless; his contribution - absolutely invaluable.

I also want to extend my gratitude to Christina Mainous for illustrating *Fireflies*.

And to Ann Sydney Taylor – who captured the cover art through her camera lens and somehow attracted a stray cat up onto the railroad tracks – my thanks for being such a creative and amazingly talented artist and friend!

I also want to thank Peggy Stamps, a brilliant, compassionate soul whose rich imagination and creativity took the story to an entirely different level. She is a woman of magical graces and genius.

Also the University of Kentucky Libraries, for use of the Belle Brezing Photographic Collection. Special thanks to Matthew Harris.

And to my friend, Dawn Bazner – thank you for the gentle nudge, suggesting that I adapt my stage-play into this novel.

Author's Notes

In 1983, I was working as in-house counsel for a Disney-owned (Shamrock Corporation) television station in Lexington, Kentucky. Unexpectedly, a child wandered into my life. Marigold (*not her real name) was a gentle, loving child whose mother (a pedophile) had held her down while the boyfriend raped her. Asked to be the little girl's Guardian ad Litem, I said "Yes" without really knowing where that spontaneous decision might lead. Where it led was into the labyrinth of what was then our Kentucky Juvenile Justice System and a wake-up call to see the children (like Marigold) who were becoming more and more invisible. As a result of taking on Marigold's case, I became actively involved in the arena of Children's Advocacy. I served on the Kentucky Bar Association's Children's Advocacy Committee and authored a chapter in the KBA handbook, *Children and the Law.*

It was during the summer of 1983 that a Futures for Youth board member asked me to consider writing a play about the famous Lexington Madam, Belle Brezing – whose own childhood had been shadowed by abuse, an alcoholic mother, rape by a pedophile and the illegitimate birth of a child with serious challenges. Despite this incredible suffering (or perhaps because of it), Belle Brezing became one of the most famous madams in the South. She was a charismatic and dynamic southern woman who rose out of poverty and a painful childhood to operate one of the most successful bordellos in the South. Her house at 59 Megowan Street was known for attracting the finest clientele; when she died both Time Magazine and the New York Times ran her obituary on the front page. And there is convincing evidence that Belle Brezing inspired the character of Belle Watling in Margaret Mitchell's book **Gone With the Wind.**

Having grown up in Lexington, I was familiar with some of Belle Brezing's colorful history. By sheer chance, I happened to grow up next door to Belle's "last paperboy." So - I accepted the invitation to write a play that would benefit Futures for Youth, an organization dedicated to helping children like the present-day *"Belle's"*. The stage-play's journey began: I climbed the stone steps, all that then remained of Belle's "gilded mansion for men", and began interviewing those who once knew the Madam or knew stories from their grandfathers. I began sifting through facts and trying to attract the story that would inspire others to see Belle (and all the other "Belle's") in a light of compassion.

In June, 1983, the play (originally titled 59 *Megowan Street)* opened at the Lexington Opera House. Produced by Actors Guild, the play sold-out all performances. By that next spring, *Belle* would be invited to Charleston where the play was performed in the prestigious Spoleto Festival. And from Charleston, *Belle* traveled to Los Angeles (first for a staged-reading) and then in 2010 to the LA Lost Theatre. Subsequent performances included a staged-reading at the University of Kentucky (Guignol Theatre) and another full production by Actors Guild of Lexington. (Eric Seale, producer). Then in May, 2013, the play *Belle Brezing* was presented at the New York National Opera Theatre. Directed by Kentucky native Shauna Horn, the play featured the soulful singing of powerful Spirituals, supervised by Peggy Stamps (Manager, The American Spiritual Ensemble.)

The play has traveled many paths. And I am grateful to all those actors, artists and directors who breathed Life, Inspiration and Soul-Magic into the stage-play. Throughout the journey of this play – through the many revisions, the late-night rewrites with the sole company of a faithful chocolate lab and loyal golden retriever, I have tried not to lose sight of the "Child-Belle" who inspired that first play. It is this child's spirit that leads me gently, quietly – to write not only facts but to try and find the essence of her story. For twenty years, after closing 59 Megowan Street, Belle Brezing, a recluse, sat alone on her second floor sun porch, sitting in her rocking chair, reading her Bible – addicted to morphine. When she died, her gravestone faced the side of her mother's stone where she had these words engraved: *"Blessed are the pure in heart; for they shall see God."*

It is for that Child – whose early life shaped subsequent decisions – that I wrote the original stage-play. And it is for that Child (and all the other "Child-Belles") that I dedicate this adaptation of my earlier stage-play into a novel. Shedding light on the connection between a wounded past and a life lived in quiet desperation, *Belle Brezing* is ultimately a story of forgiveness and personal redemption. The novel is not intended to be a biography of

Belle Brezing's life. The intention here is simply to invite the reader into the "soul" of a dying woman as she is guided by the spirit of her life-long friend, lover and soul-mate (Billy) through the "dark night of her soul" – to travel with her as she faces the demons of her past in order to forgive and ultimately love the lost Child within.

Belle Brezing, the novel, is nothing more or less than an invitation to "Awaken to dance."

Billy Mabon, 59 Megowan Street

Belle in feathered hat

LEXINGTON, KY.

Madam Jennie Hill

Bulldog sketch by Belle Brezing with her signature

Belle Brezing with umbrella

Belle Brezing with floral corsage

A girl's bedroom in 59 Megowan Street

Belle, in 59 Megowan Street parlor

Parlor, 59 Megowan Street

Parlor, 59 Megowan Street

Madam Belle Brezing's bedroom, 59 Megowan Street

ABOUT THE AUTHOR

As an attorney active in the arena of child advocacy, Margaret Price has had books published by Simon and Schuster (in the *Chocolate* series) and by the Kentucky Bar Association (*Children and the Law*). A young adult book, CHILLIPOP (about a llama and a child with Autism) was presented at the World Equestrian Games (2010, Ky.) Price's screenplay THE DOVE AND THE DANDELION, produced into a hard-hitting film, won Honors in the Louisville Film Festival. An UNGENTLE TRUTH won the Minneapolis St-Paul Screenlabs Competiton and was produced. LOOKING FOR MRS. CLAUS won second place in the San Francisco Practical Paradox Competition and was later adapted into both a book and stage-play musical (Produced.). Her popular children's book, *Smiley Pete, The Magnificent Moocher,* benefits homeless animals. Price's poem RESILLIENCE won second place in a national poetry contest (Horticulture Magazine). A Northwestern University honors graduate (Theatre) and a graduate of the UK College of Law (Law Journal; and a member of the Kentucky Bar), Price studied screenplay writing at the American Film Institute and International Law at Queens College, Cambridge. Price has sold scripts for film and television and is a member of the Writers Guild, East. She lives in Lexington, Ky. with her husband, Gary Swim and their three daughters, Meredith, Julie and Katie.